LETHAL
TEMPTATION

NEW YORK TIMES AND USA TODAY BESTSELLING AUTHOR

KAYLEA
CROSS

LETHAL TEMPTATION

Copyright © 2020
by Kaylea Cross

* * * * *

Cover Art and Print Formatting:
Sweet 'N Spicy Designs
Developmental edits: Deborah Nemeth
Line Edits: Joan Nichols
Digital Formatting: LK Campbell

* * * * *

ISBN: 979-8682921379

For Beep, my hunky Alberta cousin who fought his demons for as long as he could. You never realized what a beautiful soul you had, but your family knew. You will forever be missed.

xo

Author's Note

Mason got under Avery's skin in *Lethal Edge*, and not in a good way. If he wants to win her over, he's got his work cut out for him in this one! Hope you enjoy it.

Happy reading,

Kaylea

CHAPTER ONE

Avery stopped typing notes on her computer to snatch her phone from her desk when it rang. She stilled when she saw the number of her main police contact in Billings, and took a deep breath before answering.

She'd been waiting for this call. Dreading it for days. "Detective Dahl."

"Avery, it's Jim. I have some news for you."

"Hi, Jim. Go ahead." She braced herself for the possibility of bad news.

"It's about Mike Radzat."

"Yes." Her stomach tensed, her fingers tightening around the phone.

"The National Appeals Board met this morning, and they've made the decision to—"

To overturn the Parole Commission's decision and grant Radzat parole. So that dangerous, manipulative piece of shit could target more innocent victims.

"—deny his appeal."

Thank you, God. She leaned back in her chair, slowly

1

relaxing. "That's great news." She wanted him to stay in prison for as long as possible. "When will his next parole board hearing be?"

"Likely in another two years."

Hopefully he'd be denied parole then too. "Thanks for letting me know."

"Of course. Have a good day."

"You too." She set her phone down on her desk with a relieved sigh. Until now she hadn't realized just how anxious she'd been about the situation.

She looked up at a brisk knock on her partially open office door. Her work partner, Tate, stood in the doorway, wearing dress slacks, a charcoal-gray button-down, and a few days of bronze stubble on his jaw. His expression was somber. "We're being dispatched to a domestic violence call."

Avery pushed up from her desk and took her service pistol from the drawer, sliding it into the holster on her hip. "Where's everyone else?" They were detectives, not patrol officers, but the Sheriff's Department here was small enough that they were often spread thin, so everyone had to pitch in where needed.

"Busy."

She hurried after him down the hall toward the main doors. These kinds of calls were thankfully rare here in Rifle Creek. It had been a long while since she'd had to respond to something like this, and she hadn't missed it. She'd always hated them.

One in five officer "line of duty" deaths occurred while responding to domestic violence calls. They were by far the most dangerous kind of call for an officer to respond to, and she was thankful to have Tate with her.

They'd been partners for just over seven months now, and they'd become close right from the start. She trusted and felt safe with him. And not only was he a former Marine Raider with combat experience in addition to his years as a law enforcement officer, he was also in love with Avery's best friend.

There was no one else she'd rather have watching her back in a situation like this. "Where's the domestic at?"

"Summit Park. Neighbor called it in."

New, fairly affluent neighborhood on the ridge above the creek. Just went to show that domestic violence didn't discriminate—it affected all demographics, and all walks of life.

They exited the building into the bright October morning sunshine and hurried for his gray Ford pickup. "What was that call about when I showed up at your office?" Tate asked. "You looked relieved."

"Just got word that the inmate I testified against in Billings a few years ago has officially been denied parole."

"Radzat?" He unlocked the doors for them.

"Yeah." Serial assaulter, thief and drug dealer. "For once, our justice system got it right." Even though she'd done everything in her power to keep him behind bars, she'd been worried they might let him out early.

During the parole hearing she'd testified that he shouldn't be granted parole—ever. Mike Radzat needed to stay behind bars right up until the last day of his sentence. He'd been committing violent crimes since the age of twenty-three, and he'd only been put away for the things he'd been *caught* for.

Having worked as a patrol officer in Billings for several years prior to becoming a detective, she had arrested him at least ten times, and each crime had been increasingly violent. No surprise to her that he'd wound up being arrested for aggravated murder soon after, having carved a rival to pieces with a machete.

"How long's he got left in prison?" Tate asked as he steered out of the parking lot.

"Eighteen years." She shook her head. "He had every

chance in the world to straighten out. He came from a good family and had all kinds of support and opportunities. Instead he threw it all away."

"At least he's not getting out anytime soon."

"That's the silver lining."

They were quiet for a few minutes, until Tate turned off the two-lane highway. "So, Mason's moving in tomorrow night, huh?"

Her good mood took a dip. Oh, God, she didn't even want to think about Mason. The man unsettled and confused her. And he was about to become her basement suite tenant, because rental suites in Rifle Creek were sparse, and she could use the money. "Yeah. Now give me the rundown on this situation we're responding to."

Tate outlined what the caller had told the 911 operator about the domestic violence incident. Sounded like the middle-aged couple had been in one hell of a fight if the neighbor had been concerned enough to call the cops. Husband was a lawyer, wife an interior decorator. The caller didn't know if the wife had been injured, but had feared enough for her safety to make the call.

As they approached the neighborhood, Avery mentally readied herself for the unknown situation they were about to walk into.

"Ready?" Tate asked as he pulled up to the sprawling, two-story brick house.

"Yep." She got out and walked with him up to the front door, hand on the butt of her service weapon. The neighborhood was quiet, most of the driveways empty with the residents at work, though she noticed the next-door neighbor peeking at her and Tate through a gap in the curtains as they headed up the front walkway.

Tate rang the doorbell. Electronic, with a camera. When no one answered, he rang it again, and rapped on the door.

"Hang on," came the irritated reply a few moments

later.

"Mr. Zinke," Tate said when the homeowner finally opened the door.

Avery studied him in silence. Forty-three-year-old male, clean cut, with brown eyes and dark blond hair. Same height as her, right around six feet, with a wiry build. The dress slacks and shirt hinted that he was on his way to work.

Zinke didn't budge, the door opened only wide enough to frame his face. Avery didn't see any visible scratches or marks on it. "Yes?" he said, still sounding irritated.

Avery and Tate held up their badges. "Rifle Creek Sheriff's Department. We got a call about a domestic disturbance at this address," Avery said in a no-nonsense tone. "We'd like to speak to you and your wife."

His face tightened as he stared at her. "She's not here."

Uh-huh. Then how come both cars were still in the driveway? "Can we come in?"

He eyed them with suspicion. "What for?"

"We want to ask you some questions."

A muscle ticked in his jaw, then he relented and stepped back. "Fine, but make it quick. I need to get into the office for a meeting."

Tate went in first. Avery followed, using her heightened awareness to get a read on the situation. The wife was nowhere in sight. And the place was spotless, furnished and decorated to perfection, like a show home. "The report said you and your wife were in a heated argument."

"Who reported it?" Zinke demanded.

"I don't know. Was there an argument?" she asked.

"Yeah. So?"

Avery already disliked this arrogant sonofabitch. And it didn't bode well that his wife wasn't visible.

"Where's your wife right now?"

"Out. And it was nothing." His cheeks flushed, but not from embarrassment. Oh, no, this asshole was pissed right off at having his behavior witnessed and reported.

"Where's your wife now?" Tate asked.

"Out," he snapped, no longer even trying to maintain a civil façade. "Look, whoever reported it was overreacting. I raised my voice, so what? I was mad. It's over now."

"Do you have any weapons in the house or on you?" He wasn't wearing a holster, and there were no visible bulges in his clothing. Avery patted him down to be sure.

His jaw flexed. "In the gun safe in my office."

"Which is where?" Tate said.

He jerked his chin toward the hallway. "In there."

"Show us." They followed him to the office and verified that the firearms were all accounted for.

"I'm going to check this level," Avery told Tate.

"She's not here," Zinke snapped.

Avery ignored him and did her job, looking in each room on the lower floor for weapons or any sign that the wife was here. When she found nothing, she came back to join Tate in the living room.

"Did you assault your wife, Mr. Zinke?" Tate asked.

Zinke's face turned even redder. "*No*. Now are we done?"

A muted thud sounded above their heads. All three of them paused. Avery watched Zinke closely. "Is someone else home?" she asked.

"No. Was probably the cat," he muttered.

Right. "I'm going to look upstairs," Avery said to Tate, pushing to her feet.

Zinke shot to his, blocking her way. "I didn't give you permission."

Avery arched an eyebrow at him, not the least bit intimidated. "Under the circumstances, I don't need your permission."

Zinke made a move to block her as she stepped past him, but Tate was there, placing himself between them with a solid hand on Zinke's chest. "You stay here with me. Sit down."

Zinke glared, his eyes burning with anger. "You got a warrant?"

"Don't need one if we suspect someone might be hurt."

"I'll be reporting this," Zinke growled, jaw tight.

"Be my guest," Avery muttered to herself as she hit the stairs. She kept her hand on the butt of her pistol, attuned to every sound, watching for any sign of movement above her.

The upstairs landing led down two hallways. One to the guest suites, which were empty, and one to what she guessed must be the master.

Her pulse sped up as she walked toward the master bedroom. "Mrs. Zinke? I'm Detective Avery Dahl, Rifle Creek Sherriff's Department. Are you all right?"

No answer. But then Avery caught the faint sound of something moving inside.

She entered the room. "Mrs. Zinke?"

Silence.

Screw this. Avery drew her weapon and began a more thorough sweep. The master suite was huge, and immaculate. Sweet perfume scented the air. "Mrs. Zinke?"

The bathroom was empty. So was the walk-in closet. What the hell? She'd heard something hit the floor up here not two minutes ago, then movement.

She stopped, spotting a faint smudge of dirt in the carpet. A potted orchid rested on an occasional table above it. The stain in this immaculately kept home was like a red flag. Pointing Avery directly to the built-in cabinets beside it.

She turned toward them and crouched down to pull one of the cabinet doors open, weapon ready.

A tiny gasp answered.

Avery's heart clenched at the sight revealed in the beam of sunlight streaming through the window behind her. A blond woman was curled up in a ball inside, her face half-hidden in shadow. But the visible part of it was all Avery needed to see.

She holstered her weapon and got down on her knees to peer inside. "Tracy?"

The woman didn't answer, her face wet with tears, her left eye swelling shut. She was trembling.

Avery extended a hand toward her. "It's all right now. I'm Detective Avery Dahl. Come out and let me help you."

The woman's one-eyed gaze darted frantically around the room.

"My partner has him downstairs. You're safe now."

"N-no," Tracy whimpered. "Don't—d-don't arrest him."

Avery gestured with her hand. "Just come out and we'll talk. I need to see that you're all right." Because clearly, she wasn't.

Tracy put a trembling hand in Avery's. Avery helped her out, and smothered a sharp intake of breath when she saw the woman fully in the light.

Zinke had busted her lip open. Her pink blouse was covered in blood. A welt was forming on her cheek below the swelling eye.

Tracy sniffed and wiped gingerly at her face, her gaze on the floor.

"You're hurt," Avery said, keeping her tone gentle even as she wanted to race back downstairs to watch Tate cuff Zinke and tell him what a piece of shit he was for beating his wife.

The woman shook her head. "N-no. I slipped in the sh-shower."

"Tracy." The woman looked up at her, the shame and

fear there making Avery's gut tighten. "You and I both know you didn't slip in the shower."

Tracy began to cry softly.

Avery gently took her over to sit on the edge of the wide, king-size bed and got on her radio. She called dispatch for an ambulance, ignoring Tracy's protests. If Zinke had beaten her this badly, she might have fractures or even internal injuries that needed to be checked.

Just as she finished, Zinke's enraged voice shattered the quiet from downstairs. "Get out of my fucking house!"

Tracy jerked, her entire body going rigid. Avery grasped her hand and gave her a reassuring smile. "Listen to me. I want you to stay right here, okay? I'm going to check on my partner, and then I'll be right back. Don't move."

She turned and raced for the door. Zinke was screaming and swearing at Tate as she ran down the stairs. His enraged stare snapped to her the moment she came into view. Avery held it, a rush of triumph hitting her. "I found her and called for an ambulance," she said to Tate. "Cuff him."

Tate drew the cuffs from his belt and reached for Zinke's wrist. Zinke snarled and took a swing at him.

Tate blocked the punch and sidestepped. Zinke stumbled past him, his momentum throwing him forward as he caught himself on the coffee table, scattering a pile of mail everywhere. "You wanna add resisting arrest on top of everything else?" Tate snapped, grabbing Zinke's arm to twist it behind him.

Zinke whirled, the glint of the blade in his hand catching in the light.

Tate! Avery didn't have time to shout the warning. She launched herself at Zinke, hitting him square in the back.

They landed with a thud on the coffee table, Zinke taking the brunt of the impact. Avery instantly locked her

hands around the wrist wielding the blade—a freaking letter opener they'd missed under the mail.

She twisted sharply while Tate wrenched the bastard's other hand up and behind him, one muscular arm
pinned against Zinke's nape.

Zinke screamed, thrashing. The letter opener hit the
floor.

"I got him," Tate said as he held Zinke there, totally
calm.

Avery released what she sincerely hoped was
Zinke's broken wrist and kicked the weapon across the
floor. Then she shoved off him, heart racing as Tate kept
the asshole subdued and cuffed him.

Tate yanked Zinke to his feet and started Mirandiz-
ing him. Avery whirled toward the stairs, stilling at the
sight of Tracy standing halfway down them. Her one open
eye was wide, her tear-streaked face pale, one hand at the
base of her throat. "No," she pleaded.

At the sound of her voice Zinke's head spun around.
"You fucking *bitch*!" he screamed. "You did this!"

"Shut up," Tate growled, giving him a rough shake
before shoving him toward the front door.

"I told you to stay out of sight until they were gone!"
Zinke yelled at his wife.

Avery rushed past them to take Tracy by the arm.
"Come upstairs with me."

"No," Tracy cried, turning back toward her husband.
"Where is he taking him?"

"He's being arrested for domestic assault, resisting
arrest, and attacking a police officer."

"No, you can't," she begged. "You can't, he'll—"
She broke off, dissolving into tears.

Avery hurried her up the stairs and into the master
bedroom. Backup was on the way, should be here any minute. "I'm having some paramedics come look at you. For
now, just come sit and tell me what happened."

10

Tracy continued to cry, a devastated, heartbroken sound that made Avery's insides tighten. "He—he d-didn't mean it," she sobbed. "It was an accident."

No, it fucking wasn't. And Avery would bet everything she owned that this wasn't the first time, either. Not even close.

"I won't press charges," Tracy blurted through her tears, a hint of defiance breaking through her fear.

Avery quelled a rush of frustration. So many women refused to press charges against their abuser, for a variety of reasons. But there was enough evidence to charge and convict him, so hopefully that wouldn't matter. "Tracy. I understand that you're afraid right now, but you don't need to think about any of that yet. Right now, I just need you to take some deep breaths, calm down, and talk to me."

She sat quietly, letting Tracy calm down, waiting for the tears to stop. "There. Now please tell me what happened."

"It… It was just a s-stupid argument," Tracy began.

Avery listened, taking detailed notes. But ten seconds in, it was obvious Tracy wasn't telling the whole truth. "So you see, it was partly my fault," Tracy finished in a whisper.

"No, it wasn't," Avery said in a low voice, holding back the rest of what she wanted to say. Her phone buzzed in her pocket. She pulled it out to see Tate's message that Zinke was on his way to the sheriff's department in the back of a squad car, and the ambulance was ten minutes out.

Avery replied for him to stay outside. She didn't want anyone else to come in here and make Tracy clam up even more.

"Can I get you anything?" Avery asked her in the quiet.

"No." Tracy sighed and bent her head, rubbing her

11

fingers over her forehead. "He didn't use to be like this," she whispered. "When we first got together, he was wonderful. But…"

"But?"

"After we got married, things changed. *He* changed." She looked up at Avery, her battered face full of misery. "Does that sound crazy?"

An echo of pain twisted through Avery, an old hurt flaring back to life. Not as severe as Tracy's. But still valid. "No. It doesn't sound crazy at all."

She knew all too well how suddenly a man could change after putting a ring on a woman's finger.

CHAPTER TWO

Normally Avery was able to compartmentalize the bad things that happened in life and at work, but that situation earlier at the Zinkes' place lingered with her as she drove back into town that evening. Partly because Tracy Zinke's last comment had hit too close to home. But mostly because violence against women infuriated her.

Just a few weeks ago, her best friend Nina had been kidnapped and nearly killed by her rapist. Avery and Tate had barely found her in time, and that wasn't something Avery was going to get over anytime soon.

On the drive back into town, her mom called. For a second, she considered ignoring it, then decided against it and picked up. Her mom was like a bulldog when she wanted something. "Hey, Mom. How's it going?"

"Fine, everything's good here. How are you?"

"Fantastic." There, that sounded moderately cheerful even to her.

"Glad to hear it. You on your way home?"

"No, to Nina's." She tried to get together for dinner with her and Tate once a week, schedule permitting, and tonight was the night. Avery was tired, but didn't want to go home yet. It was lonely in her old brick Victorian without Nina there, and she hated cooking for one. It made her feel even more divorced.

"Ah, enjoy. Well, I'm actually calling about the guest list for next weekend. Annie's asked me to finalize the numbers for the caterer, and she said you responded that you're bringing a guest?"

Avery cursed silently. Dammit, with everything going on lately, the wedding had crept up on her. And she didn't want to change her RSVP now and confirm what everyone thought—that she couldn't get a man. Not that she wanted one after what she'd gone through, but that didn't seem to matter to her family. She was tired of them feeling sorry for her.

It hadn't been her choice to walk away from her marriage. Though it had been her choice to end it. Doug had killed all the love she'd once had for him. She wouldn't give him the time of day now even if he crawled to her on his hands and knees and begged her to take him back.

Thankfully, Tate had said he'd go to the wedding with her months ago when she'd first brought it up. He'd have to use a different name for the weekend, since her family knew about him but hadn't met him yet. "Yeah, that's right."

"Who?" Surprise and curiosity filled that one word.

"I'm seeing someone," she blurted, unable to come up with another plausible explanation. Dammit, she hoped Tate had remembered the dates.

"Really? Is it serious? I mean, if you're bringing him to a family wedding, I assume you've been seeing him for a while?"

Avery cringed at the eagerness in her mother's voice. "Not that long." For a cop, she was a terrible liar.

"What's his name? Where did you meet him, online? And why haven't you told me about him before now?"

Because he doesn't exist. "Through a friend. Look,

Mom, I'm running late for dinner, so I gotta go."

"Dinner with him?"

"Yes." That part wasn't a lie, at least. "I'll call you later, okay? Love you."

"All right, love you too." She squealed in excitement. "This is great, I'm so looking forward to meeting him!"

Hell. Within minutes, both Avery's dad and sister would know. By morning, half of the extended family would too, alerted through the family grapevine her mother loved to feed. "Me too. Bye."

She ended the call and shook her head at herself in disgust. "Ah, shit." Why the hell couldn't she just have told her mom the truth? Why did those stupid insecurities keep coming back to the surface when she'd worked so hard to bury them? "Tate, you better not let me down."

She released a breath and consciously relaxed her tight shoulders. Maybe Nina's eternal and optimistic romantic sensibilities had rubbed off on her lately, because she could acknowledge that deep down, she was lonely. On the other hand, she didn't believe in happily-ever-after anymore. She wasn't sure where that put her.

Good company was just what she needed to pull her out of her funk, even if the man she tried to avoid whenever possible would be there.

Mason Gallant alternately irritated and turned her on just being in the same room as her, and now they would be sharing her house, since Nina had moved out of Avery's basement suite and into Tate's place several weeks ago. Mason felt like a fifth wheel there, and Avery couldn't blame him. Besides, Tate's niece Rylee stayed there sometimes when she wanted a break from dorm life at the University of Montana.

So Avery had reluctantly offered Mason the suite, mostly because it was only temporary, until Mason got his feet under him here. She hoped he wouldn't make her regret her decision.

In spite of her vow to get over her bullshit and get in a happier frame of mind, she groaned when she saw Mason's red Jeep parked in Tate's driveway with the small trailer hitched behind it. It was probably already packed with all his stuff, ready to be moved into her suite in a matter of hours.

Her precarious mood slipped another notch.

"All right. Happy face, and pull up your big girl panties," she muttered to herself as she walked up to the front door of the gorgeous log home, bracing herself for the inevitable moment she was forced to see Mason in person again. She'd made it a whole three weeks since the last time, on the day she and Tate had found Nina fighting for her life in the woods.

The vivid memory popped into her head, bringing an unwanted wave of heat that spread through her as she thought about it. Mason had shown up at the scene soon after Tate had carried Nina out of the woods to where the emergency vehicles were gathered. Avery had been talking to an FBI agent about what had happened.

Spotting her, Mason had ducked under the police tape and walked straight at her with that sexy, confident stride that made it impossible to look away from him. He'd stopped directly in front of her, asked if everyone was okay, then shocked her by hauling her into a long, tight hug that made her whole body go haywire.

Even now the memory of it made her insides tingle. He was hot, and he knew it. Sexy as hell, and he knew it.

He was also haunted by whatever had ended his military service. That was enough of a red flag right there to make him a relationship risk.

But she'd seen the powerful and protective warrior inside him that day, and it made him even more dangerous to her. His cocky and damaged player image made it easy to dismiss him, because she had no time for that kind of male macho bullshit.

That little glimpse underneath it all made that impossible. And therein lay the dilemma.

Thankfully he was nowhere to be seen when she entered the main level, the log walls and masculine furnishings giving the home a cozy, lived-in feeling. She relaxed a little more to find Tate alone in the kitchen working on dinner.

"That's what I like to see, a man hard at work in the kitchen when I get home after work," Avery said as she walked in.

One side of his mouth lifted. "Ha-ha."

"Well, fancy meeting you here," said a bright, sunny voice behind her.

She spun around and smiled at Nina, still dressed for work in a plum-colored turtleneck sweater and gray pencil skirt that hugged her curves. "Hey, lady." She gave her best friend a hug. "Just get back from campus?" Nina taught astronomy and astrophysics at the University of Montana, a forty-five-minute drive away in Missoula.

"Yep. I grabbed our groceries at the store, and a couple bottles of wine." Her expression sobered. "Tate told me about the call earlier. You okay?"

Avery grunted. "Yeah, but it sucked."

"I'm just glad you guys are both okay. Tate said you tackled the guy."

"He deserved it."

"He totally did," Tate agreed.

Nina grinned, her brown eyes twinkling. "Wish I could've seen it."

She shrugged. "Tate could have handled him without me, I just saw the letter opener and reacted without thinking."

"Still, thank you. I love how you guys have each other's backs."

"Tate's a great cop, and an even better partner." Which was why it bummed Avery out so bad to think of him leaving soon to start his new adventure/training ranch with Mason and another military buddy of theirs.

Wow, aren't you just made of sunshine and rainbows tonight?

She pasted on a smile for Nina. "Pass me that wine." Sunshine and rainbows were Nina's territory, not hers, but she couldn't subject the others to her sour mood. "I'm also gonna need a baking pan to make my appetizer." A wheel of camembert topped with double-raspberry jam and chopped pecans, all baked in the oven until it was oozy, gooey goodness and ready to devour with crackers.

As Avery set the oven to preheat, Nina handed her a baking dish and uncorked the first bottle of wine. "Wine time," she announced, coming up behind Tate to wrap her arms around his waist.

"Rather drink you up instead," Tate murmured, curling a thick arm around his lady and pulling her in for a kiss.

Avery mentally rolled her eyes and managed not to make a face. But seriously. They were ridiculous together. She was happy for them, even if seeing them so in love made her want to gag sometimes. "I'll pour." She uncorked the second bottle and left it to breathe, then poured a glass each for her and Nina from the first. "You having some?" she asked Tate.

"Nah, I'll have a beer later."

"Hey, by the way, my cousin's wedding is next weekend. You're still good for it, right? For at least two of the three days?" It felt weird asking him now that he was Nina's man.

Tate froze in the act of seasoning the steaks to stare at her, then winced. "Shit. That's next weekend?"

A hint of foreboding curled inside her. "Yeah, why?" *Please don't say you can't make it.*

He looked at Nina, who also winced, then back at Avery. "We're meeting Nina's family over in Coeur D'Alene for the weekend. Rylee's coming with us."

Shit. "The whole weekend?" As soon as she said it, she realized how stupid it sounded. Of course the whole weekend, it was over three hours' drive away.

"Yeah. Damn, I'm sorry."

Avery maintained a neutral expression as dread swamped her. Noooo, she couldn't go to this thing alone. Her entire extended family would be there, expecting her to have a boyfriend, along with her ex and his twenty-six-year-old trophy wife, who was best friends with the bride.

God, Avery's cousin had bad taste in friends. If it wouldn't put her in the family bad books forever for ditching the whole thing, Avery would in a heartbeat. "It's...fine."

"I'm really sorry, Ave," Tate said with an apologetic look. "I didn't think it was a for sure thing, because you never finalized it after we talked initially."

"No, it's seriously fine," she said with a wave of her hand, even as dread scraped along her spine. This was her fault. She should have locked the date down with him a while back.

"What's the problem?"

She stiffened at the sound of that deep voice behind her and turned as Mason strolled into the kitchen with his service dog Ric on his heels, his mere presence making the room seem small. She was tall at a shade under six feet but he was at least six-three, and his powerful build made her feel small by comparison.

That unsettling hum started up deep inside her again like it did every time she saw him, traveling along her nerve endings like the tingle of a low-level electrical current. The man radiated an intensity that was impossible to ignore.

Today he had on a plain black T-shirt that hugged his

sculpted chest and shoulders and showed off the tats on his forearms. His well-worn, faded jeans fit him to perfection. He wore his dark hair short, his neatly-trimmed beard accentuating the clean lines of his jaw.

But as beautiful as the rugged masculinity of him was, his eyes were the most gorgeous part. Pale, piercing blue, and when they met hers it was like he could see inside her. Past the confidence she'd worked so hard to restore after her divorce, past her defensive walls to the place deep down that responded to him against her will.

"There's no problem." Tearing her gaze from him she focused on his dog instead. She crouched down and beckoned to him. Ric lowered his head and ears and rushed over, his back end wiggling, feathery tail swishing back and forth like a fan.

"Ricochet, you handsome thing. How are you?" she crooned, aware of Mason's stare on her and the nerves dancing in her belly.

Ric was far and away the best thing about Mason, a border collie-Aussie shepherd cross with silky black, white and brown fur. One eye was brown and the other blue, topped by adorable brown eyebrows that gave him so much expression. She was looking forward to him moving in downstairs.

As for his owner, Avery would be polite when they crossed paths, but continue to avoid him as much as possible once he moved into her suite. Hopefully his stay would be short and sweet.

"Pretty sure I heard a problem just now," he said, leaning against the counter to fold his arms over his chest as he watched her.

"It's nothing," she answered, wrenching her eyes away from all that muscular glory on display. She wasn't used to being around a guy like him.

She spent a lot of time with Tate, but he didn't count. Yes, he was built and a little gruff, but he was her work partner and she'd never been attracted to him like she was to Mason. She'd just have to call her mom back and make up another lie to cancel her plus one for the wedding, even though going alone was the last thing she wanted.

The thought was depressing beyond measure. She was freaking sick of being an object of pity, and had been looking forward to portraying something other than a single, forty-two-year-old woman with no life outside of her job, and no romantic prospects. It was no secret she'd become a workaholic to fill the void since her divorce, and her entire family knew it.

Dammit, she used to be fun and interesting. She loved to travel, loved animals, and she'd let work get in the way of all that. She needed to book a trip. Maybe she'd start fostering for the local shelter or something too.

"Avery needs a date for a wedding next weekend and Tate can't go with her now," Nina said to Mason.

Avery opened her mouth to deny it, but Mason turned those piercing blue eyes on her again, freezing her in place. "I'll stand in for him."

CHAPTER THREE

The look on her face would have been funny as hell if it hadn't felt like an insult.

Avery's golden eyes widened for an instant, as if she couldn't believe he'd made the offer. Then she snorted. "Yeah, no."

Mason blinked, surprised at the blunt rejection. From the first time they'd met, Avery had been a major check to his ego, and apparently nothing had changed over the past few weeks. "I'm serious."

"So am I."

He frowned at her, a little affronted by her outright refusal. "Why not?" He might have his issues, but he was a decent guy, and he wasn't bad looking. He had good hygiene, could carry on a decent conversation, and he was capable of being part of a social gathering without embarrassing her.

She stood and grabbed her wineglass. "Thank you for the offer. I just don't think it's a good idea. At *all*," she muttered under her breath as she took a sip.

Mason tamped down his irritation, aware of Tate standing there pretending to ignore them, and Nina hanging on every word.

LETHAL TEMPTATION

Mason didn't care. Avery had captured his attention instantly the day they'd met. She was tall and lean with jaw-length strawberry-blond hair and killer golden eyes. The woman was flat out sexy. She was also a cop and could handle herself, which was insanely hot.

It wasn't just looks or her being able to handle a weapon, however. Her independent nature appealed to him, because he couldn't stand clingy, and Avery definitely had her shit together. Maybe part of his attraction to her was also because she didn't seem interested, when normally he had the opposite effect on women.

Whatever it was, it didn't much matter because the woman seemed to be doing her level best to ignore him at all costs and work herself to death. She was even more of a workaholic than Tate, and that was saying something, although Nina had helped him find a much healthier balance lately.

As for him, Mason was still struggling to find his footing. He was bored, edgy and restless. Unfulfilled and searching for a purpose. He liked Avery, though. Hanging out with her for an entire weekend at this wedding and forcing her to spend time with him sounded like the best thing that had happened to him in a long time. He wanted to get her naked and under him.

"You worried I'd embarrass you?" he asked, unwilling to let it go.

She met his gaze, and in that instant the pull she exerted on him was stronger than ever. "No."

"Then why not? Because I'm moving in downstairs?"

"No." She sighed. "If it was a one-day thing, I could probably get through it with you."

Get *through* it? Wow. Talk about a swift kick in the ego.

"But it's two-and-a-half days, and I just can't. For various reasons."

23

Mason bit back another demand for her to explain herself. Evidently, he irritated the shit out of her, and at this point he wasn't sure why.

True, he'd laid the flirtation factor on when they'd first met, but he'd scaled it right back since then. Yeah, he still flirted a bit with her, because he couldn't stop himself. He'd never hidden his interest in her, even though he'd been respectful about it.

She glanced away. "Anyway, let's get this show on the road. I'm starving."

"On it." Tate took the steaks outside to grill.

Nina started prepping the veggies but Mason reached over and took the knife from her. "I got this. You go outside and relax."

"You're the best," Nina said, then fished something out of a grocery bag. "Here. Bought this for you. It's a local company in Missoula. Hope it's good."

He grinned and took the bottle of root beer from her. She'd never asked him why he didn't drink, but Tate had probably told her. It was sweet of her to remember. "Thank you."

"You're welcome." She patted him on the shoulder and picked up her wine, giving Avery a curious look. "Gonna go put my feet up for a bit. Call me if you need help."

"We've got this," Mason said, and started assembling the veggies.

Avery shot him a glance as she worked beside him at the counter getting her appie together while he chopped the peppers and zucchini. "You're good with that knife. You cook?"

"Yeah."

She stopped to stare at him. "Really? I didn't know that."

He met her gaze. "There're a lot of things you don't know about me, angel eyes."

Her mouth tightened and her eyes narrowed slightly at the pet name he'd called her before. Mason hid a smile and kept working, not in the least bit sorry. The name suited her. She had the prettiest eyes he'd ever seen.

"So, who's getting married?" he asked after a few moments of stony silence.

"My cousin."

"And you had a date originally, but now you don't?" Maybe she'd been seeing someone when the invitations had gone out.

"Tate was supposed to be my date but I forgot to finalize it with him, and now he's with Nina. And I stupidly told my mom tonight that I was seeing someone."

He arched a brow at her. "You lied to your mom about it?"

"Yep, and now I have to come clean, which is gonna suck, but there it is."

The way she said it made it sound like she dreaded everything about it and the wedding. "Why are you uncomfortable going on your own?"

She scooped jam over the top of the wheel of cheese in the baking dish. "My entire family's gonna be there. And my ex," she added. "With his pregnant and much younger new wife."

He stopped chopping to look at her, surprised. Tate had never mentioned anything about this, only that Avery's ex was a loser, and that she never dated, didn't do hookups or anything. Her ex must really have fucked her over. "You were married?"

She nodded and kept working. "This will be the first time I've had to see him since the divorce. And she'll be there too."

Hell. No wonder she didn't want to go solo. "Look, you just said you told your mom you're seeing someone. She's never met me. We could pull it off."

He braced himself for a quick and sharp denial, but

25

KAYLEA CROSS

one side of her mouth kicked up instead. "Why the hell would you want to give up an entire weekend to help me out by going to a wedding when my entire family and ex will be there?"

A witty comeback sprang to mind, but he killed it. She already kept him at arm's length and he wanted the opposite. "Because you need someone to be there for you."

She stopped in the act of scattering nuts on top of the jam, frozen for a second before she looked over at him. The surprise on her face couldn't quite mask the flash of vulnerability in her eyes.

Seeing that from this strong, put-together woman made his heart squeeze. *Sweetheart, what did he do to you?*

She looked back at her dish and scattered the remaining nuts. "Thank you. Really. But it's at a fancy guest ranch outside of Billings. The whole place was booked up months ago, and I could only get a room with one bed."

Making excuses now. "So where was Tate gonna sleep?"

"On his side, on top of the covers," she said in a no-nonsense tone.

He chuckled. "I can do that too."

"Uh-huh." She shot him an I-don't-believe-that-for-a-second look and popped her dish into the oven.

He set the knife down and put a hand to his heart, feigning hurt. "Don't trust me?"

"Not like I trust Tate."

He inclined his head. "Fair enough."

She nodded at the cutting board. "You about done there?"

"Yeah." He threw the veggies into a bowl and drizzled them with olive oil before giving them a good seasoning of salt, pepper, garlic powder and oregano. "Let's go make sure Tate doesn't cremate the steaks." He

26

grabbed his root beer and the stainless steel bowl. "After you."

She plucked her wineglass off the counter and shot him a little smile that made him hopeful the ice had thawed a bit between them. Avery Dahl wasn't like any of the women he'd been with. She was prickly and he liked that she challenged him. If he wanted her, he was going to have to work for it.

He was totally up for that mission.

He sat at the table on the back deck, talking with her and the others while Tate manned the grill. When the oven timer went off, Avery went inside to get her appetizer.

"Did Tate tell you about the call they had today?" Nina said as Avery brought her dish out for them and placed it in the center of the table.

"No, what happened?" Mason glanced between Tate and Avery.

"Domestic abuse situation," Tate said as he flipped the steaks. "Piece of shit beat his wife and made her hide upstairs when we showed up. Avery found her cowering in a fucking cupboard, too afraid to come out."

Mason shifted his attention to her. "For real?"

"Unfortunately, yes. I got her to come out, but then the husband got combative, so I went downstairs and he pulled a sharp letter opener on Tate."

"She hit him with a flying tackle," Tate said with a proud grin. "Took him down like a linebacker and busted his wrist."

"Oh, it actually fractured?" Avery asked with a hopeful expression.

"Yep, in two places."

"Well, good. Now he knows a fraction of the pain his wife's going through."

Mason liked that satisfied gleam in her eyes. Except it made him wonder what it would take to put that same gleam there in bed. Taking away her control would be insanely hot, because she wouldn't make it easy for him.

He jerked his thoughts out of the gutter. "This is why I could never be a cop. That guy would be in the hospital, and I'd be in jail."

The approving smile Avery gave him made him want more of them. "I'd bail you out." She leaned forward to hold her glass out to him.

Mason gently tapped his bottle to it and grinned, her allure growing by the second. Avery was awesome. "Good to know."

Tate's cell rang. He checked it, glanced up at them. "Work. Gotta take this." He handed the tongs to Mason. "You mind?"

"Not at all." He turned the steaks forty-five degrees to make a perfect diamond pattern with the grill marks while the ladies talked.

"What are you going to do about the wedding?" Nina asked Avery. "I'm guessing there's a reason you can't just cancel and not go?" She scooped up more melted cheese and jam. "This is delicious, by the way."

"Thanks. No, I have to go, it's a big family thing. It's just so complicated." Avery sighed, made an irritated sound and pushed her bangs off her forehead. "But that's my issue, so I'll just go and suck it up."

"I wish you didn't have to go alone," Nina said. "Walking into that kind of situation for a prolonged period, sucks."

"It's fine. I'm just…tired of the whispers, you know? Of everyone feeling sorry for me, especially when he'll be there. Of people wondering what's wrong with me, why I'm still alone, when there's *nothing* wrong with me."

No, not as far as Mason could see there wasn't. And he also understood how some of that felt. He'd struggled like hell during his transition out of the military and back into the civilian world. In some ways, he still was.

It surprised him how much he wanted to go with her to this thing and use the excuse to spend more time with her.

He took the steaks off the grill and put them on a platter to rest. "My offer still stands," he said to Avery one last time. He didn't want her to have to go alone to this thing, especially with her ex and the new wife there. "I'm happy to go and be your fake boyfriend for the week-end. Give 'em something to talk about."

She arched an eyebrow at him. "Because you've got nothing better to do with your weekend when you guys are busy getting your business set up?" Her voice was dry.

He shrugged. "Everything's kind of on hold right now. Just waiting for my immigration papers and work visa to go through, and then the final word from the bank on the financing. All of that's pretty much a done deal, but we can't move forward until it's all in place." He needed a distraction, and that's definitely what Avery was.

"What about Braxton, what's his status?"

"Still overseas." Mason had served with him on JTF2 for almost seven years. Braxton would be their third part-ner. "Hopefully he'll move down here at least part of the year once he's out of the military."

"And when's that?"

"Next spring." He loved her sarcastic edge. Loved the way she didn't back down around him, and gave as good as she got. "Anyway, think about it. I think we'd have fun."

She gave him a pointed look. "Yeah? What kind of fun?"

"All kinds of fun." He smiled at her because he couldn't help it.

She held his gaze for a long moment, then inclined her head slightly. Not a yes, but a concession. "I'll think about it."

"Okay." Battles were won with small victories, and he'd just scored one.

When dinner was ready, they all sat at the table and ate together. Avery was her witty, sarcastic self, and Mason found himself watching her more closely than ever.

After dinner she stayed to help clean up, then said her goodbyes to Nina and Tate before turning to him. "Guess I'll see you tomorrow."

"You definitely will."

At the door, she surprised him by stopping and turning around to face him, her golden eyes assessing him. "All right. If you're serious and you're really okay with it, then yes, I'll take you with me this weekend."

Mason hid his surprise while doing a mental fist pump. "Great, then it's a date."

A hint of humor danced in her eyes as she gave him a censuring look. "Don't look so smug. You might wind up regretting this after."

Nope. Not ever.

Tate came through the kitchen just as Mason was locking the door behind Avery. "What'd I miss?"

"I'm gonna be Avery's fake boyfriend for the wedding."

"Yeah? Good stuff." Tate grinned and clapped him on the shoulder. "Treat her right, man, or else."

"I will." In and out of bed.

Whatever else happened next weekend, he was going to peel away that steely exterior and discover the woman hiding underneath it.

CHAPTER FOUR

Mason's Jeep bumped along the dirt road on the way to the property they'd put an offer on for Rifle Creek Tactical. Hopefully the surveyor showed up on time, because he had a lot of other meetings to take care of regarding the business today.

With Tate still working a full-time job, Mason had taken on the tasks of website design, logos, interviewing architects and going over potential ideas for the buildings they had in mind. Getting everything set up was going to be a lot of work, but he liked to keep busy and he was also excited as hell to get the ball rolling on this thing.

"Fun, huh, buddy?" he said to Ric, reaching over to ruffle the top of the dog's furry head.

Ric glanced at him from the front passenger seat and wagged his tail, a camo bandana tied around his neck. Ric loved adventure, was up for anything, and Mason couldn't imagine his life without him.

Reaching the entrance to the property, he parked and got out to let Ric stretch his legs. The dog leaped out of the Jeep and immediately began sniffing around. He'd wander off a few dozen meters or so, then stop and look back at Mason, never straying out of sight.

Mason leaned against the front fender of his Jeep and sipped at the travel mug of coffee he'd brought, using the fancy coffee maker in Avery's suite. He and Ric had moved in two days ago now, and he'd barely seen her since. She was avoiding him, maybe even more so because of the upcoming wedding this weekend, and he intended to put a stop to it then. He wanted to get to know her better.

Right now, he had business to attend to.

The sound of an approaching vehicle drifted through the tall evergreen trees surrounding the driveway. Mason whistled for Ric, who immediately ran back and parked his hind end next to Mason's foot, staring up at him adoringly through mismatched eyes.

Mason rubbed the dog's ears and watched as a white pickup with the surveyor company's logo on the side turned into the driveway. "Morning," he said when the guy got out.

"Morning. Ready to get to work?"

"You bet." Once the official survey was completed, they would be one step closer to purchasing the property and making Rifle Creek Tactical a reality. Mason was stoked at the idea of having something concrete and fun to do again.

They walked the land together while the surveyor took precise measurements of the property boundaries and discussed details about the plans for RCT once it was up and running. Every day things were falling into place, and even if Braxton decided not to join them full time yet, Mason and Tate could run everything for a while.

Ric trotted around checking various things out, but never strayed far. The two-hundred-acre parcel was rugged and covered with a mix of evergreen and deciduous forest. Only one section had been cleared, and that's where the main lodge would be built, close to where the property hugged Rifle Creek as it rushed down the mountain into the valley.

Mason loved it. Loved being outside in nature, and he couldn't wait to get set up here to do some shooting, rappelling, kayaking and other things they had planned. Teach some courses, use his skills and expertise for the first time in too long.

It felt good to be excited about something again. For too long he'd been trapped in a dark place, and it finally felt like the light was starting to penetrate the shadows. Now he had RTC to look forward to with his closest friends—and his upcoming weekend with Avery. She wasn't going to be able to ignore him then.

He and the surveyor had just come into view of their vehicles when an old truck roared up the driveway. Mason tensed, reaching down to grab Ric's collar as an old man climbed out wearing a furious expression.

"Can I help you?" he asked cautiously, his free hand ready to draw the pistol from its holster on his hip. He liked being able to carry here with his weapons permit. The surveyor stood off to the side, watching warily.

The old man stormed toward Mason, a pissed off expression on his bearded, weathered face. "You Baldwin?"

"No. I'm his business partner." He stood his ground and moved in front of Ric, reading the aggression and rage in the man's posture and expression. "Who are you?"

"Ray Gladstone. I own this property," he snapped.

Mason frowned. "That's not what the title on it says."

The man's face twisted. "I don't give a goddamn what the paperwork says!" He thumped a finger into his chest. "I own this land, it's been in my family for five goddamn generations, and I won't sell it to *anyone*."

What the hell was this? This was the first Mason had heard of any internal friction with the owners. "Ray, the seller already accepted our offer. As soon as the bank—"

"My family can go to hell. I never agreed to the sale, so you can take your offer and shove it where the sun don't shine."

Okay, then. "You need to take this up with whoever is on the title. Not me. But it's already a done deal." Almost.

The old man's eyes widened with fury. Mason braced himself as Ray came at him, taking a swing at Mason's face, but he ducked and moved out of the way. He wasn't going to hit an old man, no matter how angry the guy was.

"Hey," the surveyor snapped, storming toward them.

Mason held out a hand to stop him, his gaze trained on Ray, who had caught his balance and whirled to face him, shaking with rage. There was no way he was getting into a fight with an old man. Old-timer had no idea he was facing off with a former JTF2 operator.

"We're not doing this. You need to take it up with your relatives," Mason told him firmly. "And if you harass me or my partners again, I'm calling the police."

Ray straightened and took a deep breath, glaring holes into Mason's face. "I'm warning you, get out of here *now*. This land isn't for sale. Not while I'm still breathing." With that he spun and stormed back to his truck.

It reversed and roared down the driveway, its tires kicking up gravel and dirt as Ray sped away.

Mason looked over at the surveyor, who looked stunned. "Know him?"

"Not really. Seen him around town at the bar a couple times. Damn."

Mason nodded. "Thanks for coming out." He let Ric in the passenger side of the Jeep, then got in and fired up the engine. A seed of worry took root in his gut. Ray might be pushing eighty, but he was mad as hell and might cause enough trouble with his relatives to get the deal pulled.

On the drive back to town he called Tate to tell him the news. "Ray Gladstone?" Tate said, sounding confused. "He wasn't listed on the title."

"I know. But you might want to talk to whoever was, to make sure this won't be a problem. He threw a punch at me."

"Wow. All right, will do. You heading back to town now?"

"No, I'm gonna take Ric for a hike first." He needed to blow off some steam and clear his head.

He drove to a spot he'd found soon after moving to Rifle Creek, and called his mom in Calgary on the way. "Hey," he said when she answered.

"Mason! How are you, babe?"

He loved that she still called him that. She'd fostered dozens of kids in her lifetime, but he was the only one she called babe. Just hearing her voice made everything better, erasing the anxiety beginning to churn in his mind. "Good. May have a little hiccup with the property we offered on, but I hope not." It was the best available piece of land in the area, and he was already in love with it. He didn't want to lose it now.

"Why, what happened?"

He explained the situation. "It's probably nothing. Just got me thinking."

"Yeah, too much, probably."

That made him grin. She knew him better than anyone, even himself. "Yeah, probably."

"You know what? You can stop worrying right now, because I have a good feeling about all this. It's going to work out and you're going to be happy there."

He shook his head fondly. "I need to introduce you to Nina. Between your gut feelings and her insane optimism, you two could conquer the world together."

"Tate's girlfriend, right? I'd love to meet her. By the way, how's the new digs working out for you and your

35

boy?"

She and Ric loved each other to a ridiculous degree. "So far, so good."

"Yeah? Landlord's nice?"

"Yeah, she's real nice." A little frosty to him, maybe, but she'd still let him rent her suite when he'd needed a place. She must like him a little. "And I think she's starting to warm to me a little. We're going to a wedding together this weekend."

Nancy was quiet a second. "Mason, you tell me everything right now."

He chuckled at the demand, easily picturing her leaning against the kitchen counter in her faded jeans and a sweater, her long gray hair up in a ponytail, all her attention on him as she stared out the window above the sink. "She needed someone to go with her. It's a three-day thing at a guest ranch near Billings."

"You're spending three days with a bunch of strangers for her?" She sounded skeptical.

"Yep."

"So then you're into her." Satisfaction dripped from every word.

Oh, he was into Avery. More than he'd been into any woman in a damn long time. If she wasn't Tate's partner, he would definitely be trying to get her into bed. Not that he was going to say that to the woman he considered to be his mother. "I'm just helping her out."

"Oh." She sounded disappointed. "So you're…not together?"

He smiled at her tone. "No." Not yet. But hopefully that would change. He was going to take advantage of their forced relationship status to see how far he could move the needle with her this weekend. He was sick of her ignoring him. He wanted her to notice him, and know he wasn't the only one affected by the chemistry between them. "But I think I just may have found my footing here."

"I think so too. But Mason?"

"Hmm?"

"If you decide she's special to you, promise me you won't walk away."

A sinking sensation filled his chest. His immediate reaction was to get defensive, to deny he would do that. But she was dead on. That's exactly what he did when things got too intense—he walked.

Until Nancy, who'd taken in another scared, angry kid and kept him despite all the shitty things he'd done, all the ways he'd acted out. Pushing her and everyone else away because to him it was a foregone conclusion that they'd eventually dump him too.

But not Nancy. She'd stuck with him through everything, had raised him with firm but kind rules and boundaries, tons of love he still wasn't sure he'd deserved, and eventually taught him to trust her. She was the only person in his entire life he'd ever felt complete security with.

She'd taught him what unconditional love meant and felt like. For that she would always have his undying love and gratitude, and she'd more than earned the title of mother. "Thanks, Mom. Love you."

"I love you too. Give Ric a cuddle for me."

"I will. Bye."

Mason continued to drive, lost in his thoughts. He'd had a few moderately serious relationships, but they always fizzled. The last time, his girlfriend had still been in love with the guy who'd come before him. Mason had come home one day to find she'd moved out. Gone back to her ex.

So even though he was more interested in Avery than he had been in anyone in forever, he wouldn't soon forget the lesson that had confirmed the deep-seated fear he'd carried since he was a kid.

Maybe he was unlovable after all.

****

Shannon waited for the guard to escort her into the prison visiting room. She followed him, unable to keep the smile off her face as she neared the small table in the room already crowded by families visiting their prisoner.

Excitement flooded her. She couldn't wait to tell Mike what she'd been working on. She'd found them the perfect starter house, a little brick bungalow at a good price, miles out in the countryside where no one would bother or judge them. If he liked it, she would go look at it today and maybe put an offer in. She could swing all their expenses on her own for a month or two, and with his impending parole, he'd be able to get a job and help pay the bills.

Her heart skipped a beat when she saw Mike already waiting for her in his orange jumpsuit. His wrist and ankle restraints had been removed. He'd shaved, looking better than he had in ages. And the way he watched her was so damn sexy she almost shivered.

"Hi," she said as she sat in front of him, only half-listening to the guard's instructions. No touching, no gifts. Blah, blah. She was impatient to tell Mike everything.

The guard retreated to stand at the side of the room, watching them. Shannon didn't care. She was just so glad to be able to talk to Mike alone after two weeks of no contact. She had no family anymore. All the men she'd been with had treated her like shit—until Mike. He'd changed her entire world, and now they were planning for their future together.

"You look good," Mike told her, his brown eyes sweeping over her face, and lower, to the cleavage her new pushup bra and low-cut top showed off. She'd worn them just for him, to show him what he could have when he got out of here.

"Thanks. You look good too." Since meeting him

online eight months ago she'd fallen totally in love with him. He was brilliant, he wasn't dangerous to her, and he'd paid more attention to her than any man she'd ever been with, even though he'd been behind bars the entire time. After being alone for so long, she would do anything to be with him.

But now that she was up close to him, she could see something was wrong. His expression was set, distant, angry lines around his mouth and between his eyes. The urge to reach for his hands was so strong she had to curl hers into fists to stop it. "What's wrong?"

His jaw flexed. "My parole was denied."

She stared at him, sure she'd heard wrong, all her dreams crumbling to dust in front of her eyes. "No."

"Yeah. Just found out the other day. I'm not getting outta here."

Grief washed through her at the desolation in his eyes. "Don't say that. You can't give up hope."

He didn't answer, and her own anger began to build. "What happened?" she asked. "Do you know?" With the amount of time already served on his sentence and his good behavior, the parole board should have granted his early release.

"That bitch cop turned the parole board against me."

Avery Dahl.

Shannon would never forget that name. That woman was the main reason Mike was in here.

Shannon pressed her lips together as hot tears flooded her eyes. She'd planned her life around being with Mike. Was working two jobs right now to save money in a special account for them. They were supposed to move in together as soon as he was released, then get married. Leave this state and start over fresh, just the two of them.

He'd promised. She'd pinned all her hopes and

dreams on him; he was the only man who'd ever understood her. The only person who'd ever really loved her, and she couldn't go on without him for much longer. It hurt too much.

"Don't fucking cry. I'm the one locked up in here, not you," he growled.

She shook her head and wiped her tears away, not bothered by his anger. He was bitterly disappointed, she could forgive him for snapping. "How much longer will you have to wait?"

Resentment burned in his gaze. "I dunno. Another five years, maybe, who knows."

Five years? She'd be almost thirty by then. She didn't want to be alone that long, didn't want to have to wait that long to start their life together.

The shocking news ruined the visit. She left twenty minutes later disheartened and sick to her stomach.

But by the time she'd reached her vehicle, she had already begun to formulate a plan. Because this wasn't right. Something had to be done.

Mike was trapped in prison. He needed her more than ever. He couldn't do anything to right this wrong.

But she could.

She had taken revenge on some enemies before. Last time she'd even torched a bitch's car, burning down the garage and half the house before the fire department put it out. No one had ever found out it was her. And that act of retribution had been in retaliation for a personal affront. Keeping Shannon's man in prison when he deserved to be set free called for decisive action.

Her mind was already racing ahead. Avery Dahl wasn't a common name. How hard could it be to find her? And once Shannon did...

Resolve hardened inside her like steel. She couldn't free Mike, but she could get revenge for him.

Avery had fucked up Shannon's life. Now Shannon

would fuck up hers.

CHAPTER FIVE

The past week had felt more like a month, but the wait was finally over.

Mason waited by his Jeep as Avery locked the front door of her red-brick Victorian house and wheeled her suitcase down the brick walkway toward him. She was dressed in a snug pair of dark jeans that hugged her long legs, and a purple sweater under her leather jacket.

She looked sexy as hell, and he couldn't wait to start their weekend together. He'd only seen her in passing since Saturday, but that all ended now.

"Good to go?" he asked, opening the trunk.

"Yes. You shaved."

He ran a hand over his smooth jaw. "Is that bad?" He'd figured he better clean up before meeting her friends and family.

"No, not at all." She started to lift her suitcase but he took it from her. "I can do it," she said in an annoyed tone.

"I know you can. But it's called manners. And since you're supposedly mine this weekend, my part starts now."

Her eyebrows drew together. "You don't need to pretend yet," she muttered, and started for the passenger side. Mason shut the back and rushed around to open her door for her. She paused and looked up at him. "And this is just manners too?"

What the hell kind of guys was she used to, if him opening doors for her was such a shock? It was just polite, and when she was with him, she should expect it. "Yep."

She climbed in and he shut the door for her before going around to the driver's side. "Where's Ric?" she asked as she put on her seatbelt.

"I already dropped him off at Tate's. He's sulking, but he'll forget all about me once Tate starts throwing the ball for him in the backyard. They're taking him to Coeur D'Alene with them."

"I doubt he'll forget about you. You guys are pretty attached to each other."

"Yep." He'd never had any pets growing up, except for the final and best foster home he'd been put in, where they'd had a little dog. When Tate had suggested Mason look into finding a therapy dog specifically trained for veterans with PTSD, he had initially dismissed the idea, embarrassed that his friend thought he needed help.

Turned out, getting Ric was the best decision he'd ever made.

The dog was his shadow and best friend. Ric slept beside him every night and woke him when he was in the grips of a nightmare. When anxiety got the better of him, Ric usually sensed it before it reached crisis point and would lean on or nudge him, helping to ground Mason along with the exercises he'd been taught to combat it.

As a result, he was doing way better now than he had in the past, though he would never be the same person he was before the horrific crash and ensuing firefight that would forever haunt him. "What can I say? I love that dog."

The hint of a smile tugged at her lips. "I know. It's super cute."

So she didn't think he was a total asshole, then. That was good. "So, what kind of music do you like?"

She shrugged. "Anything but metal. You?"

"Country, baby, all the way. That all right with you?"

"Sure."

He turned on the radio to provide some background noise as he drove. This was the first time they'd been together since dinner at Tate's a week ago. They had a six-hour drive ahead of them, and given the close quarters they would be in together for the next three days, he didn't want things to start off on an awkward note. "So did you tell your mom about me?"

"Yes. I told her we met through friends—which we did—and that we've only been seeing each other for a few weeks. That'll make our backstory easier, because it's close to the truth and the timeline works. And while we're on the topic, we should go over the ground rules."

Mason fought a smile as he headed for the highway. He'd expected her to be a little uptight about the whole thing, and would have been disappointed if she hadn't. She'd probably been second-guessing her decision to go with him since she'd made it. "I like rules." Mostly because he liked bending them until they broke.

"Good." She rubbed her palms over her thighs, then clasped her hands in her lap. "I'm not comfortable with PDAs, so don't try any."

He arched an eyebrow at her. "We've been together for weeks, you bring me to a weekend-long family wedding, and I'm not allowed to make any public displays of affection?"

"Right."

He snorted. "Come on."

"What?" She shot him an annoyed look.

"That's ridiculous. No one will believe we're together."

"Sure they will, because they know me. We'll just be subtle about it. Classy."

He gave her a telling look. "You might have noticed, but I'm not the subtle type."

Her cheeks turned a bit pink. "You can be subtle for one weekend."

She'd soon learn that he wasn't much for rule following when he thought the rules were stupid. Not that he was going to tell her that. Way more fun to let her find out on her own. "If you were mine, I'd let everyone know it."

"What's that mean?" Her tone held a note of alarm.

"It means I wouldn't be subtle," he said, throwing the word back at her.

Her fingers fidgeted in her lap. "My family's pretty conservative, and they'll all be curious about us. I'm not comfortable with—"

"Hey." He reached over to squeeze her hand. He'd never seen her like this, anxious and a little unsure of herself. He didn't like seeing her worried, so unlike the confident, put-together woman he'd seen over the past month-and-a-half. "Let's just let things happen naturally, okay? We'll play it by ear, but even if I'm not your version of subtle, I'm not going to embarrass you or anything."

She let out a relieved breath when he released her hand. "Then there's the bed issue," she went on. "I've asked them to bring a cot to our room, or put us in a room with a pullout bed for you."

He shook his head. "We've been together for weeks and I can't even sleep on the far side of the bed from you. That's cold, Avery. Why are we together again?" If she was his, no fucking way she'd be sleeping alone in the bed. He'd be touching her every chance he got, getting her worked up, making her wet and needy for him.

"Those are the rules, Mason," she said firmly. "And we'll take turns with who gets first shower."

"Or, we could—"

"*Don't* say it."

That was better, her anxiety was gone again. Damn he loved her sense of authority. It challenged his dominant side, made him want to find out what it would take to peel all that control away from her in bed.

Arousal stirred in his gut at the thought. He'd fantasized about that so many times since meeting her. Had thought about her way too much and couldn't seem to stop. "Is it your family you're more worried about seeing?"

"No. Well, yes. Kind of. But mostly my ex. Anyway, enough about me. What about your family? I don't know anything about them."

It wasn't a pretty story, and not one he wanted to share with her yet because like her, he didn't want to be the object of pity. So he gave her the abbreviated version. Maybe he'd tell her more later, depending on how things went with them. "There's only my mom in Calgary."

She nodded. "Are you close?"

"Yeah."

"Any siblings?"

Dozens of foster kids his mom had taken in over the years. He only kept in touch with a couple of them via email now. "No. So, what do you like to do for fun?"

"I thought we were talking about you now."

"Not gonna answer?"

"I like to eat."

He shot her a quizzical look and she laughed softly, the happy sound making him smile a little. "It's true. I love to eat. I just hate cooking for myself all the time," she said. "It's a drag."

"I like to eat too. See?" he teased. "We've got something in common after all."

She nodded, the hint of a smile tugging at her lips. "And we've both got great taste in friends."

"Hell yeah, we do." Tate rocked, and Nina was a sweetheart. Quirky and nerdy and she had her head in the clouds—or space—half the time, but a sweetheart none-theless.

"Tell me more about you and Tate, and Braxton. Tate's talked about him but I've never met him."

"Where do I even start?" Mason said with a fond smile.

"At the beginning. We've got over six hours to kill."

"Okay, then." He told her about how bored he'd been in the regular army until he'd finally served long enough to try out for JTF2. He'd met Braxton at Dwyer Hill in Ontario during selection. "Eventually we made the unit together. Brax is a sniper."

"Was selection as awful as I imagine?" she asked.

"Yep, and worse. But I loved it. The challenge of it. Guys started dropping out right away. We lost over twenty-percent in the first three days."

"Did you ever think about quitting?"

He'd be lying if he said no. "Once. It was the middle of January on the prairies and we'd just finished a winter training exercise. I was beat up, hungry, freezing and mis-erable. But so was everyone else, and when I looked around, it hit me again that there weren't many of us left. I decided I'd come too far and gone through too much to give up then. So I sucked it up and stopped thinking about how shitty everything seemed or felt. I did one task. Just one, then another. Then the next. And the next, until I'd made it through."

"That's pretty amazing. Tate's told me things about his time in the Marines that sounded damn awful. I admire all of you a lot for your service."

Her praise touched a hidden place deep inside him that he never let anyone see, even as it made him a little uncomfortable too. "We were all just doing our jobs." Brax was still doing his. And Mason would have given anything to be there with him. "What made you decide to be a cop?"

"I didn't, until I was thirty-two. I had a psych degree and didn't know what to do with it. I worked in a few different jobs but nothing felt right. I knew I wanted to help people and make a difference, and the thought of taking down bad guys was a major bonus. My family was horrified," she added with a chuckle.

"Really?"

"My mom almost had a heart attack. Was convinced I was going to die on every patrol I went on while I was a beat cop. I used to have to text her after each shift to prove I was still alive," she finished with a wry smile, then looked over at him. "Your mom must have worried about you a lot."

"I think she did, but she hid it well. She's a tough lady. Sent the best care packages ever, full of homemade stuff. The guys would always fight over whatever she sent."

"She sounds like an incredible mom."

"She is. She's been there for me through everything, just like all the other kids she's fostered over the years."

Avery stared at him. "You were a foster kid?"

"Yeah. But she's my mom. Without her and the military, I wouldn't be here."

"You still miss it?"

He nodded, jaw tightening. "Every day." How weird was it that he missed something that had almost killed him several times? But he did. Missed the brotherhood and the sense of belonging, knowing he was part of something elite that most people could never do.

The *hard,* was what made it great. Having all that taken away so suddenly was still unbearable some days.

"Anyway, after I was discharged from the Canadian

Forces, I was laid up for a while." Having surgeries on his knees and back from the injuries sustained in the crash that still haunted him, and he didn't want to talk about any of it. His mom and Brax were the only two people he'd ever told what really happened that day. "Once I was healed up, I decided to give contracting a shot, and that's when I met Tate. You know the rest."

"It's so strange how everyone's connected," she mused.

He changed the subject by asking her more about her work as a detective. They talked about various things, then lapsed into a comfortable silence for the rest of the first half of the trip.

After stopping for lunch at a barbecue place just off the highway, they carried on to Billings. Avery dozed for a bit until they were twenty miles outside of town.

Once they reached the city limit, she got really quiet again, and he could all but feel the tension building inside her. The guest ranch was located eleven miles outside the city.

Mason turned into the main parking lot and let out a low whistle. "Looks even more expensive in person." The pictures on the website hadn't done it justice. "So this is a low-end wedding, is it?"

One side of her mouth lifted. "Ha, no. My family doesn't do weddings half-assed." She got out and headed for the trunk.

Mason lifted her suitcase out, then grabbed his duffel and garment bag. Slinging them both over one shoulder, he shut the trunk, locked the Jeep and curled an arm around Avery's waist. She froze, looking up at him with startled, golden eyes.

He held her gaze and kept his hand firmly on her waist. "If you're going to tense up on me like that every time I touch you, we're never gonna pull this off," he murmured.

She searched his eyes a moment, and he felt that electrical current again, buzzing between them and all across his skin. Then she lowered her gaze and nodded. "Okay. Let's do this."

Yeah, let's.

The main building of the lodge was a huge, three-story craftsman-style log building with the lobby and reception rooms in the center, and large guest wings extending from either side. Private cabins and other buildings were scattered around the rear of the resort.

A dozen or so people were milling around the lobby when they entered, while the sunset glowed through the bank of massive windows that covered the back wall. A rock fireplace rose right up to the beams spanning the ceiling, a large wood fire ablaze in the grate.

Avery tensed a little and looked around. Mason squeezed her waist gently and walked her over to the front desk to check in. Several people rushed over to embrace her. Avery introduced him to an aunt, two cousins and a nephew, who all watched him with open curiosity.

"See you guys later tonight," Avery said when they were done, and turned to face the front desk.

"Avery Dahl," she said, handing over her ID to the clerk. "Checking out Sunday."

"Welcome, Ms. Dahl, we're glad to have you." The clerk typed something into his computer. "Okay, we've got you in the Ponderosa cabin. It's got an incredible view of the lake from the loft bedroom."

Avery frowned. "Cabin? No, I'm in the main lodge with the rest of my family. We're here for the wedding—"

"I upgraded us to a luxury cabin," Mason said, aware of her relatives watching and listening nearby.

Avery snapped her head around to gape at him. "What? Why would you—"

He settled his hands on her hips and tugged her close,

aware of the eyes on them. "Nothing but the best for my lady," he said, loud enough for the others to hear him, then dropped a kiss on her lips, which were still parted in surprise.

She tensed and sucked in a breath but he was already lifting his head and curling an arm around her to pull her into his side. It was no hardship for him to play this role, and it felt eerily natural to claim her publicly. He liked it. Maybe too much.

"How many beds does it have?" she said to the clerk.

"A king-size."

She frowned and lowered her voice, maybe hoping her relatives wouldn't overhear. "Is there a pullout couch? He snores."

Mason grinned and nuzzled the hair next to her temple, breathing in the clean vanilla scent of her. "You're gonna find out whether I do or not soon enough," he murmured, and choked back a laugh at the tiny jab of her sharp elbow in his ribs.

"I'm afraid not, but there's a loveseat and an armchair," the clerk said. "You could pull them together if necessary to make another bed, though I'm not sure he would be comfortable that way, given his height."

Mason straightened and pressed his lips together to keep from smiling. Avery was clearly not happy, but he was.

She let out an irritated sigh. "Will we be able to check into a different room tomorrow?"

"No, unfortunately all rooms and cabins are fully booked for the entire weekend." He gave her an apologetic look. "I'm sorry."

"It's...fine," she muttered, and handed over her credit card.

Mason caught her hand and pushed it back toward her. "It's already paid for. I'll take that," he said to the clerk, snagging the key.

Avery glared up at him. He raised an eyebrow and subtly indicated her relatives with a sideways glance. The glare disappeared, a sweet smile forming in its place, even as her eyes shot sparks at him. "Shall we?"

"Yes. Can't *wait* to get you alone." He dropped another kiss on her lips and slung his arm around her shoulders as they headed for the rear exit that would lead to the path to the cabins.

"Don't look so happy," she muttered under her breath as they stepped outside.

Mason smiled to himself and started whistling softly, smart enough not to push her more right now. This was the most fun he'd had in forever.

WHAT THE HELL just happened?

Avery felt like she'd been run over with a steamroller as she walked beside him down the pea gravel path toward the cabins, slightly dazed. She couldn't say anything to him yet, there were people around. Thankfully none of her relatives or her ex, but still.

She was acutely aware of his heavy arm curled around her shoulders, the warmth and strength of it. His body heat and crisp, clean scent teasing her.

It did things to her. Things she didn't *want* happening to her, and worse, he seemed to be enjoying this.

He'd also kissed her in front of everyone. Twice. The first time he'd caught her so off guard she hadn't been ready for it. But the second...

Shit, she was still feeling it, her lips tingling. He'd shaved off his short beard, and was possibly even more gorgeous without it. A rush of heat sped through her, pooling low in her belly and tightening her nipples. *Dammit, no.*

"This is us," he said, turning off the main pathway.

The two-story log cabin sat perched on a little knoll overlooking the lake. Trailing pink and yellow flowers spilled from window boxes along the front porch, with two blue rocking chairs flanking the front door.

It was charming. And the absolute last place she wanted to be alone with Mason.

He unlocked the door for her and she marched inside, towing her suitcase. The instant he shut it behind him, she rounded on him. "What are you doing?" she demanded.

"What?" All innocence, Mason set the key on the table by the door.

"You know what. This cabin. Why did you do this?"

He faced her, and in this cozy space being alone with him suddenly felt way too intimate. "Because I know you're stressed and wanted you to be able to relax and actually enjoy yourself a little this weekend. I thought this would give you more privacy to unwind away from everyone."

She eyed him, one hand still holding her suitcase handle. "And it had nothing to do with you wanting privacy for an ulterior motive." Because that so wasn't happening.

He grinned. "Why, would you be interested if I had one?"

The balls on him. What game was he playing? "I believe I made the rules clear. Speaking of..." She let go of her suitcase and went up the stairs to the loft.

Dammit, the king-size bed took up the entire loft, with no room for a cot, and the downstairs was too crowded for one. She'd gone through a rough time during and after the divorce. She'd been married, had devoted herself to a man who, as it turned out, hadn't ever really loved her. Now she was stuck in this private and romantic cabin with a man way too good-looking and sexy and damaged for her own good, who had heartbreak written all over him.

What the hell had she been thinking, doing this to herself?

She marched back down the stairs. "I hope you can fold up on that loveseat."

Mason set his duffel on the floor and cocked a dark brown eyebrow at her, the setting sun's rays streaming through the windows at the back of the cabin overlooking the lake bathed him in a warm glow. Outlining the mouth-watering lines of his powerful frame.

She raised her chin. "Just because you paid for this doesn't mean you're getting anything more than we agreed on."

His expression cooled, a spark of anger flashing in his eyes. "I don't want anything you don't want to give, so no worries there."

Avery checked her attitude, chastened. She'd offended him. He'd given up his weekend to help her out. And if he'd truly booked this for her to have more privacy from everyone, then she felt bad for what she'd said. "I'm sorry, I shouldn't have said that. I'm just…"

"Flustered."

She shot him a glare, annoyed that he read her so easily and that her damn cheeks were getting hot. "I'm not flustered," she snapped. "Just, whatever, let's get through this weekend and then things can go back to normal again."

She grabbed her suitcase when he reached for it and carried it up the stairs, berating herself with every step. This had been a colossally stupid idea on her part, and she had no one to blame for her predicament but herself.

Between being cooped up alone here with Mason after pretending he was her boyfriend in front of her family and dreading the moment she came face to face with her ex, she was going to need to get drunk to get through it all.

Dammit. She already couldn't wait for this weekend to be over.

CHAPTER SIX

There she was.

Shannon turned away from the lobby and walked toward the hallway leading to the east guest wing, her heart drumming hard against her ribs. She smiled at several guests who passed her, then paused, standing with her back to the wall in order to survey her target.

Avery's height and bright-colored hair made it easy to spot her amongst the people milling around the lobby. Shannon watched as she spoke with the front desk clerk.

Hatred swelled inside her. She'd found out everything she could about Avery Dahl over the past week. It had been harder than she'd thought. Searching social media and other sources online hadn't netted much. Avery kept a low profile. But her family roots ran deep in Billings.

After some digging, it hadn't taken long for Shannon to locate a cousin of Avery's, and a little bit more investigation after that had informed her about this big, fancy wedding. From other family members' social media posts, Shannon had been able to get the date and location. She'd banked on Avery being here as well, and so far, all the effort Shannon had put in and the risks she'd taken had paid off.

There was one thing Shannon hadn't anticipated, however.

Avery was with a man. A huge guy, maybe in his thirties, wearing a black cowboy hat. He radiated a palpable confidence that said he could handle himself. A cop, like Avery? And were they actually together? The online posts about the wedding she'd read where Avery's name was mentioned had made it sound like she was single.

He was big, and the way he carried himself, the way his gaze scanned the lobby, told her he was more aware of his surroundings than the average person.

Their gazes collided for a second.

Shannon quickly looked away and nonchalantly began wiping down the exterior window next to her, keeping her body angled so she could still watch them out of the corner of her eye. The man glanced away and she breathed easier.

Her question about Avery's relationship status was answered a moment later when the guy turned Avery toward him and kissed her. Avery looked a bit stiff as she stared up at him, but whatever. Maybe they'd had a fight or something earlier.

The man took the key from the clerk, wrapped an arm around Avery's shoulders and started for the door at the rear of the lobby, leading out to the grounds. Shannon was surprised. They weren't staying in the main lodge with everyone else?

She grabbed a pile of linens from a chambermaid's cart and followed them, keeping her distance so they wouldn't notice. Her stolen resort uniform helped her blend in easily, but that big guy had already caught her watching him once. She couldn't let him notice again. People dismissed her with a polite smile as she passed them, not giving her a second glance.

Outside, a gravel path split into two as it reached the main lawn in the center of the grounds, each leading away from the main lodge. To the right it led to the chapel and gazebo. To the left, a row of private cabins overlooking the lake.

Fury burned in her gut as she followed Avery and the big guy toward the cabins. They were three times the price of a room in the lodge. Avery and her man were apparently living the high life this weekend.

She maintained her distance, battling the anger with every step, her hands crushing the linens. Avery and the guy turned up the path to the second cabin from the end.

Shannon kept her face averted and continued past it, scouting out the location as she did. The Ponderosa. It was set back from the others toward the lake, making it the most private of the cabins. She could just imagine the spectacular view from the luxurious bedroom up in the loft.

She clenched her jaw as her feet crunched over the gravel. It wasn't fair that Avery got to be with her man and spend the weekend fucking him in that gorgeous, romantic cabin when Shannon's was still behind bars because of her.

At least now she could get revenge. She'd wanted a chance to ruin Avery's life, and had the skills to make it happen. Fire was one, and she'd used it in various ways over the years. Its destructive power could be used in subtle ways that still caused great fear. And she had her firearms training to protect herself if necessary.

A direct, physical attack would have to wait, however. Avery was trained, so Shannon would have to catch her with her guard down, and that would be even harder with that guy around.

When Shannon did strike, she wouldn't make it quick. First, she wanted to torment Avery, then wreck her career. Starting here.

A cold, hard smile stretched her lips. Shannon prided herself on her creative talents. And now she had a whole weekend to put her plan into action.

****

Here we go.

Avery put on her mental armor as she and Mason reached the main lodge for the family-only dinner reception an hour later. She even managed not to stiffen when he reached down to grasp her hand, but the contact sent a jolt all the way up her arm. His hand was so warm compared to hers, his strong fingers twining with hers.

"Nervous?" he murmured as they reached the massive French doors at the back of the lodge.

"No." She was totally nervous. On pins and needles at the thought of faking this in front of her family, and of running into her ex again, and Mason looking so dark and sexy and smelling so amazing wasn't helping matters—though it was a major confidence boost to walk in there on his arm. "You?"

"Nope. I've got the most beautiful woman in the whole place on my arm."

She aimed a bland look at him, but the hint of a grin on his face and the admiration in his eyes stopped her from making a sarcastic comeback. Hell. She didn't know what to do with him when he dropped the cocky front and became human with her like this.

"Don't worry, I'll protect you," he whispered close to her ear as he pulled the door open for her, sending a tiny shiver of arousal down her spine.

His tone was a little teasing, but he was serious, she realized. She softened a little more. "Thank you. I'll protect you too, from my family. They're nosy."

Relatives were all over the place as soon as they

walked in. Avery stopped to say hi to some of them, introducing Mason, then continued on to the main reception room on the opposite side of the lobby where the buzz of voices was coming from.

Her parents and sister were already at their table, and their gazes shot to Avery and Mason the moment they stepped into the room. Her mom shot to her feet, beaming at them as they approached.

"Hi, Mom," Avery said, hugging her.

"I'm so glad you're here!" She squeezed Avery, then kind of shoved her aside to look at Mason.

"You must be Mason." Her mom scoffed at the hand he extended and grabbed him in a hug instead. "I'm so glad you're here too."

He returned the embrace, grinning at Avery. "Nice to meet you."

"Not as nice as it is to meet *you*." Her mom beamed up at him. "My, she didn't tell us how handsome you were."

"Mom," Avery said on a groan, reaching out to hug her sister and dad.

"What? He is."

"Avery said I'd like you," Mason said to her mom. "And she was right."

Avery refrained from rolling her eyes and introduced him to her dad and sister. Mason pulled out her chair for her and pushed her in, trailing his fingers down the side of her neck as he moved to his own. She stiffened, sparks of heat snapping over her skin.

Her dad was watching them curiously, but her mom and sister both leaned forward to prop their chins on their hands and stare at them. "So, tell us about you guys," her mom said. "How you met, your first date."

Avery opened her mouth to respond but Mason smoothly cut her off. "We met through a mutual friend."

He gave her a heated, approving look that made her insides flutter. "And I still owe him for it."

Avery flushed a little, trying not to fidget with her hands in her lap. "He only moved into town a few weeks ago. That's why we'd never met before."

"The first time I laid eyes on her, I knew I had to make her mine," Mason said. "It wasn't easy, but eventually I managed to convince her to give me a chance."

Avery shot him a warning look but her mom and sister both sighed, utterly charmed. "You must have made a real impression on her," her sister said. "I didn't think Ave would ever risk a relationship again."

Avery shot her a quelling look but Mason nodded, his expression turning serious. "I'm grateful every day that she was willing to give me a chance." He draped an arm around her, pulling her close to kiss her temple.

Avery smothered the urge to laugh, caught somewhere between amusement and shock. Mason was coming on strong. Damn, he was good. Everything he did and said looked and felt sincere, even though she knew it was an act.

It also hurt a little, too, because even though it was all fake, deep down she'd missed this. The affection, sure, but more the feeling of being important to and valued by her partner. It's what she'd craved from her husband throughout their marriage and never gotten.

As if he somehow sensed her inner turmoil, Mason bent his head to whisper to her, his nose nuzzling her ear. "Loosen up a bit. You look freaking terrified and you're ruining the plan."

She summoned a smile and forced herself to relax, leaning into him until she was cuddled against his shoulder. Of course, that only made the tension inside her worse. Every time he got close, every time he touched her, her body lit up and tingled.

All over. In places she didn't want any tingling

where he was concerned. It made her start thinking about the idea of more with him. Sexy, erotic things she couldn't help imagining.

"Tell us about your first date," her mom said, eyes gleaming with excitement.

Mason was partway through some fictional story about going hiking for a picnic up in the mountains when the bride and groom arrived to a raucous round of cheers and applause.

Avery sighed in relief and joined in the applause. The couple addressed the guests, thanking everyone for coming and acknowledging their immediate family and those who had traveled from far away. After a short grace, people began heading for the buffet.

Mason led her to it with a solid hand on the small of her back, just inches from the base of her spine. Her skin warmed, heat spreading out in all directions and pooling low in her abdomen. It felt good. He smelled good, and shit, he was so damn sexy in the cobalt blue button-down shirt, dark slacks and his black cowboy hat.

She could feel the curious eyes on them as they waited in line. She reached for a plate but Mason beat her to it, and insisted on filling her plate for her. Avery went along with it, playing it up like it was the most normal thing in the world to have a man take care of her, when it was exactly the opposite.

On their way back to their seats, Avery caught the way her mother's face tightened slightly as she stared at someone behind Avery. Then her gaze darted to Avery, and Avery's stomach clenched.

Before she could even turn around, the familiar scent of Doug's cologne wafted to her. She tensed instinctively, her hands tightening around her silverware. Had he seen her? Was he—

"Avery."

Steeling herself, she turned to face him and pasted on

a civil smile. "Doug. Hi." He was still handsome, but thankfully this time there was no punch to the gut, no swell of hurt or sadness when she looked at him. She could feel everyone staring, though. Watching to see what happened. "How are you?" She only said it to be polite, because she actually didn't give a shit.

"Good. Busy." His smile was the same. Charming as ever. Then he glanced behind him at someone, and a sharp pain lanced Avery's chest. His wife Keely was blond and tiny and petite, the swell of her belly outlined beneath her dress. She was probably sweet and submissive, too. In short, polar opposite to Avery in every way.

"I see that." It hurt to look at her, but the damn proud smile on Doug's face made her long to scrub it off him. With sandpaper.

A strong, heavy arm wrapped around her shoulders, jolting her from her thoughts as Mason hugged her into his side. Avery leaned into him, battling the stiffness in her muscles, grateful for his warmth because she suddenly felt chilled.

Doug's gaze shifted to him, and she could practically see him sizing Mason up, looking for shortcomings as if Mason was some sort of rival.

Avery had had more than enough. "Well, enjoy the dinner." She started to step past him, eager to escape.

Doug's eyes snapped back to her, and she took satisfaction in seeing the confidence bleed from his expression. "Yeah. You too. We'll see you around."

Hopefully not. She gave a tight nod and let out a quiet breath as he and Keely walked away.

"You okay?" her mom murmured when they reached the table, watching her anxiously.

"Of course." She picked up her wine and took a sip, ignoring her ex as he crossed the room.

A strange thought hit her. *What did I ever see in him?* She pitied Keely in a way, because it was only a matter of time before he tired of her too and quit trying because the thrill of the hunt was gone. Worse, there was a child involved now and would be for its whole life.

At least Avery didn't have to go through life being tied to him that way. In a way, he'd done her a favor because now she was free. Being lonely when she was free was a whole lot better than being lonely while married.

"You did great," her sister said, squeezing her arm in support. "Very dignified. More than I would have been."

"Because she's classy," Mason said, planting a kiss on her cheek.

His lips lingered, nuzzling. Tempting her into imagining what it would be like to turn her head and meet them with her own.

Tingles scattered across her skin, fanning out in a wave that tightened her nipples and made her core clench.

God. He was only playing and she was ready to melt. It made her wonder what it would be like to feel the full power of his sensuality directed at her. Goosebumps rose and she squeezed her legs together to stem the throb there.

Mason's hand rubbed over her shoulder. "You cold?"

"A little," she lied. Try turned on. Hot, and getting hotter.

"So, Avery, tell us more about your first date," her sister said, mercifully changing the subject.

She looked at Mason, got lost for a moment in that potent, pale blue gaze. "Do you want to tell the story?"

Amusement gleamed in his eyes. "No, you tell it so much better."

She couldn't help but grin a little at him, and just like that, all the residual tension inside her eased. The worst was over. The people she loved most had met Mason, and the dreaded first encounter with Doug was over.

As the conversation flowed around the table, she began to relax even more. Mason was attentive and charming, allowing her another glimpse beneath that cocky intensity he usually wore.

He told a funny story about his time in the military and she laughed along with everyone else. The way he looked at her made her belly flip in the most delicious way, the attraction between them growing by the hour.

By the time the meal was over, she'd started to truly enjoy herself, and Mason's company. Maybe a little too much. On the plus side, she'd forgotten about Doug and Keely completely.

"Well, hate to be a wet blanket, but I'm ready for the kipper," her dad said, pushing his chair out from the table. "Think I'll turn in, it's gonna be a long day tomorrow."

Her mother poked him in the shoulder. "It's going to be a *fun* day," she corrected.

Well, it would be interesting, if nothing else. But not as interesting as the night ahead of her.

As everyone began to leave, she stood too. Mason helped pull her chair out and was right there to wrap his arm around her.

He felt so damn good, and a few times tonight as she'd watched him, she'd had to remind herself of why she needed to keep her hands off him. He tempted her in ways she'd never experienced before. Like he'd woken some dormant part of her she hadn't even known was there until now.

And now that it was awake, she couldn't seem to shut it off again.

He kept his arm around her as they stepped outside of the lodge onto the gravel pathway. The October evening was cool and crisp, with a light layer of mist clinging to the grass, and she finally felt like she could pull in a full breath again.

"How're you feeling?" he murmured.

She didn't pull away even though they were outside

and away from curious eyes, enjoying the warmth of his body and the feel of his arm around her. It was only in case someone was watching, she reminded herself, struggling a bit not to fall under his spell. "I'm good. You?"

"It went better than I thought."

She glanced up at him, amused. "Did you think it would be that bad?"

"I like your family," he said, evading the question.

"I like them too. And they liked you." Her mom practically seemed ready to accept him as a son-in-law.

"Your ex is a total fuckwad, though."

She laughed. "That's funny. But you're not wrong." When he didn't say anything else, she looked at him again. "Why, did you think it would be bad? Did you think I'd lose it when I saw him?"

"No." He stared straight ahead, avoiding her gaze. "I'm just not comfortable in crowds."

Avery's smile fell. Damn, she was aware that he battled personal demons, from things Tate had inferred and that Mason had a service dog. She'd never even considered that being around so many unfamiliar people might make his PTSD flare up. And he didn't even have Ric with him.

It made her feel selfish and inconsiderate. "God, I never even thought. I'm sorry—"

"No, it's fine," he said, shrugging it off. "But if your ex keeps trying to push your buttons while we're here, he's gonna wind up pushing mine." He gave her a pointed smile. "And then he'll wish he hadn't."

Avery stared at him, unsure what to say. Damn, when he got all protective like that, it was a hundred times harder to keep her hands to herself. To know that he cared enough to protect her and had her back was... Well, she'd never expected it, or the ache it caused deep in her chest.

The cabin windows glowed with warm lamplight as they walked up the path. Inside the Ponderosa, the staff had already been in to turn on a table lamp inside the door and light the fire in the hearth, bathing everything in warm, golden light. The entire setup oozed romance, and heightened her awareness of being alone in such an intimate space with the man she needed to keep at a distance.

She glanced up at the loft, resigned. He was six-three, she wasn't going to insist he try to squeeze onto the loveseat, or sleep on the floor. There was a comfortable king-size bed upstairs.

She looked over to find him watching her in a way that heated her insides. "Can we be grownups about this?"

His eyes gleamed with a trace of humor, and something more. Something far more unsettling than seeing Doug and Keely earlier.

Blatant desire.

He raised a dark eyebrow, his cocky attitude coming back. "You think I can't resist you?"

He was probably teasing, but she couldn't tell. Was he messing with her? He was so convincing earlier and now he was all smoldery and putting her on edge again. "Can you?"

His lips curved. "I *can*…"

The way he trailed off like that left the unspoken question *but will I* hanging in the air between them. "Fine. What side do you want?"

"Whatever side you don't."

"I don't have a side. I usually sleep in the middle," she said, heading for her suitcase.

"What? Who sleeps in the middle of a king-size bed?"

"Me." Because it had been too lonely sleeping on one side with the other empty after she'd left Doug. "But I'll make allowances for this weekend."

She crouched to open her suitcase and took out the un-sexiest set of pajamas she owned, a pair of pink flannel jammies with kittens on them. A Christmas gift from her nephew. After changing into them in the bathroom and brushing her teeth, she emerged and came to an abrupt halt when she saw Mason.

He was lounging in the armchair facing the fire, his long legs stretched out in front of him, his hands resting on his flat belly as he watched her. The flames flickered over the planes of his face and the muscular contours of his chest and shoulders.

Her belly flipped, her breath catching as heat flooded her system. For a second, she couldn't move, or think.

Shit. Maybe she was the one who would lose control.

She cleared her throat. "Bathroom's all yours."

She hurried past him and up the stairs to the loft, threw back the covers on the wide bed and crawled across to the side nearest the window. The bathroom door shut downstairs.

She lay there staring up at the wooden beams framing the ceiling, her heart beating faster. This was dangerous. She already wanted him. Having him lying a few feet from her all night was going to be torture.

The bathroom door opened. Her heart picked up speed.

He came up the stairs slowly, and a little jolt traveled through her when he appeared at the top of them wearing jeans and a T-shirt, those sexy tats revealed on his forearms. Her favorite was the JTF2 emblem on his right arm—a half-globe and half a red maple leaf melded together with an upraised dagger between them, and a scroll beneath it framing the unit motto: *Facta Non Verba.*

Words, not deeds.

It said so much about him and the kind of man he was. And she couldn't stop imagining what he looked like underneath his clothes. Couldn't stop remembering the feel of his muscular arms around her and those brief, teasing kisses he'd dropped on her earlier.

A smile tugged at his mouth when he saw her already

curled up under the covers. "You look comfy."

"I am." And anything but relaxed with him about to crawl onto the bed with her.

She'd thought she might have to reiterate the sleeping on top of the covers rule, but he surprised her by turning to the wooden wardrobe beside the bed and taking out a quilt. The mattress dipped as he climbed on and stretched out.

Avery's pulse skipped. That was a whole lotta delicious man laid out right next to her. Seemed a shame to let it—and this opportunity—go to waste.

She mentally shook herself. *Cut it out.*

"Going to sleep, or you wanna talk for a bit?" Mason asked.

"Sleep." Because she was chicken, although she'd die before admitting it to him.

"Okay. G'night."

"G'night."

He reached over and snapped off the lamp on the bedside table, but the glow from the fire below continued to flicker over everything. She'd never been in a place half so romantic, even on her wedding night.

She thought of everything he'd done for her today. How he'd put aside his own discomforts to help her. "Mason."

He opened his eyes to look at her. "Yeah?"

"Thank you for coming with me."

"You're welcome. Now get some sleep."

Avery turned over onto her other side to face the window, acutely aware of him lying so close as she stared out at the lake. She wasn't going to fall asleep anytime soon. His presence was too primal, too commanding. And she could smell him.

That clean, soapy, masculine scent that tempted her. She thought of the way he'd touched her, the way her body had reacted to the merest brush of his fingers.

And yet, as conscious and aroused as she was with him lying next to her this way…she also felt safe. Safe on a deeply subconscious level. That was new.

She might still have misgivings about this arrangement, but at least her family and ex seemed to be convinced by their charade. Now she wasn't dreading tomorrow so much anymore.

In fact, part of her wished this wasn't a charade at all.

CHAPTER SEVEN

Lying in bed next to Avery all night had been a form of torture.

Mason cracked a yawn and scrubbed a hand over his face as he loped up the Ponderosa's front steps, his T-shirt sticking to him after his early morning run around the lake.

He hadn't slept worth a damn last night. Partly because of Avery lying two feet away, but mostly because he'd been afraid to fall asleep in case he had one of his nightmares without Ric there to alert him and wake him up before it got too bad.

Instead he'd dozed off and on. While awake, he'd watched Avery as she slept. There was something deeply intimate about sharing a bed with someone and sleeping next to them. Which was why Mason never did it. When he hooked up with someone, he made sure it was a good time for all, then he left with a short goodbye before the sun came up.

His only escape this time had been a run.

He eased the cabin door open and stepped inside. Everything was quiet as he took out his earbuds and placed his phone on the coffee table in the living room.

Before he could figure out whether Avery was still in bed, the bathroom door opened and every muscle in his body tightened when she stepped out wearing snug jeans, boots and a purple sweater, her strawberry-blond hair styled to perfection and subtle makeup highlighting her features.

"Morning," she said before he could stop staring. "Did you go for a run?"

He found his voice. "Around the lake."

Her eyebrows drew together. "Did I snore or something?"

"No." He rarely slept well, and last night had made it impossible anyway. Heading out early to burn off some of the restless energy seething inside him had been a necessity. After yesterday he wanted Avery more than ever. And it was getting harder and harder to remember that this was just pretend. "You look great."

"Oh." She glanced down at her feet, her cheeks flushing, as though she was unused to receiving compliments. "Thanks."

Man, what he wouldn't have given to be able to slide his hands into her hair and kiss her right now. "What time are you meeting your mom and sister?"

She met his gaze again. "Seven. We're going to go to the spa, then have lunch before the ceremony. What are you going to do?"

"Told your dad I'd meet him for breakfast at eight."

She gave him a skeptical look. "You did?"

"Yeah, he asked me last night."

"Wow, he must really like you. He's a known introvert."

"Well, then, I'll take that as a compliment."

"You should." She turned and started to edge past him, trailing her delicious scent in her wake. "I'm all done with the bathroom if you want to shower."

"Thanks." Watching her sleep last night, all her barriers down, had roused a new level of protectiveness in him. His growing feelings for her surprised him. He'd come here as a kind of distraction, looking forward to having fun, and maybe even getting her naked at some point.

Now it felt like something more. Something he couldn't shut off and wasn't sure he wanted to even as part of him balked at the idea.

Minutes later as the hot water streamed over him in the shower, he couldn't stop thinking about her. About how she'd been naked and wet in here only minutes before. About the barely concealed hunger he'd seen in her eyes when she looked at him. The need she tried so hard to hide from him.

His cock swelled as he imagined quenching that fire in her eyes. Of showing her a hint of the dominant edge inside him that he wanted to unleash on her.

He wanted to pin her under him. Hold her down to show her his strength and demonstrate his control. Get her so hot she couldn't stand it, and then get her off—on his terms.

He wanted to drink in each and every shift in her expression. Watch her shields come down inch by inch until there was nothing left but need, and then fulfill it. Make her cling and tremble and cry out, desperate for more.

Wanting him. Needing him.

He reached down to wrap his fingers around the aching length between his thighs, stroking himself as he thought of her face. Those gorgeous golden eyes staring up into his. The softness of her lips, the way she'd melt when he kissed her, sliding his tongue inside to taste her.

The fantasy raced on in vivid, erotic detail. Him exerting his authority and control. Stripping hers away layer by layer. Making her face her desires and then surrender to them.

He imagined her gasp of mingled shock and pleasure as he reached beneath the hem of whatever dress she wore to the wedding, and cupped her heat in his palm. Imagined what she'd sound like when he made her come. Then her sinking to her knees after and taking him in that pretty, sassy mouth until she swallowed every last drop of him.

His entire body contracted, pleasure rocketing up his spine. He held his breath, locked his teeth together to smother the rough moan trapped in his throat as he started to come.

But as good as it felt, it wasn't satisfying. He wanted it to be real.

He was a little disappointed to find her already gone when he stepped out of the bathroom dressed and ready a few minutes later. The air still held the faint trace of her perfume, and it made him edgy. He left the cabin to wander the grounds for a bit before heading to the main lodge to meet her father for breakfast.

"Mason." Mr. Dahl smiled broadly at him and rose to offer his hand. "Sleep well?"

Not at all, but it had been more than worth it. "Great. You?"

He made a face as he sat. "Wife kept poking me to make me roll over. Says I snore."

Mason grinned and helped himself to the coffee already set out on the table. "How long have you guys been married?"

"Forty-two years." His eyes twinkled. "Avery rushed us along a bit."

"Really, a shotgun wedding?"

"Sort of. My wife was the one who needed convincing. She wasn't too sure about marrying a military man."

"What branch did you serve in?"

"Army. Avery tells us you did as well, in Canada."

Mason nodded. "Joined up at eighteen and stayed in until I left a few years ago."

"Ah. Avery didn't say as much, but based on how vague she was on the details, I'm guessing you weren't regular army?"

"No." He didn't say what unit he'd been with, or

what he'd done.

Mr. Dahl eyed him. "Do you miss it?"

"Every damn day."

"Me too." His grin was pure mischief. "But don't tell my wife I said that."

Mason smiled back, glad he'd accepted this invitation. Making connections with people was hard for him now. Avery's dad seemed like a great guy, and him being former military helped Mason feel more at ease. "Never."

The waitress came to take their order. When she left, Mr. Dahl shook his head. "You don't know how glad I am that Avery's with you."

That gave Mason pause. "Why's that?"

"Because you understand her, and support her being a cop. It's not an easy job she's taken on."

"No, it's not. I respect her for wanting to serve and making a difference." He respected a lot of things about her.

Mr. Dahl's face became more animated. "See, this is what I'm talking about. Have you seen her shoot yet?"

"No, but my buddy Tate says she's good." He'd like to see her shoot firsthand soon. Maybe once they got back to Rifle Creek, he could convince her to go with him to the range.

"She is. Taught her myself. Apparently, Tate sharpened her skills more, but with your background I'm betting you could take her to the next level."

"If she's interested, I'd be happy to show her some things." He smirked at her dad. "But I don't think she'll be asking me for pointers anytime soon."

That got him a laugh. "My stubborn spitfire. God, I love her. And between you and me, I'll never understand why she married that dipshit." He jerked his chin and Mason turned his head to find Doug standing over at the buffet across the room with his wife. "Must have been tough on her, to see them last night. I'm really proud of her. Of how hard she's worked to overcome everything and move on after the divorce."

Mason turned his attention back to Mr. Dahl. "She doesn't talk about it to me."

"No, she wouldn't. She's too proud. But let's just say, she struggled a lot at first. Couldn't see that it was a good thing to cut that dead weight from her life and be free of him. She can now, though."

"He was that bad, huh?"

Mr. Dahl grunted. "He never deserved her in the first place. I pegged him as a manipulative shit the first time I met him. But love is blind, I guess. Anyway, that's all done now, and we just want her to be happy."

"So do I." Her happiness was becoming more important to him by the day.

He smiled at Mason. "Glad to hear it."

The rest of breakfast passed in an easy camaraderie while they ate and shared military stories, and her dad told a few about Avery growing up. By the time it was over, Mason had a newfound respect for her and what she'd been through. Her ex was a piece of shit for hurting her, and Mason was dying to know what had really happened. But he wanted to hear it from her, not her dad or anyone else.

Her dad startled and dug his phone out of his pocket when it rang, squinted as he read the screen. "Oh. The girls want to know if we want to join them for a trail ride in fifteen minutes." He looked up at Mason. "You ride?"

"Yessir." The idea of riding was welcome, but doing it with Avery was even better, even if his knees and back would ache like a bitch afterward.

Mason was already dressed in jeans and boots, but he stopped at the cabin to get his hat. From there they met the ladies at the stable, set on the edge of the grounds closest to the main lodge.

He spotted Avery the second they crested the rise

above the stable, her bright hair all but glowing red-gold in the sun. Her face lit up when she saw him, and something deep in his chest expanded.

"Up for a trail ride?" she called out to him. Her mom and sister were with her, along with another dozen people.

"Always." He'd been born and raised an Alberta cowboy. Being in the saddle felt like home.

The trail boss gave Mason a young gelding. Avery was already mounted on her mare, so Mason swung into the saddle and nudged his horse over to hers. She looked sexy as fuck in the saddle, totally confident and at ease. "You look like you've done this before."

She smirked at him, her self-assurance a total turn-on. "A time or two. How was breakfast?"

"Great. Your dad invited me out fishing whenever I want."

Avery quirked an eyebrow. "Did he? Well then, brownie points for you." She tossed him a saucy smile and turned her horse. "Let's go, Canuck cowboy."

Even that tiny challenge revved his dominant side. Made him want to answer by dragging her out of her saddle into his lap and kissing that sassy mouth until she clung to him for support.

He nudged his horse and caught up to ride beside her. She rode like she'd been born to it, and the enjoyment on her face made him itch to reach over to grasp her reins, draw her to a halt and kiss her right there in front of everyone.

Instead he looked away and consciously relaxed his body, even as that restless, edgy hunger stirred in his gut. The rolling, golden hills and grassland surrounding them were beautiful, but the sedate pace was boring as fuck.

He longed to break free of the group and gallop across the terrain, make Avery chase him to catch up. He'd race her to a secluded spot somewhere out of view of the others, pull her off her horse and blanket her with his body right there on the grass, using his mouth and hands to take her to a fever pitch. Make her want him as much as he wanted her, then hold her there, make her wait, make her crazy with need, until she begged him to make her come.

He drew in a slow, steady breath and sought his restraint. He'd meant what he'd told her before. Nothing would happen without her consent.

But if she gave it, then game fucking on.

CHAPTER EIGHT

I f the trail ride had left him on edge, sitting beside
   Avery at the reception later that evening was way
   worse. Mason kept his fingers twined with hers as
they sat at their table with her family, conscious of every
single thing about her.

For the wedding she'd changed into an insanely
sexy, snug green dress, and added strappy black heels that
showed off the muscles in her long, bare legs. All he could
think about was taking her back to the cabin and trapping
her against the door as soon as they walked in, kissing her
until she couldn't stand up before he carried her up to the
bed in the loft and leaving her in nothing but those shoes
as he buried his tongue between her thighs and made her
lose her mind.

He shifted, his pants suddenly too tight in the crotch,
and pretended to be paying attention to what she and her
sister were talking about. She was still a little stiff whenever he touched her or showed any affection, but he didn't
think anyone had noticed because they all seemed to believe he and Avery were really together.

With every passing minute it felt more real to him
too, and he wondered if she felt the same. Not that she'd

ever admit it. Whatever her ex had done had made her close herself off from guys, and she wouldn't let her defenses down easily.

Just one more reason he was dying to get past them. And not just for a roll in the hay anymore.

His goal for tonight was simple. Keep her focused on him, not her piece of shit ex or the trophy wife who seemed determined to rub salt in Avery's wound with a snide look every chance they got.

"I'm starving," Avery finally said with a sigh. "How long until dinner?"

"Not until after all the wedding photos are done," her sister said. "And God knows how long that will take."

A few staff members were putting out some appetizers and finger foods on a table over in the far corner. Mason stood and tugged Avery to her feet. "Come with me."

She looked at him questioningly but didn't argue. "Where are we going?"

"To feed you."

They threaded their way through the tables. He spotted Doug, knew Avery had too because she went a bit rigid, her fingers locking around his. Doug looked her up and down and then dismissed her, turning back to whoever he'd been talking to while his new wife watched Avery with something like annoyance.

Mason squeezed Avery's hand. "Here." He stopped at the table to fill a plate, then tugged her into a little alcove in the corner. It was still in full view of anyone who cared to watch them, but at least now her back was to the room so she couldn't see her ex.

He turned to face her, took a grape from the plate and held it up to her lips.

Her golden eyes lifted to his, a wry expression on her face. "I can feed myself."

"Yeah, you can," he agreed. "But I can do it so much better." He slid the grape along her lower lip, anticipation pulsing thick and heavy in his veins. "Open for me."

Annoyance flashed in her gaze. She stared at him in defiance a moment, making him hide a grin, then her lashes lowered and she leaned forward to nip the grape neatly from his fingers.

He focused on her lips as they closed around the fruit, just barely brushing his fingertips. He bit back a groan, imagining feeding her something else entirely while she was on her knees in front of him.

Next, he chose a small cube of cheese. She met his gaze again. Their eyes held, the sensual tension between them rising from a simmer to just under the boiling point.

He offered her the cheese, holding it millimeters from her lips. "Take it," he murmured. A few people were watching but he didn't care, he was totally absorbed in their erotic play.

His pulse accelerated at the way Avery's pupils expanded. This time, without looking away from him, she slowly bent her head and parted her lips. The tip of her tongue grazed his skin as she sucked the morsel from his fingers.

A low, almost inaudible growl rumbled in his chest, his dick shoving hard against his fly. He'd set out to seduce her, but he was being seduced in turn. She was challenging him, pushing him. Did she realize what he wanted to do to her? Realize what he wanted from her?

Totally engrossed, he fed her other little bites. A strawberry. A tiny, bite-sized quiche. A bit of pineapple.

She swallowed it and arched a saucy eyebrow. "How do you know what I like?"

"Because I pay attention, angel eyes." To every little clue she gave him.

A cheer jolted Mason back to the present. The bride and groom had arrived to start the reception. Mason took Avery back to their table, her flushed cheeks and the way

LETHAL TEMPTATION

she darted sidelong glances at him making the anticipation burn hotter.

He wanted her. Tonight.

Dinner and the speeches went by way too slowly. He
was polite, talking with her family, but the entire time he
was focused on her. Always touching her. Making sure
his thigh brushed hers every time he shifted. Putting his
arm around her. Leaning in to nuzzle her hair or graze his
lips against her temple. She tolerated it, but he was ob-
servant enough to see it was more than that in the flutter
of her pulse in her neck or the rush of goosebumps on her
skin when he touched her.

She wanted him too.

Finally, the dancing started. As soon as the bride and
groom and parents were done, Mason stood and pulled
Avery up. "Come on."

She looked at him in surprise. "You dance?"

"Sweetheart, I've got moves you can't even imagine."

Amusement and a hint of arousal glowed in her eyes.
She didn't say anything, just followed him out to the middle of the floor amongst the other couples.

He stopped, turned her to face him and locked an arm
around her waist, pulling her forward until their bodies
almost touched. Avery stared up at him as the music filled
the air and other dancers wove around them.

Mason slowly grasped her other hand, raising it to
shoulder level. In her heels she was tall enough to look
him dead in the eye, and he liked the novelty of it. He read
the uncertainty in her gaze, and the desire she tried to hide.
She had his entire body hard already, the need to stake his
claim on her right here in front of everyone clawing at
him.

He began to move, leading her to the beat, sheer possessiveness roaring inside him. This had started off as a
kind of game for him, but now he wanted something

81

more. Starting with making her give into the need he could see smoldering in her eyes. Making her surrender to the demands of her body. Make her need him.

It was impossible to tear his eyes from hers as they danced, the heat between them rising with every second. He slowed with the music, swaying gently with her, his arm locked around her waist and the fingers of his other hand encasing hers. Avery's face was just inches from his own, her golden eyes mesmerizing. Her gaze dropped to his mouth before flicking back up, and the longing she was trying to hide undid him.

He stopped there in the middle of the dance floor to slide a hand into her hair and lower his mouth to hers. When their lips touched, she gasped and tensed for a split-second.

Mason curved his fingers around the back of her skull and angled his head, fitting their lips together. He kept the kiss slow, shoving back the raging need to take, seducing her with every stroke and caress of his lips.

Pure lust and possessiveness streaked through him like a wildfire. He held her to him, battling the need to plaster her body to him, and gave her a teasing stroke of his tongue across her lower lip.

Avery sucked in a breath and pulled her head back to stare up at him. Her irises were nothing but thin golden rings around wide black pupils, her breathing unsteady.

Fuck him. She went to his head like a drug, turning him into a raging storm of need.

She would go on the defensive now, put all her shields up with all these people around, but he'd gotten a taste of what lay beneath them, and he wasn't giving up now.

Her ex had to be the stupidest fucking idiot alive to throw this amazing, sensual woman away.

Mason was a soldier through and through. He was going to fight for her.

AVERY'S LEGS WERE a bit unsteady as they walked back to their table. Mason refused to let go of her hand and she didn't feel like fighting him, but holy shit.

She didn't care that her family were all staring at them, or that Doug and his wife were in the room. She was too preoccupied by what Mason had just done to her.

He'd turned her body against her with a single, barely PG-13 and very public kiss in the middle of the dance floor, and she'd let him. Except it hadn't been just a kiss. No, it felt like he'd just claimed her in front of everyone.

She'd never known this level of arousal before. Her body was tingly and restless. Her heart was still beating a mile a minute, and the empty ache between her legs was almost unbearable.

Over at their table her sister was grinning at her like a lunatic. Avery ignored her as Mason pulled out a chair for her, then he murmured something about getting her some dessert before leaving.

She let out a shaky breath and bunched her fingers into the napkin in her lap. It felt like her damn insides were quivering.

Her sister leaned over to nudge her. "You're looking a little flushed. Better have some water." She thrust a water glass at her.

Avery took it and swallowed a big sip, but it didn't cool her off any. Mason had her so worked up she was pretty sure she was going to stay hot for a long time. That wasn't good. What was she going to do when they got back to the cabin later? Because right now she was tempted to throw all caution aside and jump him as soon as they were alone.

Her sister nudged her again. "Seriously, Ave, *whoa*. I thought you two were going to catch fire out there."

Avery shot her an annoyed look, warning her to be

quiet.

"What?" Lindsay asked, all wide-eyed innocence.

"You know what." She glanced at her parents. They were both grinning at her across the table. She gave them a warning look too.

"All right, all right, let's go see if we can still burn half that hot," her mom said, and dragged Avery's dad onto the floor.

Lindsay looped an arm around Avery's neck. "I'm so happy for you," she squealed, practically bouncing in her seat. "He's just so…" She rolled her eyes and shivered. "Intense."

"Yeah." That was exactly the right word. Soon they would be back in the cabin alone, and there was no way she could keep her hands off him now. She deserved an award for keeping them off him *this* long.

Her sister's grin vanished as her gaze fixed on someone behind Avery. "Incoming."

Avery turned in her seat and immediately wished she hadn't. Doug was coming toward her carrying two drinks. He pretended to walk past them, then caught her eye and stopped next to their table. "You went for younger too, huh?" He chuckled as though he found the idea incredibly amusing, or maybe he actually thought he was being charming. "Good for you."

Lindsay gasped and Avery crushed the linen napkin in her fists. Wasn't it enough that he'd hurt and humiliated her behind closed doors during their marriage? He needed to do it publicly too? "Go back to your *wife*, Doug."

The way he lifted an eyebrow made her want to toss her water in his face, but he turned and walked away, leaving the stink of his arrogance hanging in the air.

"What a gigantic asshole," her sister hissed.

Yeah. Doug was both charming *and* selfish. But his verbal barbs had struck home, already taking root in her mind, dredging up all the insecurities she fought so hard to keep locked away. She was six years older than Mason, and she was rigid in a lot of ways. They were too different, and this thing between them wasn't even freaking *real*.

Whatever she thought had been building between them was only an illusion. He was doing her a favor by being here, and was only playing a part. Even if they slept together, as soon as the weekend was over, he'd ditch her, and she'd be no different than all the other women he'd taken to bed before her.

She shrugged Lindsay's arm off her. "Excuse me." On wooden legs she got up and started across the room. She needed to find the bathroom, lock herself into a stall and compose herself before coming back.

The music faded behind her as she left the reception room. Hurt and disappointment were eroding through the anger. She turned left and started down the empty hall. Five strides down it, a strong hand grasped her arm from behind.

She started to whirl, then stopped when she saw it was Mason. His face was set, his cool eyes burning with fury. "What—"

He opened a door several feet in front of them and pulled her inside. A darkened utility room filled with linens and plates.

The instant he shut the door, he spun and backed her up against the nearest shelf, his arms caging her in, his big body pinning her in place.

"Let me go," she whispered, totally off-balance. There was just enough light filtering through the tiny gaps in the wooden slats in the panel of the door to see his face.

"No." He lifted a hand and pushed her hair away from her cheek, the tender touch making her heart squeeze. "Whatever he said to you, it doesn't matter."

She lowered her gaze. "I know." But it did matter. Because in this instance, Doug had been right. Mason was younger and way sexier than her. It was never going to work.

Strong fingers caught her chin and tilted it up, forcing her to meet his eyes. "Why does it matter to you what he thinks now?" he demanded, still angry.

"Because it's incredibly hurtful and embarrassing to find out you don't mean anything to the man you said vows to—in front of everyone who's in that damn room right now."

He paused, staring into her eyes, and for the life of her she couldn't look away. "Do you still love him?"

"*God*, no." She had, once. Back in the beginning when he'd made her feel needed and wanted and important. Beautiful and desirable, even.

And then all that had stopped. He'd become emotionally unavailable, and unsupportive of her police work. As to why Doug still insisted on being an asshole to her, maybe he was jealous of Mason. Which was so fucked up, but she wouldn't put it past him given his competitive nature and fragile ego.

If she hadn't known better, she would have sworn relief crossed Mason's face. "Good. Because he's a fucking idiot for not valuing what he had in you, and an even bigger one for letting you go."

Was he just saying that? It felt so damn good to hear that from someone else, but her insides were currently going haywire with him so close, tempting her to edge nearer to the very flames that would burn her in the end.

But at the moment, Mason wanting her was a balm on her bruised self-esteem. Even though she knew it was a bad idea to act on this fire smoldering between them, she wanted him too, and wanted to feel like a desirable woman again.

He cupped the side of her face with one hand, his eyes dipping to her mouth. Her insides heated, tightened, the anticipation building as her heart thudded. She leaned forward slightly...

Then his mouth was on hers.

Avery made an incoherent sound of pleasure and gripped the front of his shirt, her entire body flooded with sensory overload. He tasted sweet, like the root beer he'd been drinking, his lips silky soft but firm. He groaned and angled his head, his tongue delving into her mouth.

Heat raced over her skin. Her core clenched, the empty ache between her legs building to an insistent throb, her breasts pressed flat to the sculpted wall of his chest.

Everywhere she touched him she met muscle. She'd never been with anyone built like him, and the way he kissed was enough to make her burn.

He teased with his tongue then took control of her mouth, leaving her panting for more before easing back to nibble at the corner of her lips. She was dizzy, breathless, clinging to him and desperate for more, the hunger inside her rising to a fever pitch.

The hand at her face eased down her neck, his fingertips stroking seductively, then dipping lower to cradle her breast. Avery gasped and closed her eyes a second as sensation shot through her, turning her nipple into a hard, aching point against his palm.

Voices outside made her eyes snap open in shock. She stiffened and stared at Mason, their faces only inches apart.

What was she doing? They were in a damn utility room. Anyone might hear them. Someone could come in at any moment. "We shouldn't—"

He cut off the rest of what she was going to say with another wicked, molten kiss, then raised his head to stare into her eyes through the shadows enveloping them. "Would I ever let you be embarrassed by someone seeing us?" His voice was deep and dark, erotic as hell with his hard body pinning her in place.

87

She could feel the tension in him, the seething, smoldering hunger, and read the possessiveness in his taut expression. This wasn't fake. He wanted her.

His jaw flexed, his eyes on hers. "No one's getting through this door while I'm standing here."

It shouldn't have swayed her, but the look on his face, the authoritative way he said it, like a vow, made something inside her sigh and flutter. Made her believe he would protect her no matter what.

The hand at her breast shifted, his thumb sliding across her straining nipple, scattering her chaotic thoughts. Her lace bra was so thin she felt every exquisite movement. She bit her lip and pushed closer to his hand, needing more contact.

"You're so fucking sexy, Avery." He kissed her again, a firm press of his lips on her chin, her jaw. The flick of his tongue as his mouth reached the side of her neck.

She shivered, her eyes falling closed once more, her body arching into his. He was hard and thick against her thigh, inches from where she craved pressure and friction. She was already hot and wet for him.

His tongue slid over the sensitive skin on her neck just as he tugged the strap of her dress down. She tightened her hold on his shoulders, holding her breath as he eased the lace of her bra down with it. He tucked the lace beneath her breast, pushing it upward slightly, framed by the soft fabric.

His thumb trailed across her exposed nipple. She sucked in a breath and bit down to trap the moan in her throat. Mason raised his head to watch her, the faint bit of light on his face making his eyes glow like blue flame.

He caught her nipple between his thumb and fingers and rolled it gently. Avery came up on her toes, a moan spilling free before she could stop it.

Mason's mouth covered hers, his tongue plunging

inside. Capturing the sound as he tormented her with his fingers.

The pressure between her legs was almost unbearable, the feel of his erection against her leg taunting her. She shifted her stance and rubbed against his solid thigh. Her whimper was drowned out by another kiss, his tongue teasing hers as he shifted to press his thigh right where she needed it.

She shuddered and clung to him, now clutching at his back. Her breathing was ragged, her heart thundering in her ears, need tearing through her. She was so wet, and getting wetter, desperate for relief.

His mouth left hers, his dark head dipping while he hooked one arm around the middle of her back, pulling her exposed breast toward his waiting mouth. Avery stifled a whimper as pleasure shot through her, every pull of that hot, wicked mouth making her crazy.

She tried to rock her hips into him but he held her fast, one hand clamped tight on her hip, the other forcing her back to curve more. All she could do was hold on and hope he didn't stop, his commanding grip turning her on even more. She wanted this. Wanted him.

He pulled down the other strap of her dress. Her other nipple tingled, her whole body tightening as she slid her hands into his hair and urged his mouth to the straining peak.

He obliged, sucking tenderly even as the pressure of his thigh lifted from between her legs. She made a sound of protest but he cut it off with another bone-melting kiss, then paused to stare at her.

His hand stroked down the side of her dress to her bare knee and gripped her thigh just above it, the heat of his palm sending a rush of sensation straight to her aching center. "You all wet, Avery?" he murmured, his lips only a breath away from hers.

She couldn't answer. Wouldn't, unsure how far she

was willing to take this. Semi-public sex while people passed by and her entire family was in the next room?

His thumb rubbed gently up and down on the inside of her thigh, a slow, seductive caress that made her belly contract. Mason watched her eyes as he slowly eased his hand upward, inching his hand along her inner thigh, and paused inches from the edge of her panties, his long fingers wrapping around her bare thigh.

He kissed her again, plunged his tongue between her lips to stroke hers, then withdrew. The way he watched her was so incredibly intimate. Like he was reveling in every moment of this and cataloguing her reactions. Getting off on them. It only made her hotter.

He shifted the hand on her thigh, grazing the backs of his fingers up the front of her panties. Avery made an incoherent sound and fought to stay still, her fingers digging into the fabric of his shirt stretched taut across his shoulder blades.

"Do you want to come, angel eyes?" he murmured.

Avery swallowed, her erratic breathing loud to her ears. She was swollen and wet. Desperate for relief, and he was so fucking sexy she couldn't think. He had her half-naked, her breasts exposed to the cool air, yet she was burning.

He really wanted her. And she believed that he wouldn't let anyone see them.

Her control teetered.

His hand moved, his fingers pressing lightly over the lace covering her swollen clit. "Do you?" His voice was a dark, velvet whisper. Sin and seduction, with the promise of ecstasy if she was brave enough to take it.

He grasped the edge of her lace thong and eased his fingers beneath it. Avery inhaled sharply, a ragged moan slipping out on the exhale. Oh, *shit*...

Mason captured the sound with his mouth, his tongue soothing hers, teasing. Making the ache in her center worse as his fingertips made contact with her swollen folds.

She fought to part her legs against his restraining hold and rock into his hand, her fingers clenching in his hair. She'd never needed like this. He'd turned her into someone unrecognizable, her entire being focused on finding the release she craved more than her next breath.

He made a low sound of either enjoyment or approval and kissed her, his fingertips unerringly finding the taut bud of her clit.

She shuddered, a soft sob ripping free. *Please. Please!*

He circled the nub, caressing it with careful pressure that made her knees wobble, his mouth slowly consuming hers. Her thigh muscles quivered, the heat between her legs growing to a fever pitch.

Avery gripped the back of his neck and pressed her burning cheek to his, panting. "Mason," she gasped out.

His arm moved. Pressure registered at her core, then his fingers slid inside her, simultaneously easing the ache and making it worse while his thumb stroked her clit. She groaned and pressed tighter to him, trembling.

His free hand skimmed up her ribs to roll her taut nipple, his other busy making her mindless. He added more pressure there, stroking over the hot glow inside her. "Ride my hand," he ordered her, everything about him rock steady. Utterly in control of the situation, and her.

Avery blindly reached down to grab the hand between her legs and clamped down on it, adding pressure so she could rock against it. Her breath halted as thick, decadent pleasure swamped her.

So close. So damn close…

Her body gathered for the final leap, her belly muscles contracting, a soft cry spilling free.

Mason turned his head and caught her mouth with

his, absorbing it, his big body caging her in as she shattered. She quivered and shook, moaning into his mouth as ecstasy shot through her.

He didn't move, didn't change anything as slowly the pleasure began to ebb, leaving her limp and gasping, clinging to him like a drowning woman. A cool draft washed over her flushed, damp skin, the confines of the utility room registering again in her consciousness.

Mason gentled the kiss, tenderly nibbling on her lower lip before raising his head.

She was too dazed to do anything but give a small groan and rest her forehead against his shoulder. He ran a hand up her back, then gently eased her bra and dress back into place. Then, curving an arm around her back, he held her close, his hand cradling the back of her head.

His other fingers were still inside her, tiny aftershock pulses rippling around them. Finally, he eased his hand from between her legs and kissed her temple. "Stay there," he whispered.

She released him and reached behind her to grasp a metal shelf for support. Her legs were wobbly as hell. The shock finally hit her, making her face even hotter, but she refused to regret what they'd just done. He'd just made her feel like the sexiest woman alive.

Water ran in the sink a few feet away. Avery finally let go of the shelf and tugged her dress back down, smoothing it over her legs. She straightened as Mason stepped back in front of her. She didn't know what to say but he didn't seem interested in that anyway, cupping her nape and kissing her slow and tender, making something low in her belly do a somersault.

Remembering how hard he'd been against her thigh a minute ago, wanting to return the favor, she slid a hand between them to press her palm against his erection. Mason groaned and licked at her lower lip, reaching down to flatten his hand over hers. He held it there and rubbed himself against her once, twice, then pulled her hand away and kissed her again.

Avery blinked up at him in surprise. Didn't he want her to make him come too?

He searched her eyes in the dimness, the hint of a smile tugging at his incredibly sexy mouth. "That's better. Now let's go back out there and hit that dance floor again."

CHAPTER NINE

Mason was strung taut for the rest of the reception, unrelenting desire pulsing through his whole body. Avery was quieter now, a little bit subdued with him, and he was positive she was counting down the seconds until they got out of here so she could start shoring up the barriers he'd just knocked down between them.

He wasn't going to let that happen. He was too hooked on her now. Every time he looked at her all he could think about was what had happened in that utility room earlier.

The way she'd felt and sounded as she finally gave into her need and let him make her come. So damn sexy he was hard just thinking about it.

She didn't know it, but she wasn't the only one rattled by what had happened. He wanted her until he could barely breathe, except it wasn't just physical now. She might not need or want a protector, but she was getting one anyway. The thought of anyone hurting her made him furious, and if her ex made another dick move that upset her, Mason would make him regret it. With his fist.

Mercifully the bride and groom finally left the reception forty-five minutes later. Mason glanced at Avery, his body aching like he'd wanted her for months instead of

94

weeks. "Ready to head out?"

Her cheeks flushed as she looked away. "Sure."

He couldn't get her out of there fast enough. After saying their goodbyes to her family, he linked his fingers through hers and walked her outside of the main lodge into the night air. It was chilly, scattered clouds obscuring the half-moon and a layer of mist clinging to the ground.

Avery tugged her wrap tighter around her shoulder. He curled an arm around her and pulled her into his side. To his surprise she slid her arm around his waist and leaned her head on him for a moment, and damned if it didn't make his chest tighten.

He'd wondered what sort of woman lay beneath her armor, and now he knew. Her combination of strength, independence and innate sensuality only made him want her a hundred times more.

The other cabins were all dark as they passed them, neither of them speaking. Mason was too focused on what would happen once they were alone to think about anything else.

He had visions of backing her up against the front door and kissing her until she clung to him like she had earlier. Rev her up until she started to melt, then pick her up and lay her down in front of the fire so he could peel that sexy-as-fuck dress and lingerie off her, and finally see everything he'd missed earlier before burying his face between her legs and making her come against his tongue this time.

"Oh, it looks so cozy," she murmured as they neared the Ponderosa, jerking him out of his fantasy.

The staff had lit the lamps again, the warm light spilling out of the front windows onto the porch. He hoped they'd lit the fire too. He wanted to see the firelight flickering over Avery's naked body.

On the porch, he released her and unlocked the door. Opening it, he froze and automatically pushed her behind him.

"What?" she said, trying to look around him.

Mason warded her off with one arm as he stepped inside, his muscles tensing. The cabin was trashed.

Avery pushed past him to see what the problem was. She stopped beside him, didn't make a sound as she surveyed the damage.

Furniture had been overturned. Their suitcases emptied, the contents strewn across the floor. His stuff was thrown everywhere. Most of hers was burning to ash in a pile in the fireplace.

"What the hell," she muttered.

Mason pushed her back toward the door. "Stay here." Before she could argue he took off up the stairs to the loft.

At the top, he stopped and let out a low curse. The bed was ripped apart. Literally. Down feathers covered everything, the duvet ripped to shreds. Someone had taken a blade to the mattress and carved it up. Bits of foam and fabric filled the bedframe.

Rapid footsteps came up the stairs behind him. Avery peered around his shoulder. "I'm calling security now."

She hurried downstairs to make the call. While she spoke to someone, Mason catalogued all the damage upstairs and down, a hard ball forming in his gut. Who had done this? And why burn Avery's stuff?

Security arrived in a matter of minutes, along with the resort manager. The three men were shocked when they saw what had happened. "The door was locked when you arrived?" the manager asked.

"Yes," Avery answered.

So whoever it was had access to the key.

"Any idea who might have done this?" a security guy asked them.

Avery glanced at Mason. "No way this was Doug. Or Keely. But whoever did this was in a rage, and it feels like it's a personal attack on me, since those are my clothes burning in the fire."

Yep, and that's what bothered him most.

Mason followed the manager and security guards while they called the cops and took inventory. They didn't find any obvious evidence about the vandal. "We'll review security footage from the camera at the front of the cabin and show it to the police when they arrive," the manager said. "In the meantime, we need to find you another room."

The entire resort was booked, so Avery's sister and family ended up moving into her parents' suite, and Mason and Avery took her room. By the time everything was settled it was close to two in the morning. Avery came out of the bathroom wearing pajamas her sister had loaned her, looking tired.

Mason couldn't shake the anxiety grinding in the pit of his stomach. They were at a fucking family wedding. Most of the guests were her friends and relatives. It should have been totally safe.

"You sure Doug or his wife wouldn't have done this?" he asked her quietly as she came toward the bed where he was already stretched out on his back. Because she was right, the damage done in the cabin was personal. Whoever had broken in had wanted to leave a message for Avery. Her clothes and personal items had been burned, nothing of his.

"I'm sure." She didn't seem shaken at all. She was calm, her jaw set. Annoyed, not scared, and he admired her for it. Avery Dahl was a strong woman. "Doug is a lot of things, but even if he still hated my guts for whatever reason, he'd never have the balls to do something like this. And Keely's not a psychopath, she's just naïve about him. Besides, this kind of damage takes time, and we were all in the reception together."

Mason wasn't convinced. Who the hell else would

have done this? "So what then, something to do with your job?"

"Maybe. I'm mulling some possibilities over." Avery pulled the covers back and slid in next to him. "Aren't you glad you came with me now?" she said wryly.

"Yes." Because of what they'd done in the utility room, but also because he'd been able to spend time getting to know her, and at least he'd been here through this tonight.

She glanced over at him, her expression unreadable. "Been a long day. Let's get some sleep. The cops will want to update us first thing in the morning." She rolled over to switch her bedside lamp off.

Mason stared up at the darkened timbers above him, a faint amount of light hitting the ceiling where it filtered in through the wooden shutters on the window above the bed, the urge to protect and comfort her coursing through him. He rolled toward her and curved an arm around her waist. Not crowding her, just letting her know he was there, and that he cared about her.

"If you're going to do that, you might as well get under the sheets," she muttered.

He did, biting back a groan as he settled in close and molded his body around hers, one arm tucked beneath her head and the other locked between her breasts. He buried his nose in her hair, breathing in the sweet, clean scent of her shampoo, vowing to protect her.

Tonight's message to her was personal. He was going to make sure she stayed safe while they got to the bottom of this.

****

They hadn't seen her.

Shannon's heart raced a mile a minute as she hid be-

hind an outbuilding fifty yards from Avery's cabin, elation building until she had to bite back a giggle. By now
they'd seen what she'd done.

Her timing had been perfect, spotting them sneaking
into that closet earlier in the lodge. It had given her the
perfect opening to go to the cabin unseen and wreck everything before they arrived. When they'd walked in,
Avery's stuff would still have been burning in the fire.
She'd delivered her message.

This hiding spot was perfect, and there were no lights
out here. She stayed in the shadows while the manager
and security came from the main lodge to check things
out.

As soon as they were inside, she darted off through
the night, circling around across a large lawn to the far
side of the lodge. The security cameras couldn't see her
here, and neither could anyone else. Even if they did, her
staff uniform wouldn't raise any suspicion.

Other staff members were leaving when she reached
their designated parking lot several hundred yards away
from the guest one. No one paid her any attention as she
climbed into her car, took the weapon from the back of
her waistband and put it in the glove compartment before
driving away.

A rush of triumph and excitement erased any remaining traces of her earlier anxiety as she hit the open road.
She couldn't wait to tell Mike about it when she saw him
next. He'd love this.

But first she had to take care of the next part of her
plan.

She turned her car to the west and took the highway
toward Missoula. The drive was long. Twice she stopped
for coffee to help keep her awake, and she arrived in the
small town of Rifle Creek a little before eight in the morning. Avery and her mystery man were hours away, giving
her plenty of time to get her bearings here.

She stopped at a local diner and took a booth near the back next to the window. The main part of town was cute, full of old heritage buildings, and quiet. Only three other people were at the diner, including one old man sitting at the counter across from her booth.

He had to be a local, because the waitress addressed him by name and didn't pay him a whole lot of attention as he bitched about something going on with his family property that some assholes were trying to buy out from under him.

"I won't let them do it," he snapped, all worked up.

"I'm sure it will all work out, Ray," the waitress said politely. "More coffee?"

He pushed his mug across the counter for her. "Why doesn't anybody care about the way things used to be anymore?"

"Some do. Now you just enjoy your coffee and your breakfast will be out in a few minutes." She patted his shoulder and turned to walk over to Shannon. "Morning. What can I get you?"

Shannon ordered blueberry flapjacks and scrolled through her messages and emails while she waited. There was nothing from Mike. Disappointment washed through her but she pushed it aside. Soon she would visit him again and she'd be able to tell him about everything she'd done.

The waitress arrived with the old man's breakfast. "Can I get you anything else, Ray?"

"Naw, thanks. Whaddyou know about that new guy in town. Tate Baldwin's friend, Mason."

She shrugged. "Not much. They've come in here to eat a few times over the past few weeks. He was living with Tate when he first got here, but I heard he moved."

"Where?"

"He took Avery Dahl's basement suite."

Shannon almost choked on her coffee. Her muscles

drew taut. Mason. Was that the guy she'd seen Avery with?

She'd underestimated what small town life was like, and that everybody knew everybody here. It was an advantage she could put to good use.

She took her coffee over to the counter and paused next to the old man to ask for a refill, immediately smelling the booze on him. Perfect. Drunks loved to talk.

While the waitress poured more coffee into her cup, Shannon smiled at Ray. He definitely wanted to talk, and right now she had the time to listen. "Morning. Not having a great day so far, huh?"

He eyed her, a thick layer of white stubble covering his face, his bright blue eyes sharp. "You heard that, huh?"

"Yeah. I feel bad for you. I grew up on a cattle ranch outside Bozeman." Not even close. She'd grown up in Billings. "My parents died in a car wreck when I was in my teens. The ranch was supposed to be split between me and my other relatives. I wanted to stay there but they insisted on selling. I couldn't afford a lawyer to fight it."

He shook his head, his expression sympathetic. "So you were kicked off your land."

She nodded and pressed her lips together, as if the memory still hurt her. "Yep."

"You new in town?"

"Yes. Just arrived, actually. Only staying for a couple days, but I don't know anyone here."

Ray patted the stool next to him. "Sit down and join me. You remind me of my granddaughter."

She smiled at him. "I'd love to."

She listened as he bitched about his situation, focused on how this Mason guy fit into the picture. Ray hated him. Shannon hated Avery.

Now she had a new plan to torment her enemy once Avery returned to Rifle Creek.

CHAPTER TEN

Light filtering into the room woke Avery. She tensed, keenly aware of the huge male body curled around the back of her.

Mason.

Her pulse skipped, her libido revving to life. He felt amazing, all warm and solid. He'd also been incredibly good to her this weekend, especially last night.

Especially in that supply room.

A heavy throb pulsed between her legs as she recalled that intoxicating mix of authority and control he'd used so effortlessly to weaken her defenses.

This level of desire was foreign and scary. She'd never felt anything remotely this powerful. As great as parts of this weekend had been with him, she would be thankful when they got back home, pretend they'd never crossed that line, and finally put an end to this charade.

He stirred behind her. She tensed a little, waiting to see what he'd do, but he only twitched once, still asleep. He probably needed it. They hadn't gotten to bed until late, and he hadn't slept well, waking a few times with violent jerks that she pretended to sleep through so she wouldn't make him feel uncomfortable.

Had the scene at the cabin triggered his subconscious and given him nightmares? She was so curious about him.

Wanted to know what had happened to him to make him leave his beloved JTF2 and the military. A man didn't put that much dedication and sacrifice in and then walk away easily. Whatever demons Mason faced, they were horrific.

She lay still, not wanting to wake him, savoring these stolen moments of being held in his arms. Soon enough reality would intrude once more and they'd have to face the rest of the world. The cops would want to talk to them again, give them an update and see if they had anything else to add to the investigation. Her family would all want to see them too, make sure they were okay.

She would do her own digging into what had transpired at the cabin. Right now, she was still unsure as to who could have done it. After that, it was time to say their goodbyes and hit the road back to Rifle Creek, where she and Mason would go back to the newly awkward relationship of tenant and landlord.

Twenty minutes later, she was too restless to lie there any longer and gently eased away from him. He woke just as she was getting out of bed, going from sleep to total alertness in the blink of an eye. "Morning," he mumbled, running a hand through his thick, dark hair, the shadow of a beard already showing on his face. "What time is it?"

"Seven. Go back to sleep if you want. I'm just gonna shower and get ready so I can talk to security."

He shook his head. "I'll come with you."

She hurried into the bathroom to shower, brush her teeth and get ready with the things her sister had given her. When she came out Mason was stretched out against the headboard, still dressed, phone in hand as he texted someone.

"Just updating Tate, telling him we might be a while longer getting back today," he said. "Apparently Ric's been pouting through their entire trip, pining for me."

"Aww, poor sweetheart. We'll get back as soon as

we can."

Those blue, blue eyes swept over the length of her, taking in the snug navy sweater dress with frank male approval that made her pulse trip. Her sister wore a size smaller than her, so it was tighter than what Avery would normally wear. "Shower free?"

"Yeah, all yours." She gave him plenty of room as he got up and passed her, unsure if she was relieved or disappointed that he didn't touch her or try to push her boundaries.

This was their last chance at being alone together in a private room here. She'd expected him to try and press his advantage after last night, that he'd sense her wavering and unleash more of that innate carnality she didn't have a hope in hell of resisting.

But he didn't. And when he stepped out of the steamy bathroom minutes later, dressed and raising his eyebrows at her with nothing but a "Ready?", she decided she was disappointed after all.

They went downstairs for a quick breakfast. Her parents and sister were there in the dining hall, all anxious about her and what had happened last night. "I'm okay, guys, really," she told them, giving them all hugs. "We're meeting with security this morning, and after I get home, I'll still be in contact with the local cops to get to the bottom of it."

She and Mason ate, then went to talk to security. Mason stood back near the door of the private room like a sentry, imposing with his muscular arms folded across his chest as he watched and listened. Avery asked the security and manager about the staff and went over the list of who had been working last night, then reviewed the video footage.

It showed someone in a dark hoodie angling up alongside the Ponderosa from the direction of the lake and

coming up the porch. Whoever it was kept their face angled in a way that no features were visible in the shot, lost
in shadow as they entered the cabin. Slender build, probably female. Height, maybe five-five to five-eight or so.

"Eleven-forty-nine p.m.," the head of security noted.
"Were you both at the reception then?" he asked Avery
and Mason.

No, they'd been in the supply room with the top of
Avery's dress peeled down and Mason's hand between
her legs as he'd made her come harder than she had in
maybe ever. "Yes."

The vandal left the cabin eleven minutes later, walking down the porch and around the side of it back toward
the lake. Avery and Mason showed up six minutes after
that. The sight of them together made something hitch in
her chest. They looked good together, and seeing Mason's
arm around her made her tummy flip.

"We've already sent this to the cops," the head of security said.

"Can you send me a copy too?" Rifle Creek had limited resources but she had contacts in Missoula or Billings
who would do her a favor and see if they could get an
enhanced image of the vandal's face. A long shot, but better than nothing to start.

"Of course. We'll keep questioning the staff, see if
they noticed anything. Again, we're really sorry about
this. Of course, there will be no charge for your stay, and
we'd like to offer you some compensation for your be-
longings."

"Thank you." She looked at Mason. There was nothing more to be done here. "Shall we?"

He nodded and opened the door for her, curled a
hand around her waist as they walked back to the breakfast room. Her family was still there. She filled them in
on the investigation, then glanced around at the other
guests. Would someone here have trashed her room and

burned her stuff? Doug and Keely were notably absent. A tiny part of her wondered if they'd had something to do with this. If not first hand, then maybe paying someone to do it for them.

At any rate, it had been an eventful weekend, and now it was time to go. She said goodbye to her family, dishing out more hugs. Her mom and sister hugged Mason, too. "Mason, I hope we'll be seeing a lot more of you from now on," her mom told him, gazing up into his eyes. "We love you already."

"Mom," Avery groaned, but he was grinning down at her mother.

"I hope so too," he said.

Her dad shook Mason's hand. "Hit me up for fishing or hunting anytime. And you take care of my little girl, all right?"

"I will, sir."

Sir? Avery's eyebrows went up, a little pang hitting her. Her family was seriously in love with him after only two days. It wasn't going to be any fun telling them later that she and Mason were no longer together.

He slung his duffel—now containing his clothes and her few unburned items too—over one muscled shoulder and caught her hand in his as they walked out to the parking lot. It was a bittersweet moment, with her anxious to get this fake relationship over with, while at the same time wishing it could have lasted a bit longer.

Which was nuts. Mason was way too complicated a man for her to get involved with in any kind of a relationship, no matter if he'd managed to slip under her skin this weekend.

At his Jeep he stopped to put his duffel in the trunk, then went around to open her door for her. She murmured a thanks and started to slide past him, but he set both hands on her waist to stop her.

Avery tensed and met his eyes, her heart drumming.

Lord, the man was gorgeous. And when he looked at her like this, like she was the sexiest thing he'd ever seen and couldn't drag his eyes from her, it felt real. "I don't think anyone's watching us now," she murmured, only part of her wanting to stop this.

"I don't care if they are or not," he said, then cupped her jaw with one hand and kissed her.

Avery dug her fingers into his shoulders, pure need slamming into her as he angled his head and deepened the kiss. Arousal blasted through her, the tender, seductive stroke of his tongue against hers making her insides clench. When he finally lifted his head moments later, she inhaled an unsteady breath, dazed.

His stare burned her. With a low sound he dipped back down for one more swift kiss, then released her, leaving her wobbly and aching for more.

"In you go," he said, his voice gruff as he handed her into her seat.

Avery scrambled into it, expelling a deep breath as he shut her door and went around to the driver's side. Jesus. The man could turn her inside out with only a kiss, and make her forget everything around her.

They'd definitely blurred too many boundaries this weekend. Where did they go from here? Where did she *want* to go from here?

She couldn't stop thinking about it as he drove them to the highway and started back to Rifle Creek. If she was smart, she would pull back and get them on the same footing they'd been on as of Friday morning. But she wasn't sure how the hell to do that when all she could think about was what he'd made her feel and how much she still wanted him.

Which begged the question, why had he done that last night? Her mind chewed away on that one as the miles ticked past.

"Your family's awesome," he said. "Mind if I take

your dad up on his offer and go fishing or whatever some-time?"

"Sure, if you want. But let me tell him first that we're not together anymore."

Mason glanced over at her, and the possessive light in his eyes simultaneously thrilled and shook her.

She frowned, caught off guard and unsure what to make of that look, or her own jumbled feelings. "Can I ask you something?"

"Yeah."

"Why did you do that last night?"

"Do what?"

"You know what." *Make me give in and then make me come.* She wasn't going to freaking say it. If it had been an ego thing for him, she didn't need to give him any more reason to gloat.

"Because I wanted to."

"And why was that?"

His jaw tensed, his hand shifting on the steering wheel. "Because I hated seeing that asshole make you sec-ond-guess yourself." He said it without looking at her, his attention on the road. "And because I wanted to hear what you sound like when you come."

A secret thrill ran through her, and she immediately scolded herself. The man's sensuality was lethal. She needed to start putting the boundaries firmly back in place. "Well, obviously that was a one-off. Because it can't happen again."

"It can't?"

"No. When we get back, it'll be just like it was be-fore. We're acquaintances, and you're also my tenant."

"Think we're more than acquaintances at this point, Avery," he said quietly.

She flushed and flailed around for a witty comeback. All she could come up with was a list of rules she blurted at him.

No more touching. No flirting. No funny business. No hanging out alone.

"Mason?" she pressed when he didn't respond to any of it.

"I heard you," he answered, jaw tight.

"And?"

He glanced at her, gave her a sexy look that had her toes curling in her high heels, and kept driving. "I heard you. But I'm hoping you'll change your mind."

Of all the things he could have said, that was the last one she'd expected. "I won't." She couldn't.

Flustered, she abruptly changed the subject. "By the way, you didn't seem to sleep that well last night. Did you have nightmares?" She winced inside. That hadn't come out with a lot of tact.

His hand tightened on the steering wheel. "Sort of."

"What were they—"

"You want to go back to being acquaintances, so how about we drop this."

Okay, she deserved that. And hell, he'd gone out of his way to help her out this weekend. "All right. You're right, I'm sorry. But it's not because I don't care."

He nodded once. "I'll tell you about it eventually. Just not today."

"All right, fair enough."

The rest of the drive was a little strained, making it seem even longer. By the time they got to her house, she was anxious to escape and get space from him. Things were already complicated. She didn't like complicated. She'd had her fill of it already for one lifetime.

"Well," she said as she climbed out. "Thanks again. I owe you."

"Avery."

She stopped and made herself face him. "What?"

His eyes were cool. "You don't owe me anything. Remember that."

Something in his tone, his expression, sent a shiver through her. It felt like he was telling her that if she wanted more, she would have to come to him.

While he went around back to the suite entrance, she approached her front door with some apprehension, wondering if it had been trashed as well. But when she stepped inside, she let out a sigh of relief to find everything as she'd left it.

Except for her and Mason, that is. And the unsettling feeling that they had already slipped past the point of no return.

****

They'd only been home for four hours, and yet it seemed like an eternity since he'd seen Avery.

Mason was waiting out in the driveway when Tate's truck pulled up. He grinned and bent at the waist when the rear cab window opened and Ric flew out of it, a black-and-white, furry missile as he darted at Mason. "Hey, buddy!"

Ric got within seven feet of him and launched his body in the air. Mason caught him with a laugh and ruffled his fur, kissing the top of his head. "You missed me, huh? But I missed you more." Sleeping with Avery had been no hardship, but Ric would have woken him before his dreams turned into nightmares. He was embarrassed that she'd known he'd had any.

But if he wanted her to let her walls down, then he was going to have to let his down too. It wouldn't be easy, but Avery was worth it.

"I've never seen such a sad animal in my life," Nina announced as she got out of the front passenger seat. "I seriously could barely get him to eat the whole time. I had to lie on the floor with him and feed him by hand."

"And she fell for it," Tate said, getting out his side.

"Well, he doesn't look any worse for wear. Do you, buddy?" Mason grinned and angled his head to avoid the frantic, ecstatic licking, Ric's whole body practically vibrating as his tail thumped against Mason's hip.

"Everything go okay?" Tate asked.

"Yeah." Great in certain areas. "Well, mostly." He set Ric down and the dog immediately plastered his side against the front of Mason's legs, staring up at him.

Tate frowned. "Why, something happen?"

Mason hadn't told him the reason he and Avery would be coming home later than originally planned. "Tell you inside." He'd been hoping for more alone time with Avery tonight, but of course she was intent on avoiding him now.

She couldn't avoid him forever, he lived freaking downstairs, and there's no way she could pretend that last night didn't happen. It was all he could think about, the way she'd felt, the shocked little inhalation when he'd first slid his fingers into her slick folds. The way she'd trembled and softened, clinging to him as he muffled her little gasps and cries with his kiss.

There was something between them whether she wanted to admit it or not, and he wanted to see just how deep it ran. And if he wanted more from her, then he had to give her more of him in return.

The front door opened. Avery's gaze collided with his, held for a second before she looked past him to smile at Tate and Nina. "How was Coeur D'Alene?"

"Awesome." Tate slung an arm around Nina's shoulders and tugged her into his side as they came up the front walkway.

"Glad to hear it. Where's Rylee?"

"We dropped her off at her dorm on the way home. She had a good time, but she's got a lot of homework to do tonight. Something about a sadistic astronomy professor," Tate said.

Nina playfully elbowed him in the stomach. "I'm not sadistic. And I already went over the math with her again to make sure she had it down. She's gonna ace this assignment."

Inside they all sat around Avery's living room. It was cozy, painted a deep turquoise color, with tufted leather furniture that suited the Victorian feel of the house without being overly fussy, even with the throw pillows women all seemed to love.

She flipped a switch and turned on the gas fireplace, filling the room with a warm glow. It reminded Mason of the cabin, and what had happened last night.

"So, weekend went okay?" Tate asked as Avery handed him a beer and Nina a glass of wine.

"Went great, mostly," Mason said, watching Avery. She blushed and avoided his gaze.

"Why are you blushing?"

"I'm hot because I'm next to the fire," she said with a glare at them. "I'm forty-two, people. It's called perimenopause."

Whatever, angel eyes. You can't stop thinking about my hand between your legs.

"What were you going to tell us before?" Tate asked him.

Mason shared a look with Avery. She lowered herself onto the loveseat opposite the easy chair he was in. "There was an incident last night." She told them what had happened.

"Did you see the video footage?" Tate demanded, frowning.

She shot him an annoyed look, displaying that sharp edge to her that Mason had managed to soften. He loved that even more. "Of course I did. They couldn't identify who it was, but they're cooperating with the local cops in the investigation, and I'll be checking for any updates."

"Was it your ex?" Nina asked with a worried expression.

"No way. He doesn't have the guts, or any reason to get back at me. I don't know who it was."

"His wife?"

"Doubt it," Avery said.

A hard knot of anger burned in Mason's gut that anyone would threaten her or want to hurt her. And he still wasn't convinced it wasn't her ex or the wife, no matter what she said. They hadn't been in the reception room the entire time last night, and they easily could have gone to the cabin while he and Avery had been busy in the utility room.

"Anyway, I'm dealing with it, and whoever it was is far away from here. I'll fill you in on everything later. Now tell us what you guys did in Coeur D'Alene," Avery said.

They visited for the better part of an hour, then Tate motioned for Mason to follow him into the kitchen. Mason's curiosity was piqued.

"What's up?" he asked when they were alone.

"Did you notice anything at the wedding? Anyone watching her?" Tate said.

"No, except for her ex. He made sure he gave her a few jabs to the self-esteem." It still pissed him off.

"You think he or his wife did it?"

"Not ruling it out. If it turns out he did, I'll make him regret it."

Tate's eyebrows went up. "Wow, you sound protective of her all of a sudden."

Yeah, because he was. And he also felt more possessive with her than he had with any other woman.

Mason grunted and shoved his hands into his pockets while Ric leaned against the front of his legs, gazing up at him. His dog freaking rocked. "He's an arrogant fuckwad, and I'm glad she dumped his sorry ass, because she deserves a whole lot better than him."

Tate laughed. "You're preaching to the choir, buddy. Listen, I'll go over everything with her tomorrow, see if we can generate any leads to follow up on." He clapped a hand on the side of Mason's shoulder. "So over the weekend I did a little digging of my own into the seller situation on the property."

"And?"

"And Ray's problems with his family go back at least a decade. Infighting over his father's will and the distribution of assets. Let's just say there's no love lost between him and the others, but the seller assured me there was no problem on their end. Once the financing's approved, the sale will go ahead without any issue."

Some of the tension in him eased. "That's good."

"Yeah. Let's call Brax and tell him the news." He pulled out his cell and dialed up their buddy. "It's four in the morning his time. He needs to get his lazy ass up."

Mason propped a hip against the countertop and leaned close to Tate so their faces were in the shot when Braxton picked up a few moments later.

"What the hell," their friend grumbled, rubbing a hand over his face as he lay in his bunk, his face barely visible in the dimness inside his barracks. "You guys know what fucking time it is here?"

"Rise and shine, sleeping beauty," Mason said in a chipper voice. "We've got news."

"Unless we won the lottery and I'm now set for life, go the hell away and let me sleep."

"It's almost as good," Mason promised.

Mason listened as Tate filled Braxton in on the latest, but only part of his attention was on the conversation. The rest of it was thinking about Avery in the other room with Nina. Women liked to talk things out, and tended to tell their best friends everything.

He wished he could be a fly on the wall to find out what Avery was saying to Nina right now.

CHAPTER ELEVEN

Nina waited until the guys were in the kitchen before rounding on Avery. "So? What's going on? Because that's some serious sexual tension going on between you guys."

Avery couldn't smother a chuckle. Nina was adorable and a loyal friend. Avery couldn't lie to her. She sighed, wondering where to begin or how to put her changing feelings into words. "He's...different than I thought he was."

Nina leaned forward more, hanging on Avery's every word. "Different how?"

"He's got layers."

"Sexy layers?"

"Those too. But more... He's got a lot more depth than I thought. He was good company. He was amazing with my family. They're all in love with him. I'm dreading the moment I call to say we're not together anymore."

Nina smacked her on the knee. "Yeah, but what about *you* guys? What happened?"

"There's chemistry," she admitted. Insane, mind-melting chemistry, especially when he turned on the seduction.

"Hell yeah, there is," Nina agreed, her eyes gleaming.

"Not that it matters, because nothing's going to come of it. Too many caution flags for me to ignore." Well, nothing *more* would come of it. While she loved Nina, she wasn't going to share the intimate details of what had happened between them. That was private.

Nina nodded, her expression sobering. "He's wounded inside. At least, that's the impression I get from what Tate has told me."

Aren't we all? "Yes. And I can't get involved with someone like that. Not to mention he's now my tenant. If things got awkward, it would be bad, because even if he moved out, I'd still have to see him because of you guys."

"I can understand that."

Avery shrugged, even as an invisible weight filled her chest. "It's not going anywhere, so don't worry."

"I'm not worried. You've got your head on straighter than anyone else I know. It's just…I dunno, I guess I was hoping for better news."

"Because you're a hopeless romantic." Avery must have some of that in her too, because that weight she felt was definitely disappointment. "Anyway, what's going on with your work these days?" she asked to change the subject.

Nina brightened, becoming animated as she shared stories about her classes and a few of her students. Avery made a conscious effort to stay present and pay attention, but her mind kept circling back to Mason. Ignoring him wasn't going to make the desire go away. Having him downstairs was a constant reminder of what she could have if she was willing to risk it.

He was wounded, but she had her own emotional baggage. A relationship with him was out of the question. But what if it was something else?

Maybe it could just be physical.

Uncertainty squirmed inside her as the thought formed. She wasn't wired to have just a physical affair,

KAYLEA CROSS

but maybe in this instance she could make an exception. She couldn't see Mason objecting, and the idea was far too tantalizing for her to ignore.

Since the divorce, she'd shut her physical and emotional needs off, to protect herself. It would be smarter to go back to merely being his landlord, but it was a little late for that after what they'd done last night.

Maybe she'd been cautious for long enough. Because from what Mason had already shown her, risking more heartbreak might be worth it to have him for even a little while.

****

"Survey's complete, and everything looks good. We should hear from the bank in the next day or two," Tate was telling Braxton, who still looked half-asleep on the phone screen.

Mason had steeled himself prior to the call, but it was still hard to see his buddy over there in the thick of the action while he was here. It made him feel like more of an outsider. As if he was trapped on the other side of a window, looking into the world he'd once been a part of and was now barred from.

He told himself to get a grip. The physical and emotional trauma of what he'd gone through made it impossible to be part of that world anymore. He knew it logically. But Jesus, he missed it like hell. Missed what Brax still had. A sense of purpose, being part of an elite unit and being able to make a difference in the world.

He shifted his attention from the phone to the living room. From his vantage point in the kitchen he could just see Avery's profile as she leaned forward to talk to Nina, the firelight gleaming on her red-gold hair.

She was so damn beautiful. He wasn't ready to let her go. Far from it.

118

The threat against her still weighed on his mind. Being downstairs from her was a relief. If anyone tried to target her here, they would have to get through him first, and that wasn't happening. Mason would do whatever it took to keep her safe.

What was she telling Nina? Anything about him? He'd bet she'd left out the best parts of the weekend. He didn't think she would disclose that kind of thing, even to her best friend.

What was really going on in that pretty head? She felt something, he knew she did, and it only made the strange new yearning inside him stronger. He couldn't wait for Tate and Nina to leave because he wanted to talk to Avery alone again. He wasn't ready to back away, he wanted her more than ever. He wanted to be with her, to be part of her life and be the one she turned to for whatever she needed.

He'd already managed to get partially past her walls. Now he needed to get all the way inside.

"Yo, Mase, you still with us?"

Mason jerked his attention back to the phone to stare at Braxton. "Huh? Yeah."

"Tate just said everything looks like a go once we get word from the bank, so it's pretty much a waiting game now."

"Yeah, that's—" He broke off at the sound of a familiar alarm in the background. His body tensed, and in his mind, he was right there with Braxton, reflexively reaching for his own rifle as his buddy rolled out of his bunk.

"Gotta go," Brax said.

"Stay safe, man," Tate said just as the screen went blank.

Mason couldn't get a word out. His heart was pounding, his throat dry as a chaotic barrage of memories hit him. Ric sat up and pressed against Mason's legs, staring up at him questioningly, sensing something was wrong.

Mason walked away, hurrying into the bathroom and locked the door. Ric whined and scratched at the other side to be let in. Mason kept the door shut as he stood there in the darkness, not wanting any of the others to know something was wrong.

Shit, his hands were shaking. His body was convinced he was back over there in the middle of a combat zone, enduring the incoming fire with Braxton.

He closed his eyes and took slow, deep breaths until the worst had passed. Opening them, he flipped on the light and ran the hot water. Catching sight of himself in the mirror, he stopped.

He looked pale, with stark shadows under his eyes. Partly because he was tired, but that didn't explain the haunted look in them. Hopefully tonight he'd get a solid sleep, because he needed one. Insomnia and exhaustion always made his symptoms worse.

When he had everything back under control, he splashed some water on his face, dried it off with the hand towel, then opened the door. Ric swished his tail back and forth, his ears perked as he looked up at Mason. "Good boy," Mason told him, scratching his fluffy ears. Ric loved him no matter how fucked up he was. Mason tried every day to be worthy of it.

They entered the kitchen just as Nina and Tate were getting ready to leave. Avery stood in the living room doorway, her long, lithe body outlined by the flickering firelight.

"Call me first thing when you hear from the bank," Mason told Tate, pretending nothing had happened.

"Will do. Have a good night." He and Nina left.

Avery closed and locked the front door behind them, then turned to face him, her gaze sweeping his face. "You look tired."

"I'm all right." He turned away and went back to the

kitchen to take care of the glasses and bottles.

"I'll do those."

"It's no big deal." He needed a minute to fully come back to the present, and he wanted the excuse to spend more time with Avery, even if it was just being here in the kitchen with her.

He washed the crystal wineglasses by hand, giving them to her one by one to dry. Wiping his hands on a dish-towel, he watched as she lifted up on tiptoe to put the glasses away in a high cabinet, the stretch making the hem of her top ride up to expose several inches of flat, smooth stomach.

Mason moved toward her like he'd been drawn there by a magnet, powerless to resist the pull. He was all twisted up inside, fighting the blackness just under the surface, waiting to drag him under. He didn't want to go down to his suite or be alone yet. Avery was the only one who could push back the darkness around him.

She closed the cupboard and came down from tiptoe, catching his stare. A silent tension took hold, buzzing deep in his belly.

He should keep his distance now, but he was too damn selfish to allow it. He craved her like he craved air to breathe. She made him feel alive again in a way he hadn't in years.

Mason closed the distance between them with a sin-gle step, taking her face in his hands as he backed her up against the counter and brought his mouth down on hers. Her tiny gasp of surprise gave way to a quiet moan that made every muscle in his body go taut. Her arms wound around him, pulling him flush to her.

The darkness in him clawed at the surface, wanting out. Wanting Avery. To consume her. Make her his in every way. Strip her right here and lift her onto the coun-ter so he could drape her legs over his shoulders and get her off with his mouth. Then carry her to her room, pin her to the bed and do it all over again, plunge into her until she was sobbing his name, her nails digging into his skin.

He pushed it back, desperate for the light she radiated. He wanted inside her body and heart. Craved it with a desperation that shook him.

Her arms were tight around him, her fingers pressing into his back while their tongues twined and teased. Mason rocked the ridge of his erection against her lower belly, a low groan rumbling up from his chest.

Stop. Stop this now, or you'll lose her.

He didn't know where the thought came from, but it was loud and clear in his head. If he pushed too hard, she would run, push him away and withdraw her light from him.

That stopped him cold.

With one last hungry kiss he forced himself to stop and lift his head. He stared down into those smoldering golden eyes, both of them breathing hard. Both of them wanting more.

Summoning all his strength, he let her go and stepped back. "Sleep well, angel eyes."

He left without looking back, but once he was down in the suite with Ric, his predicament became clear. That kiss had solidified what he'd instinctively known from the beginning.

There was no way in hell he could bear to lose her now.

CHAPTER TWELVE

The quiet, residential street a few minutes from downtown Rifle Creek was empty of traffic when Shannon turned onto it in her rental car. At eight-thirty in the morning on a Monday, everybody was either at work or busy with their weekday routines. Perfect for her purposes.

According to her research, Avery's house was half-way up this road. She slowed as she approached it. A red-brick Victorian, with a tiny front porch and a turret on the right-hand side.

The houses on either side of it were close, but not so close that you could reach through a window and shake hands with the neighbors. Both neighbors might be retired because their vehicles were still parked in the driveway.

Impatience swelled inside her. She was in a piss-poor mood and tired after a shitty night's sleep.

She missed Mike. It had been over a week since she'd last heard from him, and she wasn't sure if it was because they'd suspended his email or phone privileges, or what.

She wanted to see him as soon as she was done here in Rifle Creek, so she could tell him in person what she'd done. He'd be so proud, to know that the woman he loved was willing to even the odds a bit on his behalf. She was thinking of going after other targets after this too. Figure out a way to hurt everyone who'd put him behind bars.

Shannon stared up at the house as the resentment swelled. She couldn't target Avery here, it was too dangerous. The woman was a cop. But Shannon's background had given her a lot of useful tools to draw from in this situation.

She was great at lying and blending in. Just look at what she'd done with old Ray in such a short time. He'd spilled his guts to her about everything going on in his whackadoodle family, and vented all his rage and hatred about this Mason guy who had shacked up with Avery.

The driveway was empty, and there wasn't a garage, so both Avery and Mason must be gone for the day. She could drive around and find an inconspicuous place to park, then double back on foot and case the house more thoroughly.

As the thought circled through her brain, she became aware of a slight tingle at the base of her neck. Glancing to her left, she glimpsed an elderly woman standing in the front yard of a brightly-painted Victorian house across the street from Avery's.

The woman stared suspiciously at Shannon from under the brim of her floppy hat, gardening shears poised above the neatly-trimmed hedge.

Hell. Freaking small towns and their freaking nosy neighbors who noticed anything out of place. Like her and the rental car. The woman would know Shannon wasn't a local, and the way the lady stared was starting to make her nervous.

Looking away, she continued on up the street at a leisurely pace, watching the old lady in the rearview mirror. The woman stared after her for a few moments, and Shannon had a moment's unease that the old busybody might have memorized her plate number.

Another meeting with Ray was in order. She would

tease more intel out of him while she formulated a plan for her next move. Targeting Avery was tricky, and much easier if she was alone, without her lover around. But Shannon had to be prepared to do it no matter what.

Whatever it took to even the score. If Mike wasn't being released then she had nothing left to lose.

****

It was just after noon when Avery finally got the call from the Billings PD about the incident at the guest ranch. "Any new evidence?" she asked.

"Unfortunately, no," the woman answered. "I'm sending you the security feed as requested, so you're welcome to have your own people look at it. The angle of the suspect's face makes it impossible for the camera to get a good look, but we believe it's a female."

"A pregnant female?"

"That wasn't noted during the analysis."

So it definitely wasn't Keely, because she had a pronounced baby bump. Not that Avery had really thought it could be her. "Did anyone on staff have any further information?"

"No, and none of them could identify the suspect on the video. Although officers did find a wig along with a staff uniform in a Dumpster a block from the hotel. Unfortunately, the resort management and security could not identify anyone in uniform that night as an imposter."

"Can you send me pictures of the wig, so I can look for it in the security footage?"

"Of course. But as this was an isolated, small incident and no one was harmed, with our limited budget we won't be able to follow up with any DNA testing."

"I understand."

"If anything else comes to light, we will alert you immediately."

"All right, thank you." She ended the call with a sigh, thinking. The wig wasn't much to go on, but it was better than nothing.

She'd been hoping the Billings PD would be able to find at least a few leads to narrow things down, but she knew all too well about what it meant to work with a limited department budget. Only priority cases warranted that kind of money being spent, and she was okay with that.

However, since the damage in the cabin had seemed like a pointed and personal attack, Avery would continue to do some digging on her own.

She leaned forward to shift her keyboard closer to her and pulled up her email. The attachment containing the security feed and the image of the wig came through. She opened them, then watched the footage several times looking for the wig and other things. A few female employees had similar hair color to the wig, but they all wore their hair up or in a braid, so it was impossible to tell if any of them had the wig on.

So much for that.

She went back to analyzing other things. The suspect's build definitely appeared to be female, and Avery agreed that the woman wasn't visibly pregnant. But that somehow made this worse. If it hadn't been Keely lashing out in a kind of jealous rage the other night, then who was it? Unless this had been a case of mistaken identity.

Avery's gut said that it wasn't. And she'd already asked Mason, ruling out the possibility of this being an ex of his, targeting her because Avery was with him now.

She looked up at a rap on her door. Tate walked in carrying a takeout box. "Brought you lunch."

"You're awesome." She inhaled the familiar scent. "Oooh, Poultrygeist?" Rifle Creek's supposedly haunted restaurant that specialized in all kinds of chicken dishes. But their fried chicken was the *best*.

"Yep. Here." He slid a container of fried chicken

across her desk and parked himself in the chair opposite her. "So, you hear anything from the Billings guys yet?"

"Yep, just. Nothing helpful, but they've got a wig and a uniform we can analyze with our unlimited forensics budget."

He grinned and bit into his sandwich. "I'll get right on that." Reaching for the coffee cup in front of him, he eyed her as he chewed.

"What?" she demanded, frowning at him.

"Nothin'."

Avery eyed him a second, then got busy diving into her fried chicken. Seriously, Poultrygeist fried chicken was the best in the whole universe. Crispy and flavorful on the outside, and tender and juicy on the inside. "Aww, you even sprung for an extra breast instead of the usual breast and thigh."

"Yeah, so don't say I never do anything for you."

"I would *never* say that," she professed and took another bite of chicken.

"So how're things working out with Mason?"

She paused to look at him, his casual tone belying the frank interest in his gaze. "Why, did he say something?" She couldn't help the slight defensive edge to her tone. If Mason had bragged to Tate, she'd kill him.

"No."

Wait. "Did Nina tell you about…"

"Sort of."

Shit. "Seriously?" Whatever happened to the best friend code?

He was still watching her. "Are we going to talk about it, or…?"

"Nope."

"Okay." He opened his mouth to say something else, but his phone rang. He dug it out of his pocket, glanced at it, then answered. "Detective Baldwin."

He held Avery's gaze as he spoke to whoever it was

on the other end. "Okay. We can be there in about twenty minutes."

Avery quickly polished off her piece of chicken and wiped her hands on the wet wipe. "What's up?"

"Remember the stolen ATVs reported last week? Patrol officer may have found a witness."

Perfect. No more talking about Mason. She stood, chucking the wipe in the trash bin beneath her desk. "Let's go. We'll take my vehicle."

She drove to the address, a remote cabin high up in the hills above Rifle Creek. "This witness saw the theft happen?"

"Guess we'll find out."

A patrol car was parked out front. Avery got out and walked beside Tate up the front steps to the door where the officer was there to greet them. "Mother called in saying she thinks it might be her son, or his friends."

Avery and Tate went inside to speak to her. Mrs. Steiner was upset, her eyes red-rimmed from crying as she sat on her sofa and told them her suspicions. "He's still a good boy in a lot of ways," she said of her fourteen-year-old son, Trevor. "He's just become mixed up with the wrong crowd. You understand how hard high school can be on kids. And ever since his father left, he... We've been...struggling." She wadded up the tissue in her hands, looking ready to cry at any moment.

Avery jotted down a couple of notes before continuing. Tate was busy looking around for evidence. "Did you see him or the others with the ATVs? Or just hear about it?"

"A friend of his showed up the other day with one. The family is struggling financially. The father's a real drinker, and hasn't had a job in a long while. Anyway, the son came here to show Trevor his 'new toy,' and I couldn't help but notice how new and expensive it looked."

"Did you ask him where he got it?"

"Trevor did. The boy said he'd borrowed it from a friend, and that he had others if Trevor wanted one. I didn't realize they were stolen, but then I saw the article in the paper this morning and thought it might be..."

"Where is Trevor now?"

"I don't know. He left for school at the usual time and then they called to say he was absent." She sniffed and ran the soggy tissue through her hands. "I think he must have heard about it on social media and is trying to hide."

Tate came back into the room and gave her a subtle shake of his head to indicate he hadn't found anything useful. Avery gave Mrs. Steiner a polite smile. "We appreciate you calling this in."

She nodded. "I don't want my boy to be in any trouble. If he's done wrong, then I want him to take responsibility and make it right."

That was so refreshing, to hear a parent say that. "I understand. If you don't mind, we're going to have a look around the premises now to see if we can find any sign of the missing ATVs here. If you hear from Trevor, please let us know."

Mrs. Steiner escorted them to the front door. Halfway down the steps, Avery glanced over at her vehicle and froze. "Are you *kidding* me?"

"What?" Tate said, but Avery was already rushing down the stairs.

"Shit," she muttered, quickly circling around to check the back. All four tires had been slashed, the rims sitting on the pine-needle-strewn ground.

Tate looked, turned around and headed right back up the steps without a word. Avery loped after him, fuming. The mother answered the door, her expression blank. "Is something wrong?"

"Yeah, someone just slashed all my tires while we

were inside talking to you," Avery said.

The woman gasped. "Oh, no…" She glanced past Avery to look at the vehicle.

"Mrs. Steiner, we're going to need to talk to your son. Immediately," Tate said in a low voice.

The woman wrung her hands, distress clear on her face. "I've already called him twice and texted him. He won't answer."

"Well, he's gotta be close by," Avery muttered, and went back down the steps. Tate followed, and just as they got close to the side of the house, the sound of a small engine starting up caught their attention.

"I see him," Avery said, and broke into a sprint as a flash of red appeared between the house and the shed. She raced for the ATV, the rider's face hidden by a black helmet. Tate darted past her and cut left as Avery angled to get in front of the ATV.

She ran through the trees, then veered right, stopped directly in front of the vehicle's path. The kid shot out from behind another outbuilding, saw her, and swung a hard right to avoid hitting her.

Dirt kicked up from under its tires, and the driver eased back on the throttle. Giving Tate just enough time to act.

He caught the kid around the ribs in a flying tackle and knocked him clear off the vehicle, which stopped suddenly. They hit the ground with a thud and rolled.

Avery raced toward them, knelt down and grabbed one of the kid's arms as Tate eased off him into a kneeling position. She straddled the kid's hips and pinned his arms behind his back, pushing back her temper as Tate reached down to remove the helmet.

A pair of frightened, hostile brown eyes glared up at them both. "What the fuck is wrong with you?" he snarled.

"Watch your mouth," Avery snapped, and yanked

him to his knees. "Where'd you get this shiny new ATV from, Trevor?"

"A friend lent it to me. Get off!"

"Hey." Tate got in the kid's face as Avery put the cuffs on him. "Settle down. You've been caught with stolen property, and my partner's tires were just slashed. Know anything about that?"

"I didn't slash any damn tires!"

A door slapped shut behind them. Mrs. Steiner appeared on the side of the porch, her hands over her mouth in distress, eyes wide.

"He's all right, Mrs. Steiner," Avery called up as she stood and hauled Trevor to his feet. "But we're going to take him into the station now for questioning, if you'd like to come."

"Yes, of course." She rushed to the stairs.

"As soon as we get a ride," Tate muttered under his breath.

Trevor twisted his head around to glare at his mother. "You did this? You *narced* on me?"

"Trevor—"

Avery gave him a shake. "Quiet. You've put your mother through enough already."

"I didn't slash anyone's tires," he insisted, mouth pinched.

Tate was on his phone. He took hold of Trevor's elbow and walked him toward the driveway. While they waited for their ride, Avery called for a tow truck. Minutes later the same patrol car from before pulled up.

Avery opened up the back passenger door, giving Trevor a quelling glare as Tate put him in the back. She slammed the door and marched around to the front passenger seat, fuming inside. First the cabin and her stuff burned, now this. It pissed her off to be someone's target. She wasn't a fucking victim, and wasn't going to just take whatever this person dished out.

Avery was going to find out who it was, and end this.

"I'll drive you home after work," Tate said from the back.

"Thanks." Trevor seemed guilty enough to her.

But at the station, he held firm during the questioning. He admitted he'd been part of the theft ring, but swore up, down and sideways that he'd never been anywhere near her vehicle.

Avery's irritation turned to unease as she shared a look with Tate. If Trevor hadn't slashed her tires, then it meant she had a faceless enemy watching her every move.

CHAPTER THIRTEEN

When Mason saw Tate's truck pull into the driveway that evening and Avery climbing out of it, he knew instantly that something was wrong.

He dropped the Frisbee on the front lawn, gave Ric the command to stay and hurried to the driveway. "What's happened?" he demanded.

She shot him a look that warned him to keep his distance. "Nothing, I'm fine."

Bullshit. Her face was drawn. Something had definitely happened. "Then where's your vehicle?"

"In the shop getting new tires."

Mason glanced away from her to Tate, who gave him a wave and started reversing out of the driveway. Mason absently waved back and returned his attention to Avery. "What happened?" he repeated in a less demanding tone.

She sighed and strode for the brick walkway that led to the front door, briefcase in hand. "Someone slashed my tires while I was conducting an interview."

He frowned. "Where?"

"Up in the hills at a suspect's house." She started to pass him, but he caught her elbow, bringing that irritated, golden gaze to his.

Mason wasn't fazed. She could be annoyed all she wanted, but if her safety was in question, he wanted to know what was going on. "Did you catch whoever did it?"

"No." She looked frustrated and tired, as though she hadn't been sleeping well.

He'd love to think it was because she couldn't stop thinking about him, but he had a feeling the incident at the cabin was weighing heavier on her mind than she would ever let on, and now someone had slashed her tires. The behavior was escalating and had now followed her home.

"We were up there to talk to a teenage kid about some stolen property. I was interviewing the mother, and when we came back outside, I saw my tires were slashed. Tate and I caught the kid and took him into the station for questioning. He confessed to his part in the theft, but was adamant that he had nothing to do with my tires. And he says if one of his friends did it, he wasn't aware." She didn't sound convinced.

Yeah, given the timing, it was too much of a coincidence for the incident at the cabin and the tires not to be related. This was definitely personal, and whoever was responsible had a fondness for blades or sharp objects. That bothered him. This was a definite escalation and it made him even more protective of her.

Avery would never admit to being upset. So Mason stepped forward and drew her into a hug.

She stiffened a little and opened her mouth to no doubt tell him she was fine. He cut it off with a kiss. Nothing like the one from last night. This was soft, tender. All about comfort and protectiveness instead of dominance and seduction. It was just…real and heartfelt.

When he lifted his head, she stared up at him, her amazing eyes searching his. He'd missed her today. Wanted to spend more time with her, take her mind off everything. "You hungry?"

"No, not really. I had a sandwich about an hour ago."

"I didn't get Ric out for his hike yet today. Want to join us?"

She seemed skeptical of the offer. "Really?"

He brushed a lock of hair off her cheek. It was shiny and soft and smelled good. He loved the feel of it between his fingers. "Yeah."

"All right. Gimme two minutes." She stepped around him and headed inside, reappearing shortly after wearing jeans, a dark green sweater and a light jacket. "Ready."

He put her in the front of the Jeep and made Ric get in the back. Ric immediately stuck his head between the front seats to rest his chin on Avery's left shoulder. She grinned and reached up to scratch his ears. "You're such a lovebug."

Mason smiled. "He's a suck."

"And you love it."

"Yeah."

"So where do you usually go hiking?" she asked as he pulled onto the street. They waved at Bev and Pat across the street, out working in their front garden.

"Up near the property we're closing on. There are some great trails, and I want to know the lay of the land there better."

"All right."

They didn't talk much on the drive up. He parked at the side of the dirt road near one of the trail entrances. When he opened the back, Ric bounded out and darted into the trees, then stopped to watch them, waiting.

"He's so well trained," Avery said.

"He's smart. Sometimes I think his IQ is higher than mine."

One side of her mouth curled upward. "Nah, I think your IQ is pretty high."

Mason reached for her hand. She glanced at him questioningly but didn't argue or pull away. He considered that progress.

They fell into a comfortable pace together, her long legs meaning he didn't have to shorten his stride. Ric trotted up the trail a ways, scouting things out, then stopped and circled back.

Mason patted him and Ric was off again. "He does awesome recon patrols."

Avery chuckled. "I love how much you adore him. Big, tough guy with a squishy spot for animals."

He didn't deny it, because it was true. Ric was family. "Yeah? You like that?"

The smile she gave him hit him straight in the heart, open and sincere. "I do."

He kinda did too.

The sun was just about to set, the last, deep, golden-orange rays filtering through the base of the tree trunks ahead. They slanted across the forest floor, casting a pattern of light mixed with long, purple shadows from the trees. The air smelled of pine and cool, crisp autumn air, faint birdsong echoing around them.

"It's so peaceful here," she murmured, tipping her head back and closing her eyes.

It was. A big reason he liked to get outside and away from everyone for a few hours at a time, to center himself and recharge. Being surrounded with this kind of beauty was good for the soul, and God knew his still had a lot of healing left to do.

"I'm curious about what you told me about your mom," Avery said, her gaze on Ric as he loped ahead. "Why did you end up in foster care?"

He didn't like to talk about it, but he was glad she'd been thinking about him, and if he wanted more than her body then it was only fair that he open up a little about his past. "My birth mom was a single parent. She had a hard life, and repeated the cycle by becoming a raging alcoholic and drug addict." Surprisingly he didn't feel awkward or ashamed telling her, maybe because she was a cop and would have seen plenty of shitty situations involving kids.

She turned to him. "Oh, I'm sorry. How old were you when you were taken from her?"

"Six. Probably two or three years too late, to be honest."

She nodded, watching him. "Was your mom the first foster home you were placed in?"

"No. I bounced around to a few places through elementary school, and they even moved me to different towns. I wasn't an easy kid. Had a lot of anger and trust issues. I was defiant and closed up, and had a temper. I got into fights a lot."

"You were hurting and probably didn't feel like anyone really loved you. Of course you were going to act out." She squeezed his hand, and made his heart clench in turn. She was totally right. That's exactly how he'd felt, on top of being lost and alone.

"They finally sent me to Nancy, who took on high-risk kids. Best thing that ever happened to me. She was the only one who saw through the attitude and acting out. She stuck it out, stuck with me, refused to let me keep repeating my old patterns, and made me into a better person."

"I think I love her. A loving foster parent is worth their weight in gold, and then some."

"They totally are. I never knew what a real home was until her. Then, after high school I joined the military, and that became my family too."

She glanced at him. "It must have been hard for you to have to leave it."

"Real hard."

She nodded, switching her focus to Ric as he trotted back toward them, his tongue lolling in a grin of doggy bliss. "Tate never told me what happened to you."

His insides automatically tightened. "I was in a helo

crash."

"You don't have to talk about it if it's too hard," she said gently.

It would always be hard. But he wanted her to know. Because he wanted her to understand him and why he was the way he was. "We were coming back from an op. Three of us, and some U.S. Green Berets in the back of a Chinook. Tango on the ground got off a lucky shot with an RPG and brought us down."

He pulled in a deep breath and ordered his muscles to relax. He was safe with Avery out here in the woods, not back in that hellscape no matter how much his mind tried to insist he was. "The crash was...bad. Both pilots were killed. All of us were hurt. Some of the guys in the back were trapped. Then the fuel ignited." He'd never forget that terrifying *whoosh* and the blistering wave of heat.

"Oh, God." She was staring at him now, her fingers tight around his.

"I was hurt pretty bad, but I wasn't trapped, and I knew we only had seconds to get out. I managed to drag one guy out, went back for another, and as soon as we got clear, the enemy ambushed us."

"Mason," she whispered, her face full of anguish.

He either got this out now, or never at all. "We were pinned down. The three of us had to defend the aircraft with only the weapons and ammo we had on us. The helo was engulfed in flames. We could hear the guys trapped inside screaming, but couldn't get to them, it was just too hot and the firefight was too intense."

Avery stopped. She turned to face him, sorrow filling her eyes. "I'm sorry, I shouldn't have asked you about it."

"No, it's okay. I want you to know."

She searched his eyes a long moment, then reached up to wind her arms around his neck and press her body to his in a hug that almost made his heart implode.

He wrapped his arms around her back and rested his

nose in her hair as he exhaled, soaking up the comfort she offered even as his pulse increased. This was the real Avery. The soft, kind soul beneath the sarcastic edge and shields. And man, he had no defense against her whatsoever.

"How long were you out there?" she murmured into his neck.

"Thirty-seven hours. The enemy kept coming back with little pockets of reinforcements. I got hold of a functional radio I found in the debris field and finally got us some air support. Warthogs came in and strafed the enemy positions, then circled us until the medevac finally arrived. But not before the enemy got one of us."

She made a sympathetic sound and rubbed his back in a soothing motion. "How bad were you hurt?"

"Broke my back in two places, messed up both my knees. Minor burns on my arms. I had a few surgeries, spent a few weeks in the hospital and then started rehab."

She hugged him tighter. "I'm so glad you made it."

Mason closed his eyes, her words hitting a tender spot deep inside. For so long he'd grappled with survivor's guilt. Wondering why he'd lived when almost all the others hadn't. "Thanks. I'm starting to be too."

She lifted her head to stare at him. "Starting?"

He nodded, holding her gaze. She was beautiful, inside and out. "Until I came here, I felt lost. The world just didn't make sense to me anymore. I didn't understand people, and they didn't understand me."

"I can see why you'd feel that way. Not a lot would make sense after going through something like that."

"No." He smiled a little, his chest seeming lighter now that he'd told her. "I'm better now than I used to be. Ric's helped me a lot."

"I'm glad."

He was done talking about himself. "Now, your turn to tell me something."

She looked surprised. "Like what?"

"Like what happened with Doug."

She grimaced at his name. "To give you the back-story, I didn't want to get married in the first place, but he just wouldn't give up. He was relentless, wooing and courting me, doing and saying all the right things. So I finally said yes. Things were good at first. But within a year of getting married, I was miserable." Her expression was wistful.

"Did he cheat on you?"

"Not that I know of. He just…stopped caring or trying at some point early on. Almost as if he wasn't inter-ested anymore because he'd won me, and the thrill of the chase was over so he was bored and didn't have to try anymore. I knew we'd made a big mistake."

His loss, my gain. Mason would fight for her, always.

She shrugged, heaving a little sigh. "He wouldn't talk to me about it, would just gaslight me and tell me it was all in my head, because he didn't want to admit we were a failure. But it wasn't just all in my head, and finally one day I woke up and realized it was never going to change. I decided I wasn't going to stay married to some-one who didn't want or really love me, so I kicked him out and filed for divorce."

Mason shook his head, dumbfounded. "Like I said before, he's a fucking idiot. But I'm glad you ended it. You deserve so much more than that." She deserved better than him, too, but he hoped she would overlook his short-comings and give him a chance.

Her lips curved. "Thanks, I think so too."

He cupped her face in his hand and kissed her. It started out sweet and tender, but quickly turned to some-thing more. She pressed to him and curled a hand around his nape, her tongue gliding along his. Mason gripped her hip and pulled her tight to his erection, straining against his fly.

She moaned and pressed her face to his chest. "God, Mason, what do you even want from me?"

"You sure you want me to answer that?"

She lifted her head and met his eyes. "Yes."

All right, then.

He curved his hand around the back of her head, his heart thudding, his body on fire. "I want your heart to beat faster when you see me. I want you to get all hot and wet whenever I get close. I want you to crave me the same way I crave you." *I want you to let me in.*

Avery stood frozen, staring at him in shock. "I..."

He dropped a kiss on her lips, trying to lighten the mood. "You asked." He wasn't sorry he'd told her. He just hoped he hadn't scared her away. "Come on, let's head back."

She didn't pull her hand free when he took it. They reached the end of the trail and turned onto the road where he'd parked his Jeep. Ric paused a few yards in front of them, his ears perked, nose quivering as he sniffed the air.

Mason stopped Avery, automatically stepping in front of her as he looked around for any sign of a threat. When his gaze swept over his Jeep, he cursed and stalked forward, ready to draw his weapon from the holster on his hip.

Avery was silent as they read the message someone had sprayed onto the side of the Jeep.

Get Out Or Die.

CHAPTER FOURTEEN

T
o hell with this.
Avery whipped out her phone and strode up the road into a small clearing for a better signal to call Tate, watching for any sign of trouble as Mason prowled around, his face livid. "Tate, I'm with Mason up at the trailhead near the property you guys put an offer on. Someone spray painted a warning on his Jeep while we were on the trail."

She turned to Mason, now standing next to her, and put Tate on speaker. "Any idea who might have done this?" she asked him.

"Ray," he growled, still looking around. "Old bastard must have followed us here."

"He lives in a trailer over on Ridgeline Drive," Tate said.

Not far from here. It was possible he'd seen them and waited for them to disappear up the trail before vandalizing Mason's Jeep. "We're heading over there now," Avery told him, heading back to Mason.

"That's a conflict of—"

"I'm just gonna talk to him. If I need you to come up, I'll call." She ended the call and strode to the Jeep with

Mason.

The short drive took them further up into the hills, to an area Avery had only been to once before. Ray's trailer was parked apart from the others.

"His truck's not here," Mason said.

She got out and marched up to the door with Mason right behind her, but there was no answer. They circled the trailer, looking for any sign of him. "Probably hiding out, waiting for us to leave," she muttered.

"Or he's at the bar in town." He caught her shoulders and turned her to face him. "Look, let's just head back home. The old man is just angry and frustrated. I'll file a report, and then Tate and I can deal with him in the morning."

"Are you sure? Because I'll go find him now."

A smile softened the rugged planes of his face, his cool blue eyes warming, even more vivid against the dark stubble on his face. "I know you would. But yeah, we've got this." He set a hand on her waist as he led her back to the Jeep. It made her think of what he'd said on the trail.

I want you to crave me the same way I crave you.

She did. So much it frightened her. He was damaged inside. Would he ever be able to give himself emotionally to her? She'd committed herself to one emotionally unavailable man already, and never wanted to go through it again.

It wasn't until Mason reached over to curl his hand around hers that she realized she'd been rubbing it up and down her thigh. "You're quiet all of a sudden," he said.

"Just thinking." About what would happen once they got home.

He had her all twisted up inside. One minute she was convinced he was just trying to get into her pants, and the next he made himself vulnerable by sharing the most intimate details of his past trauma.

It was like she had emotional whiplash, and they'd

been dancing closer to the edge every time they were alone together. Once they got back to her place, she wasn't sure she had the strength to stop what would happen between them. And honestly, she wasn't even sure she wanted to stop it.

Ric nudged the side of her face with his nose, breaking her from her thoughts. She laughed and reached up to ruffle his fur. "Hello, cutie."

"He knows you're upset."

"I'm not upset."

Mason lifted an eyebrow at her. "Ric's never wrong about that. And you don't need to hide anything from us."

It made her feel bad, especially after the way he'd opened up to her earlier. She flushed and mumbled some excuse, torn between pulling her hand free and never wanting to let go. Mason had a lot more depth than she'd ever dreamed, and that made him so much harder to resist.

"Thank you for bringing me," she said as they reached her neighborhood. "I'm sorry about your Jeep."

"I'm glad you came. And it's all right, I'll take some pictures, file a report, then get it fixed up."

"Tate's neighbor does body and paint work if you—" She broke off, a gasp tearing from her when she saw the patrol car in her driveway and the front windows of her house all broken. "What the *hell*?"

Mason grabbed her arm before she could jump out of the Jeep. "Stay here."

Like hell. "I'm not staying—"

He slammed his door and was already rounding the front of the Jeep. She jumped out and hurried after him, taking in the damage.

All four of the front windows were smashed. Two were missing their upper halves entirely, and the other two had holes punched in them, fractures radiating out like spider webs.

"Avery, hey," the patrol officer said.

"Hi, Bill. What the hell happened?"

"Your neighbor heard glass breaking and saw a car take off up the street. She—"

"Avery!"

She turned to find Pat hurrying across the street toward them, gray curls bouncing, a piece of paper in one hand and a basket in the other. Her quiet sister Bev stood by their garden gate in front of the blue and purple Victorian house, holding a rake in front of her like a weapon, as if she expected the vandal to come back at any moment and was prepared to do battle to protect the neighborhood.

Avery turned her attention back to the eldest sister. "Pat. Did you see what happened?"

"Yes, dear. It happened about fifteen minutes ago. I called you straight away and left a message."

Avery pulled her phone out. Sure enough, there was a voicemail. Damn. "I was in an area with no service when you called."

Pat stopped in front of her, gray curls bouncing, eyes alight with indignation and concern. "I first noticed someone stop in front of your house earlier today as well when we were out in the front garden. The car slowed down and the driver appeared to be looking at your house. I didn't recognize the car, so I watched, and the driver kept going. But then fifteen minutes ago I heard the glass break and ran to the front window in time to see someone in a dark hoodie-thing throw something through your last window."

Avery set her jaw. "You didn't happen to notice the make and model of the car, or a plate number, did you?"

Pat lifted her chin, her gaze sharp. "Of course I did. But I only got the first part, because it took me a few seconds to find my glasses to see properly. And I wrote the one from this morning down too." She handed Avery a piece of paper with the numbers on it.

This was one of the benefits of having nosy, elderly

neighbors who noticed everything. "Thanks, Pat. This is fantastic."

"You're welcome." She looked at the house and shook her head. "I'm only sorry it happened at all."

"At least now with your information we might be able to find out who it was."

"I hope you will. Do keep us in the loop, dear. Oh, and this is for you and your new tenant." Her eyes gleamed with interest as she glanced at Mason, still standing on the front lawn surveying the damage. "From us."

From her sister Bev, she meant. The resident baker. Avery took the basket with a smile. God, she loved her quirky sister neighbors. "Thank you."

"Want me to run those plates?" the patrol officer asked her as Pat walked back across the road to her sister.

"I'll handle it."

"Okay. Then I'll check the backyard, make sure no one's hiding out back there."

"Sure." A hot ball of tension gathered in the pit of her stomach. She walked around the house to look for more damage, but didn't see any. When she headed for the front door, Mason was there to stop her. "Let me go in first."

She glared and opened her mouth to blast him.

"Please. I need to make sure you're safe."

The annoyance drained away, the sincerity in his eyes reaching into her chest with invisible fingers to squeeze her heart gently. "I'm a cop, in case you've forgotten. And this is my house. I go first." She stepped past him.

Mason followed, none too happy but not arguing. The change in him as they entered the house was stark and fascinating to witness. His expression was set, the look in his eyes and his posture all shifting into operator mode as he drew the pistol from the holster at the base of his spine and opened the front door to make sure it was safe.

LETHAL TEMPTATION

Avery wished she had her weapon too, every sense on alert. "I'll check upstairs. You check down."

The front windows appeared to be the only damage to the upstairs as she walked through to her bedroom and grabbed her service weapon. Moving fast, she hurried back to the kitchen and the stairs leading into the suite, her body tense, leg muscles coiled and ready to spring if Mason was in any kind of danger.

He'd flipped on the light, revealing the changes he'd made since moving in. It was tidy. The living room walls were studded with various swords and other bladed weapons, all arranged neatly on their mounts. Some he'd told her he'd made himself.

He'd set out a few framed photos on the table and mantel as well. She noticed one of him and some buddies standing armed in full combat gear, and one of him and a gray-haired woman who she guessed must be his foster mom.

Upon initial inspection the suite didn't appear to have suffered any damage, and he confirmed it when he finished his sweep and came back a minute later. "It's clear." He holstered his weapon and she did the same. "Wanna head back up?"

"Yes." She spun and jogged back up the stairs to confront the damage to her living room as she filed the report with Bill, then called Tate. In the meantime, Avery took pictures of everything and made voice notes on her phone.

Tate arrived several minutes later, his face grim as he took it all in. She worked with him on looking for more evidence, then he left to go talk to her neighbors.

Avery paused to crouch down next to one of the four bricks the vandal had used to bust the windows lying on the hardwood floor. This one had a small piece of paper tied around it.

Avery put on the latex gloves the officer gave her and

untied the paper, aware of Mason standing at her shoulder. A handwritten note in red ink covered the page.

You ruined everything. Now I'm going to ruin you.

If she'd been upset before, now she was shaken. Someone was out to get her. Someone who had violated the sanctuary of Avery's home.

Trevor, or one of his friends? Ray? Mr. Zinke? Someone else?

She handed over the note and bricks as evidence, then saw the officer out. Shutting the door, she confronted the mess in her living room, exhaustion and a trickle of fear running through her.

A strong hand landed on her shoulder. "I've got this. You go call your insurance company."

His offer was sweet, and meant a lot to her, as did his willingness to help. "No, I'll clean up first." She went out to the shed to get her wide broom and shovel. Together they worked to scoop all the broken glass and other debris onto a tarp.

Tate came back just as they were finishing up. "Bev and Pat across the street confirmed their story. Pat made it to their front window just in time to see someone in a black hoodie throw a brick through your last one, then jump into a black Jetta and take off. You wanna run the plate while I grab some plywood for your windows?"

"Sure, thanks."

While she called someone to run the plates, Mason finished sweeping up, then dragged the tarp down the steps and outside. Turned out the black Jetta had been reported stolen a few hours earlier. And the first vehicle Pat had noticed earlier today belonged to a Shannon Torbert out of Billings.

Avery called her contact there to alert him to the new developments, who promised to inform her if he found anything of interest. And she would start looking into this woman personally first thing in the morning.

Tate arrived with the plywood. He and Mason boarded up the broken windows while Avery called her insurance adjuster, then Tate promised to pick her up first thing in the morning to take her into the office.

"Find anything?" Mason asked her once Tate had gone.

"Possible suspect to look into."

He set his hands on her hips and turned her to face him, his gaze intent. "How are you, really?"

"Getting pissed."

He cracked a grin. "That's good." Then his expression sobered, his thumbs stroking the sensitive hollows just above her hipbones.

Heat pooled low in her gut. Latent sexual energy hung in the air between them, but there was a tenderness in his gaze along with the heat that turned her inside out. When he cupped the side of her face in his hand and kissed her, she allowed herself to melt into it. Allowed herself to cling to him, absorbing his strength, the distraction he offered.

Too soon he ended the kiss and tucked her face into his chest. "I'm here for you, okay? No matter what."

"Thank you," she whispered, her heart squeezing. That scared her even more. She couldn't resist this tenderness from him.

"I'm sleeping in your guest room," he told her. "Until this is over."

"Okay." Badass cop or not, having him across the hall would make her feel better tonight. "Thank you."

She went to her room alone, conflicted about what she wanted. She'd seen so many sides of Mason tonight. A surprisingly vulnerable one, as well as protector and comforter.

If she wasn't careful, Mason would steal her heart and she might never get it back.

****

Shannon smiled to herself, imagining Avery's reaction when she got home. She'd left the note just to fuck with her.

Avery thought she was a do-gooder, doing her duty and protecting others by locking up people. But Mike was only a threat to his enemies, no one else. And his enemies deserved to suffer.

She drove to an empty parking lot along the downtown strip and parked behind a building to eat her takeout dinner, waiting. Plotting. Working out exactly how she was going to pull this next part off.

She glanced in the rearview mirror at the can of gasoline in the back, her heart beating faster. In a few hours she would put it to good use.

CHAPTER FIFTEEN

Mason lay flat on his back in Avery's guest room, staring up at the ceiling. It was almost midnight now. She was asleep in her room, and he'd give just about anything to be in there with her. This entire stalker situation was weighing on his mind. He needed to make sure she was safe.

Lying across the foot of the bed, Ric snorted and rolled onto his side, then dropped right off into doggy dreamland again. Mason gingerly shifted his legs under the covers so as not to disturb him, thinking about Avery and their conversation earlier.

Talking about his past with her had actually been a relief. That terrible event was always with him, even on the good days. The horror of it built and built inside him, and then invariably he'd have an episode. They weren't as bad or as frequent as they'd been before he got Ric, thankfully. He no longer had nightmares every night, and the panic attacks were rare now.

It was a relief that Avery knew his secrets. He was already falling for her, and refused to let her distance herself now. His previous relationships had never worked out because he'd never clicked with anyone before. Until

Avery.

Ric lifted his head and perked his ears. Mason sat up to stroke his head. "Go back to sleep, buddy," he whispered.

But Ric rolled to his belly and lay there, head cocked as he stared at the door. Then let out a low woof and jumped down to stand in front of it.

Mason's stomach muscles grabbed. He snatched his pistol from the bedside table and got up, yanking his jeans on. Ric was still poised by the door, ears up. "What did you hear, buddy?" Wasn't Avery. Ric wouldn't have been concerned if it was.

He passed a reassuring hand down the dog's back, then turned the doorknob and stepped out into the hallway. It was dark, the only light coming from the moonlight spilling through the kitchen windows. Ric scampered ahead, running into the kitchen to stand by the door leading to the back deck.

Mason raked his gaze over every corner of the room before turning his attention outside. As soon as he opened the door to the deck, Ric ran out and began sniffing around it.

Mason made his way down the stairs from the deck, weapon ready. The entrance to his suite was undisturbed. He swept around the perimeter of the house next, then came back to check the backyard. Ric was sniffing around the fence line. Mason watched him closely, but the dog didn't bark or show other signs of agitation.

"Mason?"

He spun to find Avery coming onto the deck, a pistol in her hands. "Everything's fine," he said. She didn't look scared, she looked ready to kick ass. Her being able to handle herself was one of the sexiest things about her. "Ric heard something, but whatever or whoever it was is gone now."

She stood at the deck railing and looked around.

"You sure?"

"Positive. I've checked everything." But according to Ric, something or someone had definitely been moving around out here.

"Okay." She lowered the weapon to her side.

He crossed the yard and loped up the steps with Ric bounding after him. Mason stroked the dog's head. "Good boy." Then he faced Avery. She looked like an avenging angel standing there with her fiery hair and creamy skin glowing in the moonlight. "I'm going to install some cameras tomorrow," he said quietly.

"You don't have to do that. I can hire—"

"I'll take care of it."

She nodded slowly. "All right. Thank you." She sighed and gestured at the open doorway behind her. "Feel like a root beer?'

He smiled a little. "Sure."

"Good."

He followed her into the kitchen and locked the door to the deck behind him. She got two bottles of root beer for them from the fridge and returned to the kitchen table. He liked that she hadn't turned on any lights. The faint moonlight coming in through the glass gave this a surreal quality, made it more intimate.

She unscrewed the tops of both bottles, handed him one and raised her own. "Cheers."

He touched the neck of his to hers with a soft clink. "Cheers."

She took a few sips before speaking again. "Is the root beer thing because of your family history?"

"Sort of. Mostly it's because I know I could be like her."

Her golden eyes were illuminated by the moonlight slanting across her face. "Your birth mom?"

He nodded. "And after I was released from the hospital, things got bad. I drank way too much, could feel

153

myself slipping into a place I was never going to be able to climb out of if I got in any deeper. That was when I realized I had to cut the booze off completely, and my meds too."

"You're not even taking any antidepressants anymore?"

She sounded surprised. "Just a daily furry one." He rubbed Ric's head with a fond smile. "Best antidepressant in the world has four paws and a wagging tail."

"I can believe that." She angled her head slightly, her lips tilting upward as she looked at him. "Not to sound trite, but I'm really proud of you for overcoming everything you have."

Her praise warmed him from the inside out. "Yeah? Well, thanks."

They finished the pop in comfortable silence, sharing glances and smiles every so often. With each minute that passed, the pull between them magnified. He wanted to gather her into his lap and taste the sweetness of the root beer on her tongue, peel that snug T-shirt and her shorts off so he could taste her all over. The other night at the wedding hadn't been nearly enough.

Avery stood, watching him with a look he couldn't decipher, but it made his heart thud and his dick harden. "Mason."

The need to reach for her was so strong he had to curl his fingers into his palms to stop it. "Yeah?"

"Come to bed with me."

Every muscle in his body drew taut. Staring at her, he slowly rose to his feet. "Be sure this is what you want," he said in a low voice. He wanted this more than his next breath, but refused to be something she regretted in the morning. "Because I won't be able to hold back with you."

She shook her head, the moonlight making her hair glow like flames. "I don't want you to hold back."

Mason pulled her close and brought her flush to the front his body, letting her feel every inch of what she did to him. He searched those unearthly golden eyes, anticipation hummed in his blood. Seeing no sign of hesitation from her, he took her face in his hands and found her mouth with his.

Hunger roared through him, so intense it stole his breath. Avery seemed to melt into him, a soft moan spilling from her as he kissed her. Her hands dug into his shoulders, holding on tight.

Mine. She's mine, *dammit.*

Mason banded an arm around her hips and hoisted her off the ground. She immediately wrapped her legs around him, stroking her tongue against his. She tasted of sweet root beer and pure need, one that he was going to satisfy completely.

He carried her down the hall to her room and laid her on the bed, the sheets striped with moonlight coming through the blinds above it. Avery made a sound of protest and held onto him when he stood.

"I want you naked," he rasped out, reaching for the bottom of her shirt. She helped him peel it off her, and a low, dark groan rumbled out of his chest when her breasts were finally bared to him. He pressed her shoulders down flat and cupped her breasts, rubbing his thumbs over the rigid nipples. Tight and candy pink, begging for his mouth.

He bent and took one into his mouth, stroking his tongue across it as he sucked. Avery mewled and arched her back, her hands sliding into his hair. Loving her uninhibited response and that neither of them had to be quiet this time, he played with her other nipple with his fingers, tracking every restless movement she made.

She let go of his head to reach down and push her shorts over her hips. Mason helped her, dragging them off her long legs, then gripped her knees and applied pressure to the insides. "Open for me," he said, his voice deep as the hunger inside him.

Avery slowly parted her thighs, allowing him to see the tender, flushed folds between her legs. He groaned deep in his chest and stroked his right hand up her inner thigh, the tips of his fingers brushing the soft flesh between.

She sucked in a breath, her legs tensing. Mason pried his eyes from the beautiful place between her thighs and raked his gaze up the length of her naked body to her face. Her cheeks were flushed in the moonlight, her eyes heavy with need.

Holding her gaze, he stroked his fingertips over her folds, his dick throbbing at the way she gasped and bit her lip. Watching. Waiting.

Avery lowered her lashes. He went to his knees beside the bed, ignoring the ache in them as he slid his arms beneath her thighs and lifted her calves over his shoulders. Her abs contracted, drawing his gaze back to the red-gold patch of hair covering her mound, and the succulent, pink flesh he was dying to taste.

Holding her hips, he kissed her stomach, trailing his tongue across that satiny flesh, then licking at the hollow of her hipbone. She squirmed but he held her fast, the need to pin and satisfy her driving him.

Leaning down to kiss that tender, secret place between her legs, he reveled at her liquid moan as he settled his mouth on her and stroked his tongue up the length of her folds. Her fingers dug into his head, urging him on. He licked her, delving deeper, up to tenderly circle the tight bud of her clit. Stroking, caressing, then down to plunge into her warmth.

Avery gasped and clutched him tighter, lifting her hips into his mouth. He wanted her mindless with sensation, drowning in the pleasure he freely gave, while he enjoyed the sweet-tart flavor of her arousal, her shallow breaths.

Over and over he aroused her, licking her clit, then sliding his tongue deep. Lost in her.

"Mason," she breathed, her thighs trembling on his shoulders. "Please get inside me."

Yes. This first time he wanted to be buried deep inside her, holding her down so he could stare at her face when he made her shatter.

He closed his lips around her clit, sucked and flicked his tongue tenderly until she was moaning uncontrollably. Wet and swollen and ready.

Shoving his jeans down, he lowered her legs from his shoulders and had just enough blood left in his brain to remember to grab the condom from his wallet before reluctantly lifting his mouth from her core.

Avery was panting, her hands grabbing at his shoulders as she sat up to fuse her mouth with his. He plunged his tongue deep, gliding it along hers. Her touch burned like fire as her hands roamed over his chest and down his stomach. The breath exploded from him on a tight hiss when her fist closed around the aching length of his swollen cock.

Ah, God... "Stroke me," he rasped out, wrapping a hand around hers, caressing himself with her soft palm.

He groaned into her mouth, a shudder ripping through him. Pleasure streaked up his spine, sizzling along every nerve ending. He'd fantasized about this so many times over the past six weeks, but her touch felt even better than he'd imagined.

But he wanted more than her hand around him. He pulled it away and quickly rolled the condom on. She grabbed the back of his neck, pulling him in for a hot, desperate kiss. Mason growled and pressed her down onto the bed, immediately covering her with his weight.

She moaned and wrapped her legs around his, rocking against the ridge of his cock. Mason nipped at the edge of her mouth, her jaw, nibbled and licked his way down her neck and then paused to tease each pointed nipple, his hips rocking slow and sure against her core. Rubbing his length against her swollen clit.

Avery whimpered and brought him even closer, her hips wriggling.

Mason clamped a hand around one to still her, then lifted his head and braced his weight on one forearm. Avery stared up at him in the moonlight, her eyes half-open, heavy with pleasure and need.

His for the taking.

With deliberate slowness he reached up to grab her wrists and pressed them flat on either side of her head, his fingers locking around them. Avery's eyes opened wider but she didn't struggle.

"Don't move," he grated out. The need for control, the need to possess her, was like a living thing inside him. He held her absolutely still underneath him while he eased into position, the head of his cock nestled against her entrance.

"Mason." She strained under him. Restless and needy, but not fighting his grip. Making the fire inside him burn hotter.

"Stay still." He dropped a tender kiss on her parted lips, a thrill running through him as she allowed him to exert his dominance over her.

Avery closed her eyes, her eyebrows drawing together as her body quivered beneath his. "Don't," she whispered.

He lay on top of her, unmoving. Aching. "Don't what?" he whispered back, kissing the edge of her lips, anticipating the moment when he drove into her.

"Don't make me need you."

His heart thundered out of control, raw possessiveness streaking through him. He wanted her to need him. In every way there was.

Their faces were only inches apart, his mouth hovering over hers. "I have to," he answered. It was the only way he knew how to make her need him in return.

AVERY HADN'T COUNTED on this. On being out of her mind with need, while Mason watched every shift in her expression.

She felt like she would splinter apart, that he was the only thing holding her together. The way he pinned and dominated her should have felt wrong. She should fight it, hate it.

But she liked it, the dark edge of it, and knowing she was in his hands. And that scared her.

Her heart raced, the feel of him holding her down sexier than she'd ever imagined. This was a power dynamic shift she'd never experienced before, and it shocked her how much she wanted it. Having her control stripped away, giving it to Mason this way, the blend of force and tenderness making her insides quiver and the pulse between her legs unbearable.

He was a wall of heavy, solid muscle on top of her. With every subtle movement of his body he rubbed against her swollen clit, the tantalizing pressure and heat of him lodged against her opening driving her insane.

He was forceful, yet generous and gentle, and it cut through all her defenses as nothing else could have. She was melting, her body awakening in a way it never had before, unable to move, having no choice but to surrender to him.

It was so freaking hot.

"I'm gonna make you come so good, angel eyes," he murmured, his mouth teasing hers, the slight scrape of his stubble against her skin heightened.

Avery lifted her head to deepen the kiss but he eased back, his fingers tightening around her wrists. She whimpered in frustration even as a hot thrill shot through her.

She wanted him inside her, wanted him adding friction where she needed it to send her over.

"Please," she finally whispered, unembarrassed to voice her need aloud.

"Look at me."

Her heart trembled in fear, but she forced her eyes open and stared up into those smoldering blue eyes. As soon as she did, he shifted his hold to take both wrists in one hand and she didn't even think to move them.

She held her breath as the heat and pressure between her legs increased. Her inner muscles contracted as he slowly buried his length into her.

A gasp tore from her. The friction, the incredible fullness made her clit ache. She could only lie there, quivering, poised on the edge of something beautiful as he slid a hand between their bodies to rest against her clit.

She whimpered and rocked against it, desperate for more friction where she needed it. He made a low sound full of satisfaction and kissed her.

Soft, tender kisses when she needed deeper. Slow, gentle strokes inside her when she wanted hard. Tantalizing contact against her throbbing clit. Teasing her. Making her insane with need.

The pressure built inside her, drawing every muscle taut, her skin slick with perspiration as she quivered and strained, unintelligible sounds coming from her. "Mason," she choked out, unable to stand it a second longer.

"Give it to me," he rasped out, and gave her everything she'd been craving all at once.

She sucked in a breath as pleasure swamped her, then released it on a sob as the orgasm built and built and built. Her whole body arched when it finally hit.

Her cries rang unchecked as it tore through her in decadent, velvet waves, Mason's strength and weight keeping her safely in place as she flew. She sagged as she

160

came back to earth, gasping and trembling all over, forcing her eyes open to look at him.

Mason was staring down at her, his face tight, eyes burning with something she couldn't begin to name while he held her down and began to ride her harder. Faster.

Avery watched every moment, watched the tension build in him, his eyes squeezing shut, all those gorgeous muscles standing out in sharp relief when he finally reached the edge. Her only regret was being unable to touch or kiss him through his release, but as soon as the last shudder faded, he let go of her wrists and came down on top of her with a ragged groan, burying his face in her neck.

Instantly, Avery wrapped her arms around him to stroke his shoulders and back, his smooth skin damp, and kissed every bit of him she could reach. Her fingertips found and traced the long surgical scar down the center of his spine.

She stroked it, wishing her touch could take away his pain and everything he'd suffered. Something major had shifted inside her, and now she needed his reassurance as much as she'd needed release a minute ago.

As if he sensed it, Mason lifted his head, cupped the side of her face and kissed her tenderly, first her lips and then softer ones across her face. Avery held on and soaked up every caress, some part of her desperate for this. She was glad he wasn't looking at her face right now because she was afraid of how much she'd already revealed to him.

But rather than gloat or say something cocky as he drew away, he eased onto his side and pulled her to him. His strong arms cradled her, one big hand curved around the back of her head to press her cheek to his thudding heart, holding her like she was the most precious thing in the world to him.

Avery pressed close, the backs of her eyes beginning

to sting. Oh, damn. They were way beyond the point of no return now.

She gasped as the bed shook, blinked to find Ric curling up in a ball at the foot of the bed.

"You okay with him sleeping up here with us?" Mason murmured drowsily.

Aww. "Sure." She loved that Mason planned to stay here with her for the whole night.

But she worried that if he broke her heart after this, it would never heal again.

CHAPTER SIXTEEN

Avery had expected to wake up next to Mason, so it surprised and disappointed her to find the other side of the bed empty when she opened her eyes. It was still early, weak daylight coming through the gaps in the blinds above the bed.

The house was still and quiet. Maybe he was down in his suite showering and getting ready for the day.

They definitely needed to talk. She was already emotionally involved and had to know where they were going, find out if they were even remotely on the same page if she wanted to protect her heart.

She got up and put her robe on, stopping in the en suite to brush her teeth before venturing down the hall. The kitchen was empty. Rather than being relieved at not having to see him and talk about last night, her heart sank a little.

She glanced at the table, her belly flipping at the way he'd picked her up and carried her to her room last night. Where he'd proceeded to blow her mind.

A wave of arousal swept through her as she remembered it. She tore her gaze away and started for the coffee maker, only to pause when she spotted the gift he'd left.

163

A to-go cup from her favorite coffee place sat on the counter, along with a chocolate croissant from the bakery in town—also her favorite—and a note. A little smile tugged at her lips as she picked it up and read it.

Morning, angel eyes. I'm out running errands but thought I'd drop this off first. Have a good day, can't wait to see you tonight.

She lowered the note, a bittersweet pain lancing her chest. It was a small gesture, but the thoughtfulness behind it touched her more deeply than he would ever know. Such a simple thing, yet after having known her for less than two months he'd already paid attention to what she liked, and had done this for her of his own accord.

Whether she wanted to face it or not, everything had changed between them last night, and his sweetness this morning solidified it. She'd been trying to put Mason in a box for her own convenience, and because it made it easier to distance herself from him emotionally. But there was no avoiding the truth now—that he didn't and never had fit into the box she'd made for him in her mind.

She drank her coffee and ate her croissant, savoring the flaky, buttery layers of the dough with the strong, bittersweet dark chocolate, thinking about Mason. Going forward without settling things between them would be disastrous.

When she was finished eating, she called her insurance company and hit the shower so she'd be ready when the restoration people arrived. The talk with Mason would have to wait until tonight.

The glass company showed up right on time, with the new windows they'd managed to get from a warehouse in Missoula last night. She went over everything with the head installation person, then walked back into her room to call Mason. Not to have the talk they needed to, just to hear his voice.

Nerves buzzed in her stomach as the line rang, her

pulse picking up.

"Morning."

Just the sound of that deep, sexy voice had her insides fluttering, and the nerves fell away. "Morning. Where are you?"

"Picking up a couple things in town, then meeting with the bank and going over initial pricing, licensing and scheduling for Rifle Creek Tactical."

"Ah. I wanted to call and thank you for the present. That was really nice of you." She felt spoiled, and kind of liked it. Doug had been nothing like this.

"It was nothing."

"It's not nothing. Not to me." She'd spent years with a man she'd vowed to love and cherish until death do them part, and received piss all in return for her efforts. Mason had already shown her more care and consideration over the past week than she'd received in the entirety of her lonely marriage.

He grunted, as though uncomfortable with her gratitude. "Glad you liked it. Did you talk to your insurance company again?"

"Yes. The crew is here now, replacing the windows. They should be done within the hour."

"Good. You heading into work after that?"

"Yes, Tate knows I'm coming in late." Hell. Warning herself not to get any more attached to him didn't seem to be working. But whatever happened, she needed to keep her heart out of the mix. Mason was sexy and protective and could be sweet and charming, but that didn't mean he wouldn't break her heart in the end. She had to be strong, practical, and accept that this might only be a physical—and temporary thing. "What's your favorite dinner?"

"My favorite *ever*?" He sounded surprised by the question.

"Ever."

"I dunno. Probably homemade spaghetti and meatballs with marinara sauce. Why?"

That was easy enough. "How 'bout I make it for you tonight? I'm planning to be home from work by six. Is seven okay for dinner?"

"Seven's perfect, especially if it's just the two of us."

"Three of us. You have to bring Ric too."

"Hear that, Ric? You get to have a meatball tonight." The tags on Ric's collar jingled in the background, and she could just imagine Mason ruffling his fur. "Can I pick you up some wine or anything while I'm out today?"

"How about more root beer? I kinda liked how that went last night."

"Did you?" His sexy voice held a satisfied edge. "I did too."

She shifted on the bed, all but squirming at the thought of a repeat performance tonight. Except this time, she wanted to go down on him and feel his hands bunch in her hair as she sucked on him. She wanted to be in control and make him to be the desperate one. "See you at seven."

"Looking forward to it, angel eyes."

She hung up, smiling to herself, but the sound of the workers repairing her windows in the living room wiped it from her face. It was a reminder that nothing in life was certain. She decided she was going to enjoy Mason for as long as this lasted. And with him to look forward to tonight, she had lots of work to get done first.

She got up and strode out of her room, impatient for the workers to finish so she could get into the office. Someone had targeted her, three times now, and there was no guarantee it was over.

Avery was sick of this shit. She wanted her normal life back. She was going to find out who'd done this to her, and put them away before it got any worse.

166

LETHAL TEMPTATION

****

Yeah, this was just what she needed. Coming here had been the right decision.

Shannon parked her car in the prison parking lot hours later and climbed out, exhausted, frustrated, but filled with anticipation. She didn't know how, but Mason must have heard her last night. Or his dog.

She'd waited until the middle of the night, until she was as sure as she could be that he and Avery were both asleep. So she could set the fire and take off. But just as she'd crept around the back of the house with the can of gasoline, she'd seen a flicker of movement through one of the windows.

She'd had no choice but to abort the mission and leave. Being on foot made it ten times as risky, and she'd barely made it out of there before Mason and the dog came out. She'd heard them as she was scaling the neighbor's fence.

Not wanting to risk being seen by anyone when she was so close to achieving her goal, she'd decided to get out of town for a day or two. Not having heard from Mike lately, she'd driven back to Billings to surprise him with a visit today. It would lift both their spirits.

Excitement bubbled in her as she waited in line for the security check and registration. Since it was a weekday, the line of visitors was small.

She bit her lip, anticipating the look on Mike's face when they brought him out to find her waiting at a table for him. It would brighten his day, and hers. If it was safe, she couldn't wait to tell him what she'd done, and what she planned to do next.

It took a while for her to be processed, and then she was escorted to a waiting room until her appointment time arrived. A guard came for her. She shot to her feet, her pulse accelerating as she stepped into the visitation room.

Searching the space, she stopped, her feet sticking in place when she saw Mike at the far side. A horrible, crushing pressure filled her chest.

He already had a visitor at the far table in the corner. A young blonde, who was leaning forward in her low-cut, skin-tight top, laughing and tossing her hair to give him a better view. And Mike was eating it up, his eyes locked on the woman's tits, a half-smirk on his handsome face.

Fury rushed through Shannon, melting away the icy shock. Who the fuck was that bitch, and why was she here to see Mike?

The guard held a hand out to stop her from moving. Shannon stood there, practically vibrating with impatience, the anger starting to morph into hurt.

Another guard near Mike's table stopped the visit. The blonde said something else to Mike, smiled and blew him a kiss before standing. She swung her purse over her shoulder and turned toward the exit.

Shannon locked onto her with a lethal glare. The blonde must have felt it, because she met Shannon's gaze, smirked and sashayed past in a cloud of cheap perfume, looking all too fucking pleased with herself.

"This way," the guard muttered.

Shannon lifted her chin and marched over to Mike's table. He was watching her now, seemed surprised to see her.

"Shan. What are you doing here?" he said when she got close, his expression unreadable.

Torn between hurt and anger, she slapped her purse down on the floor and refused to sit while the guard moved away. "Thought I'd surprise you. And it looks like I did."

He seemed taken aback for a split second, then he grinned, his eyes gleaming with amusement. "You're not jealous, are you?"

That gave her pause. "No. But who the hell was

that?'

"Doesn't matter."

"Oh, it matters." She'd put herself at great risk for him, and he was repaying her by cheating on her with some skank?

"Don't worry about it. She's nothing. I didn't ask her to come."

He was lying. She knew what she'd seen, and that bitch was totally into him. Which meant he must have encouraged her. "Did you tell her not to come back?"

"I will."

Shannon wasn't convinced. Her stomach hurt. "Are you seeing her?"

Mike shrugged, watching her in a way that was a little disturbing. His stare was intense. Scrutinizing her. "I can't see her if I'm in here, can I?"

Far from being reassuring, his offhand response devastated her. She'd done all this for him, made all these plans, risked her own freedom, and he didn't even care about her. Not really. God, she was such an idiot.

"Shan. Sit," he said softly, staring up at her with those dark brown eyes. "I'm glad you came."

There was a lump in her throat. She swallowed it down, gathered her pride and forced back the tears blurring her eyes so he couldn't see them before sitting calmly across from him. They stared at each other in stony silence for a full minute.

"I didn't know she was coming. I didn't ask her to," he repeated, then softened everything with a cajoling smile.

She drew a breath, made sure the guard closest to them couldn't overhear, and lowered her voice just in case. "You don't know what I've done for you. What I've risked for you."

He leaned forward slightly, his eyes shining with sudden interest. "What have you done for me, baby?"

She wanted to tell him, but she was too choked up and angry. "How many others, besides me and her?" She wasn't an idiot. If he was romancing another woman besides her, then there had to be others.

He eased back, his expression cooling. "Does it matter? You're the only one I care about, and I'm stuck in here for at least another five years," he muttered.

"Yeah, it matters."

He watched her for a long moment. "So. You gonna tell me what you meant before? About what you did?"

"No." Not here, and not now. He didn't deserve to know. He didn't deserve *her*.

She got up abruptly. "I'm leaving."

"Wait."

She didn't.

"Wait, when are you coming back? Shannon!"

She took savage satisfaction in ignoring him as he called her back. She kept walking, head held high even as hurt and rage scalded her insides.

Once she got to her car, she sat in it for a while, not trusting herself to drive just yet, swamped by a sense of disillusionment. How could she have gotten herself into this situation? How could she have yet again given her heart to a man who didn't want it?

She replayed this most recent visit over in her mind, then backtracked through the entirety of their relationship. Every phone call and email and letter. Every visit, every word he'd said to her. And the combination of lust and pride on his face when they sat face to face.

He'd said the blonde and the others didn't matter. That *she* was the only one he cared about. She wanted it to be true. She *needed* it to be true.

She kept coming back to the way his eyes had lit up with that weird, almost fanatical gleam when she'd told him he didn't know what she'd done for him.

What have you done for me, baby?

"Oh my God," she whispered, goosebumps breaking out all over her as sudden understanding dawned.

He was testing her. Waiting to see if she really loved him.

He wanted her to prove it to him.

The pulse in her throat throbbed, everything suddenly becoming clear. This was a test of loyalty. He wanted to see how far she'd go to prove her love and devotion to him. Once she did, he would be hers forever.

Her hands shook slightly, elation humming in her bones as she drove out of the parking lot. The other night she'd only planned to set fire to the house to terrorize Avery, force her to lose her home during restoration and reconstruction—if there'd been anything left to save by the time the fire department got there.

She'd been toying with Avery so far, fucking with her, unsure what to do next. Now Shannon realized what she had to do.

She would kill Avery, and prove beyond a doubt to Mike she was the one he was meant to be with. It was the only way to win him back.

CHAPTER SEVENTEEN

Today had pretty much sucked so far.

Avery muttered to herself as she set aside one file and took out another to finish up. What she really wanted to be doing was finding out who the hell this Shannon Torbert was, and why the psycho had targeted her. Instead, as soon as she finished one thing that landed on her desk, another came in. All. Day. Long.

Avery prided herself on being focused and hardworking in her job, but right now she was distracted, unable to concentrate properly. She wanted to put her stalker behind bars and get her life back to normal, and she also wanted to be with Mason. When that was done, she planned to talk to Nina about him, but didn't know whether she should since he was Tate's best friend and it put Nina in an awkward position.

She was all tangled up inside, veering from wanting to jump his bones as soon as she saw him tonight, and wanting to pull back to protect herself from hurt later on. The thing was, she'd come to the realization that it couldn't just be physical for her. Her feelings were definitely involved at this point. So if things didn't work out she was going to be hurt regardless.

She needed to talk to Mason about it, not Nina, no matter how scared she was of being disappointed.

Her phone buzzed with a new text message. Her heart jumped when she saw Mason's name on the screen. *What do we need from the store for dinner? I'll go grab it.*

"Good, because I'm not nearly done here yet." She listed the handful of ingredients for him, glad to be spared a stop at the store. *Thanks for this. I'll be home just after six.*

No problem. Drive safe. Looking forward to being alone with you.

Oh, my. She started to respond, then deleted it. The phone slipped. She caught it before it fell, and cursed when she saw she'd accidentally sent him a heart eyes emoji.

"Hell." So much for playing it cool.

Embarrassed, she set her phone down on her desk, trying and failing to ignore the twinge in her chest. Ah, damn. How the hell was she supposed to pull back from him or keep her distance when he did and said things like this?

After another hour she gave up all pretense of caring about her remaining workload and called her contact in Billings. He hadn't been able to look into Avery's suspect yet. She wound up trying to dig up info about the woman on her own.

Two more hours and a lot of dead ends later, she headed outside to her car, frustrated and pissed off. Thankfully her car was right where she'd left it, and was fully intact, including the tires. She drove home through the light rain pattering her windshield, the sky a dark, dull gray.

Mason's Jeep was parked on his side of the driveway. Just seeing it helped lift her mood.

Butterflies danced in her belly at the thought of seeing him in just a few moments. On the drive home she'd made up her mind to just roll with it for now and talk to him about their status later, once they'd taken the edge off in bed. There was no way she would be able to concentrate on such a serious conversation before then, and the truth was, she dreaded things not going the way she hoped when they did talk, so she wanted to delay it.

She opened her front door and stopped, surprised to find him on a ladder installing something overhead. "Hey."

He smiled down at her, making her insides all gooey. "Hey. How was your day?" He went back to work with the screwdriver.

"Good." She got preoccupied with watching the way his arm muscles flexed as he turned the screwdriver. Lord, the man was built, and she couldn't wait to feel him on top of her again. Or behind her. Yum. "Is that the security camera?"

"Part of it. I've already installed a couple cameras on the front and back of the house. This one works with your doorbell so you'll be able to see whoever's at your door by checking your phone, and the camera's hidden." He tightened the screw and eased back to study his handiwork. "That should do it."

Avery shook her head. "Mason, thank you, I—" She stopped, inhaling something rich and aromatic. Definitely Italian spices. "Did you cook?"

He chuckled as he climbed down the ladder. "Yeah. Told you I could. Did you forget?" He tucked the screwdriver in his back jeans pocket and walked to her, then closed his hands around her hips in a possessive hold that made her shiver with longing.

"I think so." God, she couldn't think around him.

His blue eyes held a knowing gleam. "Maybe you've got something else on your mind?"

"Apparently."

He grinned. "Good, me too," he murmured, and covered her mouth with his.

Avery dropped her keys and bag to wind her arms around his neck, plastering herself to his body. *Mine, mine,* her mind chanted, her body suddenly greedy. She'd gone so long without this.

Mason sucked at her lower lip, nipped it gently and pulled back. "Save that thought. Dinner's ready."

She couldn't help but grin. "I can't believe you cooked for me."

He gave her a funny look as he steered her into the kitchen with a hand on her waist. "Why not?"

"Because I was going to cook for you. And you've been busy all day with business stuff, and the cameras."

He stopped in the middle of the kitchen and turned to face her, two-hundred-plus pounds of deliciously sexy male. "Because you take priority for me, and I want you safe."

Oh, hell... She stared at him, not knowing how to respond.

He caught her hand, tugged it. "Let's eat, I'm starving."

She stood there while he plated up two servings of spaghetti and meatballs, and followed him to the table he'd already set. With freaking candles. "Mason," she murmured, touched but floundering. She didn't know what to do with all this. "What are you doing to me?"

His expression turned serious. "Showing you you're worth it."

It felt like a giant fist had just clamped around her heart. Mason seemed to be showing her he was serious about her.

"This is my mom's recipe," he added. "One of the first things I learned to make of hers before I moved out," he added, setting her plate down for her and pulling out her chair as if they were in a fancy restaurant. "Hope you'll like it."

Avery had to swallow the lump in her throat before picking up her fork. "I already love it, thank you."

His eyes warmed as he smiled at her. "You're welcome."

They chatted about their days while they ate, but Avery couldn't really concentrate. "This is incredible. You stuffed the meatballs." He'd even picked her up a bottle of her favorite wine.

"Yeah, you roll a little bit of mozzarella and parmesan into the middle of them. Glad you like it."

She liked everything about this. A great, home cooked meal and a romantic table set for just the two of them. Anticipation charging the space between them. She could see he wasn't like her ex, but just how far was she willing to take this when there was still so much uncertainty?

Suddenly, she couldn't take it anymore. The anticipation was killing her, and not in a good way. She set her fork down and rubbed her palms over her thighs. "We need to talk about how this is going to go."

He paused to look up at her, his fork spearing a meatball on his plate. "This. You mean us?"

"Yes. I don't want things to be awkward later. I mean, you live here now, this is a small town, and you're also Tate's best friend. So it's not like we can avoid each other forever if things don't work out."

He didn't look away. "Define 'things.'"

The urge to backtrack was tempting, but she had to get this out. Had to be honest and real with him before one or both of them got hurt. "I'm not okay with this just being physical. I thought I could do it, but I can't." *Not with you.*

He stared at her, his eyebrows pulling together. "What does that mean?"

She sighed and screwed up her courage even though

her insides were quaking at the very real possibility of rejection looming before her. "My life before you showed up? I knew how to do that. I was an expert at it, and was prepared to do it forever. And then you came along, and now I don't know what the hell to do with all this." She gestured between them with her hands, unsure how to put her feelings into words.

"Good, because I don't either."

His quiet response surprised her. "You don't?"

He shook his head, set down his fork and reached for her hand, curling his long fingers around it. "But I want to learn how."

Her heart rolled over in her chest and landed with a little thud.

"If it makes you feel any better, I'm in uncharted territory with you."

A lopsided smile spread across her face. "Yeah, that kind of does make me feel better, actually." A familiar ringtone filled the air. She checked her phone without thinking, because she was on call. She was always on call. And when she saw her partner's name, a spurt of disappointment hit her that she had to answer and interrupt this conversation. "It's Tate. Hang on a sec." She pulled it out of her pocket and answered.

"We've got a situation," he said.

She sat up straighter. "Why, what's wrong?"

"There's been a domestic disturbance reported. Ray has barricaded himself in his trailer, threatening to kill himself if the police won't leave him alone. He'll only deal with you and me, apparently."

"What the hell did he do now?" she asked. Mason had only gotten his freshly-painted Jeep back this morning.

"Got into a brawl with some family members at their house, and took off. Good chance he's drunk."

"And armed," Avery muttered, getting to her feet.

Mason was right with her, following her to the front door. "I'll pick you up in a few minutes," she said to Tate, since he was on her way. Disconnecting, she turned to Mason. "Sorry, duty calls. Ray's barricaded in his trailer, threatening to kill himself and will only talk to me and Tate."

Concern knit his brow. "Want me to—"

She laid her fingers across his lips and smiled. "No, you can't. But I'd love it if you were still here when I get back." She kissed him, hope making her heart feel lighter than it had in years. They would finish their talk later, in bed. Once both of them were too tired to move. "And that'll be as soon as humanly possible, because I want you so damn much…"

Surprise lit his eyes, a grin curving his mouth. "Guess I'll make dinner for you a lot from now on."

Snickering, she kissed him. "See you."

He took her head in his hands, deepened the kiss for a few dizzy seconds. "Hurry back, and be safe."

"I will."

She drove to Tate's, thinking about Mason's parting words. It felt incredible to know he cared about her so much. Doug had never told her to be safe before a shift. He'd hated that she'd become a cop after they were married, and never let her forget it.

Tate was waiting for her outside his house. He hopped in the passenger seat and slammed the door shut. "No updates. They're waiting for us up there now."

She turned the vehicle around and headed toward the hills above them. "What the hell's Ray's problem now? Still about the property?" He still wouldn't admit to tagging Mason's Jeep.

"I'm guessing so. His sister's on scene, waiting to talk to us."

The rain was coming down in a steady shower now, making the beams of her headlights glisten on the wet pavement. When they arrived on scene at Ray's trailer, three squad cars were there. Four officers, and a civilian woman in her fifties who turned out to be Ray's little sister.

Avery and Tate spoke to her, getting the intel they needed. As expected, an argument about the land sale had erupted in the middle of a family birthday party.

"He was irate," the sister told them, shaking her head. "He'd been drinking, of course, and he just got out of hand. No one could settle him down, not even me. He started throwing punches at my brothers, and my nephew when he stepped in to break it up. It was chaos."

"And then he left?" Avery asked.

"Yeah, he just got in his truck and took off, yelling about how we'd all be sorry when he was dead. I ran out to my car and followed him here. I pleaded with him to let me in but he refused, crying and threatening to shoot himself."

The woman was understandably agitated, her concern for her brother real. Avery walked her over to one of the patrol cars. "Sit in here where it's warm and dry while we go talk to him."

The woman—Catherine—grabbed Avery's arm. "Please. Please don't let him hurt himself. He's a good man underneath all this."

"I know. We'll do everything we can to make sure he's safe."

Joining Tate, they went to the trailer's front door while the other officers stood back near their patrol cars. "Ray," Tate called out. "This is Detective Tate Baldwin. My partner Avery's here with me. You wanted to talk to us?"

An anguished sound came from within the darkened trailer. "I can't talk to no one." It sounded like he was still crying. "Not after what I done."

Avery stepped closer to the door. "Ray, it's Detective Dahl. Will you please come out and talk with us? It's not that bad. No one's hurt bad enough to need medical attention, and your family isn't going to press charges. They're worried about you. So please, just come out so we can make sure you're okay."

Silence answered.

Avery looked at Tate, contemplating their next move. Then muffled footsteps shuffled toward them. She and Tate both drew their weapons and held them pointing at the ground, waiting on either side of the door.

A lock scraped, then the door cracked open. Illuminated by the patrol car headlights, Ray stared out at them from red-rimmed eyes. "I ain't armed," he muttered, and pushed the door open.

Seeing that his hands were empty, Avery relaxed a bit but still didn't lower her weapon all the way. "Come outside, Ray."

He did, standing under his tiny porch with his head hanging low while rain dripped off the eaves.

"Why did you want us specifically, Ray?" Avery asked. Given the history between him, Tate and Mason, it was best she do the talking here.

"Because." Ray pulled in a shuddering breath, sniffed, and raised his head to look at them. First her, then Tate. "I owe you an apology," he said to Tate. "Wanted to give it in person."

Okay, this was…not what Avery had expected. At all.

"I was so worked up about the land being sold, I never realized what a shit I've been until tonight," Ray continued, his expression woeful. "That land's as good as sold, ain't it?"

Tate nodded. "Seems that way."

Ray nodded too, then dropped his gaze to his boots. "I'm still mad as hell at you and your buddy for buying it. But you done it fair and square, so I want to say I'm sorry for my actions before. And for tonight." He swallowed, his shoulders hitching. "I was drunk and wasn't thinkin'. My f-family's all I got left, and I..." He covered his eyes with a hand, silent sobs shaking him.

Avery couldn't stand it. Maybe her feelings for Mason were making her soft. "Your sister's still here, Ray. Did you want to see her?"

His head snapped up, his eyes searching the yard. "Catherine? She stayed?"

"Yeah, she's real worried about you."

He pressed his lips together, fat tears rolling down his cheeks. "I want to see her."

It was about the best ending they could have hoped for. Catherine ended up taking her brother home with her. Ray was still calling out apologies as she put him in her car.

"That went well," Tate said as they got into Avery's.

"Tell me about it." She glanced at the dashboard clock. It was almost ten now. "How quick do you think we can get the paperwork done and go home?"

He raised an eyebrow at her. "Why, you in a hurry to get there?"

"Yes." She had Mason waiting for her, and that was more than reason enough to hurry.

By the time she arrived home ninety minutes later the rain had stopped, and the house was dark. She stepped inside the front door, disappointment hitting her when a quiet stillness settled around her. There were no lights on. Had Mason gone to bed?

Maybe he was in *her* bed.

She hurried to her room, but it was empty. She walked back to the stairs leading to the suite, wondering if he'd gone down to his place, then caught a slight movement out of the corner of her eye and whirled to face the kitchen.

But it wasn't a threat. Through the door to the back deck she saw Mason sitting out there on the top step, his back to her as he stared out into the yard, his arm around Ric. He was hunched over. Almost as if protecting himself from something.

Her heart twisted. Even from this distance she could tell something was wrong. That he was hurting.

She started toward him without conscious thought, needing to ease his suffering.

MASON TURNED HIS head when Ric alerted him there was someone behind them. Avery opened the door and stepped out onto the deck. "Hey," she murmured softly.

"Hey." He didn't have it in him to get up and go to her right now. "Everything go all right?"

"Yes. Sorry I took so long, we had to file the paperwork before I could come home." She sat beside him, studying him with worried eyes. "I'd ask if you're okay, but I can see you're not."

He didn't see the point in lying to her. He didn't want to lie to her ever. "Yeah, not really."

She eased closer and wrapped her arms around his ribs, leaning into him. "Thinking about things you'd rather not remember?"

He nodded, glad he didn't have to explain. That she got it. "I fell asleep for a bit, then wished I hadn't. Ric woke me up." But not before he'd been transported back into his personal nightmare.

His skin still crawled with the memory of his comrades' terrified and agonized screams as they burned to death in that wreck. Nothing in the world would ever make him forget that sound. The sickening helplessness.

She made a sympathetic sound and rested her head on his shoulder. "What can I do to help?"

He placed his hands over hers where they rested over his sternum. "You're already doing it." Just having her close helped chase away the ghosts in his mind.

Avery nestled closer and relaxed into him. Mason relaxed too, pulling in a deep, steadying breath. He was off-balance, unsure if he was ready for what he was feeling for her, because it was twice as intense and powerful as it had been with his ex, and he'd sworn he'd never make himself that vulnerable again.

But every minute he spent with Avery, the potential cost became more worth the risk. He couldn't shut off his feelings now anyway, it was too late. Until her, he'd doubted his ability to love. Or that he was worthy of being loved. Not anymore.

The only thing he could do now was go forward and hope he didn't fall off the cliff he was poised on and smash against the rocks waiting below.

Slowly the restriction in his chest eased, making it easier to breathe again. The specter of his nightmare began to fade under the warmth of Avery's concern and comfort.

In those long minutes they spent together in the cool, damp air staring up at the night sky, she taught him the meaning of true intimacy. About being silent and comfortable together as she slowly broke down his inner walls with gentle and sincere affection.

Overwhelmed by his feelings for her, Mason gathered her into his lap and tucked her head under his chin. She sighed and nestled into him, running her fingers over his chest and arm. He closed his eyes, absorbing the moment while the crickets sang softly around them.

The sense of peace and acceptance he experienced in those moments with her stunned him. She was the only one who had ever been able to quiet his mind just by being close. Without a single word she'd calmed him, grounded him in the here and now instead of the past.

He nuzzled her cheek, waiting for her to turn her face to his. The kiss was slow, tender. Unbelievably erotic.

With only a single kiss she had him wound tight as a cable, his heart thundering against his ribs.

Avery made him feel seen and accepted, baggage and all. She made him feel like he mattered. Like he still had something to offer.

She made him feel like he was still worthy. Maybe even worthy of being loved.

Mason inhaled, a painful pressure expanding his ribs. He would do fucking anything for her—except let her go. He just couldn't.

Because he was in love with her.

It rocked him, but he couldn't deny it was true. He needed her. Would never stop needing and wanting her.

Without a word he gathered her up and stood, lifting her to his chest. She stroked the back of his hair, a gentle smile on her lips. He kissed them, drinking in the tenderness she offered, aware of how precious a gift it was.

He carried her inside, nudged the door closed after Ric and strode down the hall to her room. This was her most private space and he wanted to explore this new, tender intimacy with her in more detail.

Even as they undressed each other he felt the difference. The emotional shift inside him. This was no longer about the thrill of the conquest, of making her want him, or even the wielding of the control he enjoyed. It was about having this amazing, strong and caring woman surrender herself to him because she trusted him.

That changed everything. *Avery* had changed everything.

He was deep in unknown territory now. Whatever the future held, he just prayed he wouldn't screw up and lose her forever.

CHAPTER EIGHTEEN

A tall stack of blueberry pancakes and a side of crispy bacon had never looked so good to him.

Mason poured syrup over them, his mouth watering. He couldn't remember the last time he'd been so hungry for breakfast. Or the last time he'd been this happy. It felt like a literal weight had been lifted from his chest. The whole world seemed brighter, the horizon before him full of possibilities.

All because of Avery.

"Wow. That's a lotta syrup," she said from across the café table, voice dry.

"I burned off a lot of calories last night. And this morning," he added with a smug grin at her, enjoying the way her cheeks turned pink.

"You did," she conceded. "Guess I did too."

He stopped pouring to stare at her in disbelief. "You *guess*?"

She grinned and took a sip of her coffee. "Okay, I did."

"Damn right." He'd made sure of it. Twice. And he'd taken her out for a breakfast date this morning because he wanted to show her it wasn't just sex he wanted. He wanted to spend more time with her with their clothes on too, and while he was still concerned about the threat hanging over her, installing those security cameras had eased his mind a lot.

He dug into his pancakes, watching Avery as she ate her omelet, and thought about what he'd done to her last night. How intense it had been while he'd teased her clit with his tongue, her hand gripping the headboard above her because he'd ordered her not to let go of it.

Watching her submit, her willingly putting herself into his hands, had been the biggest turn on. He'd kept teasing her, pushing her right to the edge before backing off, waiting until she broke and begged him to let her come before thrusting deep inside her.

Even that hadn't been enough. He'd draped her long legs over his shoulders and folded her up underneath him, desperate to get as deep as possible, wanting her eyes to be blind with pleasure, her entire body trembling when he finally let her come.

Everything about last night had been a revelation. An awakening, like part of him had been asleep until now. They hadn't talked more about their relationship yet, but he was going to bring it up soon. He wanted Avery, as much of her as she was willing to give him.

Her expression changed suddenly. Tightened as she looked at something over his shoulder.

Mason immediately turned, silently cursing as Ray walked in.

The old timer stopped dead when he saw them together, his eyes widening. He clenched his jaw and stood there stiffly, his cheeks flushing.

"Morning, Ray," Avery murmured.

Ray's gaze jumped to her. He nodded once, then focused back on Mason. "Having a celebratory meal out, are you?"

Jesus. He thought Avery had said Ray was all apologetic last night. "Just having pancakes," Mason answered calmly, refusing to be baited.

Ray stood there quivering with indignation for a moment, his whole face changing color, but the pain in his eyes was real. "Hope you choke on 'em," he said, and stormed back out.

Avery sighed as people around the café began murmuring amongst themselves, shooting glances at them. "Want me to go talk to him?"

"No. Let him be." Guy had issues and clearly wasn't handling the loss of the property well. Mason actually kind of felt bad for him. Even if he had tagged the Jeep. Mostly he just wanted this finalized and wrapped up. "No idea what the holdup is with the bank. I've submitted everything they asked for. It shouldn't be taking this long." Every day that passed without the sale being finalized made him worry that something had gone wrong.

"I'm sure it's just a red tape issue, and don't forget it's a small town. Things move slower here. The sale will go through, and then you'll have more work than you know what to do with."

"Can't wait. I'm doing up a marketing plan today and starting to source some supplies."

"I love that my man's a go-getter." Her lips curved as she chewed a mouthful of toast.

My man. He loved how that sounded. It gave him an overpowering urge to reach across the table, take her face in his hands and kiss every inch of it right here in the middle of the restaurant. "You sure you have to go into work this morning?"

She chuckled. "I'm sure. Why, you had something else in mind?"

"Maybe." He wanted to take her back home and savor her bite by bite.

"Uh-huh, *maybe.*" Her eyes gleamed with humor,

and interest. "But I have to get my ass in gear. Got bad guys to catch and files to finish. Including one on whoever busted up my windows, and hopefully find enough evidence to ID my psycho stalker."

There hadn't been any further incidents at her place since, and with the security cameras installed he didn't expect any. "I'll have dinner waiting for you when you get home."

"See, I could really get used to this set up."

"Good." He opened his mouth to broach the subject of their relationship, but she pulled out her phone to check it.

"New file from the Billings PD. I gotta get going into the office." She shoveled a few more bites into her mouth, then reached for her bag, but he grabbed her hand to stop her.

"I got this."

"You sure?"

"Positive. Go."

Smiling at him, she slid out of the booth. Mason caught her forearm and tugged her toward him. "See you when you get home," he murmured.

"You'll get to see *all* of me when I get home," she whispered back, then cupped the side of his face in her hand and leaned down to kiss him. Right there in the restaurant, in full view of everyone. Mason thought his heart would explode. "Bye," she whispered.

"Bye, angel eyes. Go get 'em."

He watched through the window as she sauntered to her vehicle. Damn, he had to be the luckiest son of a bitch on the planet to be with her.

She unlocked her door, saw him looking and blew a kiss. Mason pretended to catch it and press it to his lips. Then, waggling his eyebrows, he shaped the fingers of his left hand into a circle and thrust his right index finger in and out of it.

Avery laughed and got in her car. Mason grinned, his heart full to bursting. Things were looking up. He just hoped he could win her heart, because she already owned his.

****

Hours later near the end of the day, Avery still didn't have a clue about who was harassing her. And that pissed her off.

"What am I missing?" she muttered to herself, toggling between various screens on her computer as she reviewed all the evidence she'd gathered so far. Shannon Torbert had no arrest records, and neither Avery nor her Billings contact had come up with anything of use so far. Avery had to keep digging on her own.

As part of her own investigation she'd made a list of every possible person she could think of who might consider her their enemy. Most of the cases she dealt with here were pretty mild, but there was a handful that might have the potential for trouble. If anything panned out, she would pass pertinent intel to the investigating detective handling her case in Billings.

Including the Zinke file. Although Mr. Zinke was currently dealing with assault charges brought against him by her department. As he would have just as much of a grudge against Tate as he did her, it didn't make much sense that he would be the one targeting her.

Same for Ray. He'd been embarrassed and remorseful last night, and fairly civil to her this morning, before giving Mason that parting shot.

Which left only a handful of others on her list, all from her time on the Billings force. And one name stuck out far more than the others.

Going with her gut, she picked up the phone and called her contact in Billings. "Hey, when you've got five minutes, could I trouble you to send me a list of whoever's visited Mike Radzat since his parole was denied?" It was the only lead that made any kind of sense to her. And since he was still locked up in prison, the only way he could get to her was through someone else. Who, though?

"No problem. I'll compile a list now and send it over."

"Great, thanks." She hung up and reviewed her list again, growing more and more certain she was onto something with Radzat.

"How's it going, Sherlock?" Tate asked as he walked in.

"Slowly. But I think I've got a promising thread to pull on now," she said without looking up from her screen.

"Yeah? What've you got?" He pulled a chair around to sit next to her and study her screen.

She reviewed everything, explaining her theories.

Tate nodded. "Yeah, I'm gonna agree that we can rule out Zinke and Ray for sure. Of the two of us, both of them would come after me, not you."

"Exactly. I'm thinking it has to be related to Radzat. With his parole denial, the timing is right." A ding signaled an incoming email. "Here's the list of who's visited him."

She opened it and read the names. "Wow, seven women, huh? No guys." She shook her head. "No way they're all related to him. I don't recognize a single name."

"It's crazy to think there are women out there looking to hook up with a convict."

"Nuts," she agreed, and called her contact back. "Thanks for the list. Any way I can get an image of these women? It's related to a case I'm working on."

"Sure. Give me a few minutes."

Avery ran the women's names in the meantime, and

found nothing of interest in the database about them. Whoever they were, none of them had criminal records.

"Can you run more background and credit card info on these three while I check out the other four?"

"Sure." He wrote down the names. "You guys are still coming over for dinner tonight, right?"

She looked over at him, caught off guard. "What?"

"The barbecue. My sister's coming down to stay with us for a bit. Remember? Nina's picking her up in an hour."

Shit, she'd completely forgotten Tala was coming from Kelowna today. "Yeah, we'll be there." She needed to remind Mason.

"'Kay." Tate's hazel-green eyes lit with interest. "Anything you want to share before then?"

Her face heated. She didn't know exactly where she and Mason stood at the moment, and she wasn't about to admit to Tate that they'd slept together. "Not really."

His expression turned serious. "Look, I just gotta say this, and then we'll leave it alone. Mase is awesome in a lot of ways and I love the guy like a brother, but you need to know he comes with a certain amount of baggage that isn't going to magically disappear. So just…you need to know that going in, that's all."

"I know." She was willing to deal with the baggage if it meant being in a committed relationship with him. The question was whether Mason would allow it.

"Okay," Tate said with a relieved smile. "Just looking out for my partner."

Thankfully she was spared any further awkward conversation by a new email hitting her inbox. "Got the images."

They studied them together. "These five could easily be the woman at the resort," Tate said a minute later.

"They could," she agreed, analyzing their builds. The two remaining women had completely the wrong build to be her suspect.

Tate squeezed her shoulder and rose. "I'll start on these three now and get back to you. If you need anything else, holler."

"Thanks." She loved and respected Tate for trying to protect her. But Mason was already deep under her skin and in her heart. It was too late to protect her now; if Mason dropped her it was going to hurt like hell.

She expelled a breath and started digging deeper into her list of the remaining four female suspects, still preoccupied with Mason. The man had managed to turn her inside out in the matter of a week. As it was, she was going to have trouble keeping her hands off him in front of the others, and was a little worried that he would have no such compunction.

After tonight, Avery had a feeling their secret wouldn't be a secret for long.

CHAPTER NINETEEN

Tala was glad she'd made the decision to come down here for a few days. Part of her job as big sister meant making sure her brother never got hurt again, so ever since Tate had told her about Nina, she'd been dying to meet his new lady.

Today had taken any worries about Tate off her shoulders. Within fifteen minutes of Nina picking her up at the airport that afternoon, Tala decided her brother had chosen wisely. A few hours later, and she already loved Nina to pieces. How could she not?

"I'm so glad you're here," Nina said to her with a happy smile, as she, Tala and Avery helped themselves to some nibbles at the coffee table in Tate's cozy but rustic living room while he and Mason dealt with dinner.

"Me too. I'd come down to visit a lot more, but my training schedule's kicking into high gear."

"Yeah, how's that going?" Avery asked, helping herself to a chocolate-dipped piece of pineapple.

"Good. Hard, but good. Though ever since getting this thing, nothing really seems that bad by comparison." She shifted the prosthetic where her right foot and lower leg used to be.

Four years now. She would never regret her service to her country, but she did still miss her foot. Crazy to think how much her life had changed since that horrible day. She'd survived so much, including the latest blow of seeing her baby girl move down here to go to college. Tala missed her like crazy.

"I'll bet," Avery said, and Tala noticed her eye kept trailing over to Mason, who was in the kitchen laughing at something Tate was saying. She thought she'd felt some sparks striking off those two, and she was never wrong about that kind of thing. Her own romantic life was nonexistent, since the only man she wanted had no clue and was usually thousands of kilometers away from her at any given time.

"How long have you been doing biathlon?" Nina asked, cradling a glass of white wine in one hand.

"Just over a year now. Hoping to make the para national team next season, though I'm considered kind of long in the tooth as far as biathlon goes. That's my goal, anyway." She hated talking about herself, though, and she was more interested in Nina and what was happening with Avery. "So, nothing more on whoever's been stalking you?"

Avery glanced at her from the loveseat across from the sofa she and Nina were seated on. Tala had met her twice before, and had talked to her on the phone dozens more. Avery was a levelheaded badass, and Tala was thrilled that Tate had been partnered with her. "Not yet. Hopefully soon. Tomorrow I'm following up on some leads my contact in Billings uncovered today."

"You'll track 'em down," Nina said with absolute confidence. "But enough of that—Tala and I are dying here. What's going on with you and Mason?" She popped a grape tomato into her mouth, eyes wide with curiosity.

"Dying," Tala agreed, leaning forward. "So spill." She'd already been here when Avery and Mason arrived thirty minutes ago, and had picked up on the vibe between them almost instantly. "I've known Mason for years, and always hoped he'd pick someone good for a change. And you're definitely one of the good guys," she added with a grin.

Avery cleared her throat and raised her wineglass to her lips. "Not exactly sure what's happening yet," she mumbled, taking a sip.

It was clear enough to Tala. That boy was seriously into Avery, and Tala couldn't be more thrilled. Avery was exactly the kind of woman Mason needed. Someone strong and independent, but also kind and patient. Someone who appreciated all his mostly good qualities, and was willing to work with the rest.

"Okay, fair enough," Nina said. "But you're into him, right? Because you look like you're seriously into him."

Avery shrugged, trying to downplay it. "Yeah."

"I love it." Her voice was rich with satisfaction.

Avery shot Nina a frown. "Why do you love it?"

"Because while you're opposites in a lot of ways, you also complement each other well. Exactly like Tate and me." She beamed at Avery. "Plus, I think you're good for him. And I *know* he's good for you." Her grin made it clear she meant between the sheets.

"Definitely," Tala agreed with a decisive nod. "He needs someone steady and solid."

Avery smiled at the compliment. "And do you think he's good for me too?"

Nina's gaze shot to Tala, worry in her eyes. "He won't hurt her, will he? Because Avery's already had her heart trampled on once."

Avery grimaced. "Nina, jeez."

"Well, it's true."

Tala reached out to take Avery's hand and squeezed it in reassurance. She liked Avery, and Mason deserved to find happiness. They could make it work if they were willing to put their pasts behind them. "He's a good guy with a big heart. Just look at how he treats his dog."

"I know. It's the darkness in him that worries me."

Tala sobered and withdrew her hand, easing back into the sofa. "Did he tell you about what happened?"

"Yes."

Tala blinked in surprise. "Then that's huge." Veterans didn't talk about that kind of shit with anyone they didn't trust. And if Mason had made the effort with Avery, then that spoke volumes about his feelings for her. This relationship had serious potential, and Tala hoped it worked out for them.

Avery shifted on the loveseat and stared into her wineglass. "Just trying not to get ahead of myself."

Nina shrugged like it was no big deal. "Falling for someone is always scary. It's a leap of faith. If your gut says it's right, then it's right, and all you have to do is make the jump."

The words hit Tala hard. She liked to think she was brave, but the reality was, she was too chicken to make her own jump. Too afraid of being rejected and ruining everything.

Avery gave Nina a bland look and Tala shook her head. "Is she always like this?" Tala lifted her chin at Nina.

"Honestly? Yeah. She's our little miss ray of sunshine. Can put a positive spin on pretty much anything." She playfully touched the tip of Nina's nose.

Nina wrinkled it and leaned away. "It's a gift. But I'm not a dog. You don't get to boop my nose. Boop his," she said, nodding at Ric, who was sitting at Avery's feet with his chin resting on her knee, gazing up at her with hopeful, mismatched eyes.

"This one's in love with you already," Tala said with a grin, and she had a feeling his master wasn't far off that mark either. "I can't believe how attached to you he is. Usually he's stuck to Mason like Velcro."

"It's because he knows I'm weak and will feed him treats," Avery answered, sneaking a cucumber slice to Ric. "Anyway, did you guys get to see Rylee after you got into Missoula?"

The mention of her daughter filled Tala with warmth. "Yes, she came with Nina to the airport to pick me up. We dropped her off at campus on the way through town. She's coming up here this weekend to spend a couple days with me, and I can't wait."

"She's a great kid."

"She is." Having her move so far from home had been a huge and painful adjustment. Tala was mostly rolling with it, but it wasn't easy, especially after her daughter had been drugged by the same psycho that had killed her roommate, and nearly killed Nina weeks ago.

Thankfully the bastard was now dead. Tate had taken him out and saved Nina. Tala had been relieved, but the empty nest thing was real, leaving a hole in her heart *and* her life. It sucked. Her job and rigorous training schedule were the only things keeping her sane at the moment.

"And she's got a knack for astronomy too," Nina added with a smile.

"Maybe that has something to do with her favorite professor," Tala said on a laugh. Her stomach let out a loud growl and she glanced toward the kitchen. "I traveled all day, and at this rate I'm gonna freaking starve to death before they get food to us. Back in a minute."

She got off the sofa and strode for the kitchen, the tiny hitch in her gait from her prosthesis barely noticeable as she headed for Tate and Mason. "You guys working in here, or just talking?"

They both whipped around to stare at her with identical guilty expressions, bottles in hand. Tate's a beer, and

Mason's a root beer. "Both," Tate said. "Everything's under control."

"Good, because my stomach's about to eat itself from starvation. Need a hand or something?" She raised an eyebrow.

"No, we got it." Her brother whipped back around, and soon the kitchen was a flurry of activity.

Avery came up beside her, a smirk on her face. "Love how you just snap them into action."

"Must be a military thing," Nina mused, watching the boys work as she stuffed a piece of chocolate-dipped fruit into her mouth.

"More like a big sister thing," Avery said. "There's nothing Tate wouldn't do for her. If she told Tate to stand on his head, he'd do it without even asking why." She shook her head. "It's adorable how much he hero worships you," she murmured to Tala.

"Well, that goes both ways," Tala said with pride. "My brother's awesome. And now he's got an awesome girl," she added, wrapping an arm around Nina's shoulders.

Within minutes, the guys had the meal ready. Having successfully completed her supervision, Tala gave Avery and Nina a wave. "Get in here and grab a plate before I eat it all."

Avery went to stand in line behind Nina, but Mason had already filled her a plate and handed it over with a private smile that made Tala bite back a snicker. "Enjoy," he murmured to Avery.

"I will." She took the plate without reacting, trying to play it cool. But the pink in her cheeks gave her away, and Mason sat next to her at the table. *Right* next to her, so that their shoulders touched. If he thought he was being subtle, he was mistaken.

"So, how's the business plans coming, you guys?" Tala asked as she helped herself to some veggies and oven-roasted chicken parm. Rifle Creek Tactical was a great idea, and both Mason and Braxton would be solid business partners for her brother. She just hoped Tate stayed on as a detective here until the business took off, because startups were always risky.

"Couple of snags to get past, but otherwise good," Tate answered, passing Nina the chicken. "Mase has been working on the possible programs and price points."

"Speaking of," Mason began, "if the idea of managing the place is still too much, maybe you'd be interested in doing some cross-country skiing courses through the winter instead? I was thinking we could combine it with a winter/mountain survival component. We could even market a class specifically geared for women, since they might be more comfortable with you instructing them than any of us."

The offer surprised Tala. Tate had asked her several times if she wanted to be part of it, but she hadn't thought about it seriously because it was still early stages, nothing had been finalized, and she lived in Canada. Taking on a managerial role remotely wasn't an option, yet moving down here meant upending her entire life. Not to mention the strict immigration procedure for trying to get a Green Card.

"I'd love to teach a class like that, as long as I could make it work with my training schedule." It would also allow her to see Rylee, and she was all about finding excuses to make that happen.

"Great. I've been interviewing architects for the main lodge project. Got some blueprints today if you wanna see 'em."

"Love to. Have you shown them to Brax yet?"

"No, I was gonna wait until I heard from him."

"Why don't we call him now?" Finding excuses to contact Braxton was something else she was all about, and this one had landed right in her lap. "It's just about time for reveille over there."

"We woke him up early last week and he wasn't too happy about it," Tate said, helping himself to one last scoop of potato casserole.

"He won't mind," Tala said, eager to see and talk to him. They were on friendly enough terms, but this way with everyone else around, it wouldn't seem weird or desperate if she called him to say hi. "Here, we'll use my phone for a video call."

She pulled it out and dialed the number, which she'd memorized by heart within minutes of getting it last year. Until then they'd mostly resorted to email, and had only seen other in person twice when Braxton had come to Kelowna with his unit for mountaineering training at SilverStar.

The ring tone filled the dining room. "H'lo?" a sleepy male voice answered.

And there he was. Gorgeous, quiet, serious Braxton. The man who had been there for her during her darkest hours. The man who had literally held her life in his hands, and refused let go until the medevac crew had flown her back to base.

She'd already had feelings for him before that day. Not surprisingly, they'd become a thousand times more intense since.

"Hey, it's me," Tala said, her heart thudding as his shadowy face came into view. She'd love to wake up to that face every day, but that was a secret she could never tell, for a lot of reasons. He was one of her brother's best friends, for one, and things could get hella messy if they crossed the line. "You still sleeping?"

"Yeah." Covers rustled in the background as Braxton sat up in his bunk. "Time is it?"

"Time to rise and shine," Tala said cheerfully. "I'm in Rifle Creek at Tate's place, and the gang's all here. Say hi to everyone." She turned the phone so he could see them all.

"Hey, Brax," Mason said as the rest of them waved.

Braxton lifted a hand and blinked sleepily at them, his bare, solidly muscled chest and shoulders visible above the covers. A chest she'd been fantasizing about for over four long years now. *Yum.* "Hey. What are you guys doing?"

"Just finished dinner. How are things there?" Tate asked.

"All right." He squinted at the camera. "I hear Mase, but I can't see him."

Tala angled the phone more. "There."

Mason put on a cheesy smile. "Morning. And say hi to Avery." He slung an arm around her shoulders and pulled her in tight to his side. Claiming her in front of them all.

Tala grinned at him in approval. *Way to go, Mase.*

Avery smiled too, her face flushing. "Hey, Braxton."

Braxton stared at her for a moment, then the sleepiness seemed to clear from his dark brown eyes, a slow grin curving his mouth. "Hey. Anything new with you guys, Mase?"

"Yep. All good things," he answered, hugging Avery to him. "Got some blueprints I wanted to show you. An idea for the main lodge."

Braxton opened his mouth to say something but Tate's phone rang, covering whatever it was.

"It's my banker. Must be back from his trip," Tate said, looking up at the others. "Hopefully calling with good news." He walked away as he answered, his voice trailing off as he moved to the next room.

"They approve the sale?" Braxton asked, wide awake now.

"Hope so," Mason said, craning his neck to see Tate.

"How are things there, Brax?" Tala asked.

A light came on in the background, illuminating his

handsome face, and the crooked smile he gave her had her insides curling. "Pretty quiet right now."

"That's good." She worried about him constantly over there.

Tate walked in, his expression giving nothing away. Tala hated it when he did that, because even she couldn't tell what he was thinking. "Well?" she demanded. "What did they say?"

Tate slid his phone away, a smile spreading over his face. "Congrats, boys. Soon as Mase and I sign the final papers, we're the proud owners of Rifle Creek Tactical."

Mason whooped, hugged Avery and jumped up to grab Tate. He slung an arm around Tate's shoulders, then faced Tala's phone. "So, Brax. When you comin' back, man? We need you down here to help us get this thing up and running."

Braxton grinned, his teeth bright against his tanned skin. "Workin' on it."

Mason looked at Tate. "What are we waiting for? We've been on pins and needles waiting for him to get back from his trip and make a decision. Call him back and see if he'll agree to let us sign tonight."

Tate grinned. "Now?"

"Why not?"

Tate shrugged. "All right. Hang on." He called the banker back, spoke for a few moments, then ended the call. "It's a go. We're meeting at his place in twenty minutes."

Mason let him go and held out a hand for Avery. "Come on. Let's go do this."

She placed her hand in his, smiling. "Okay."

"Tal, keep Brax on the line. I'll text you when we sign," Tate said, hooking an arm around Nina's waist as they all headed for the door.

And just like that, Tala found herself alone with the object of all her romantic fantasies still on the screen.

BRAXTON'S HEART DID a slow, painful roll as Tala's face came back into view a second later. Her chocolate-brown hair was loose and shiny around her shoulders, and he could see the golden flecks in her big brown eyes. "Hey," he murmured. "They all leaving?"

"Yep, already heading out the door. It's just you and me."

He wished he was there in person to make the most of that.

She got up and walked somewhere. He recognized the old logs and white lines of chinking in between them in the walls of Tate's living room, from the original cabin built well over a hundred years ago. "So, when are you coming home?"

"If all goes well, a few more months. Maybe by spring."

"Oh." Her face fell a little. "That long?"

His heart tripped, that stupid bit of hope that refused to die flaring to life again no matter how hard he tried to snuff it out. Did she miss him just because they were friends? Or was it something more? Did she ever lay awake at night thinking of him, dreaming about them being together? If she had, she'd never given any indication of it.

Realizing he was staring, he cleared his throat. At least the other guys were out of the tiny room they were all bunking in, so they had a little privacy. "Right now, I'm supposed to get a couple weeks' leave over Christmas. I was planning to come down there to see the guys if it all works out." He wished he could reach through the screen and touch her. "Will you be there?"

She nodded and sat. There was a fire going somewhere close by, because the light of the flames flickered over her face. She was so fucking gorgeous he could only stare.

It had been way too long since he'd seen her in person. They'd become pretty close since she was wounded. She was one of the few of people he considered a real friend, along with Tate and Mason.

Mostly they kept in touch via email or text, and she'd occasionally send him a cute picture of her amputee teddy bear, Mr. Stumpy on his latest adventure. They didn't talk on the phone or video call much. That might be for the best, since he wasn't exactly a conversationalist, but he loved getting to hear her voice and see her face. He missed her so damn bad, and had thought so many times about telling her how he truly felt the next time he was back home and could get out to Kelowna to see her.

If he ever worked up the balls to tell her, he would do it in person.

"I was thinking of it, yeah. Sounds like Rylee wants to stay here for the holidays rather than come home to Kelowna, so I thought I might come down here and train for a bit over the holidays."

Biathlon. She'd picked it up late last year as a hobby and fallen in love with it. Now she was gunning for a shot at the Canadian Paralympic team. Braxton was so fucking proud of her for working so hard and going after her dreams. After overcoming all the obstacles life had thrown at her, she deserved every happiness she could find. "Good, hopefully I'll get to see you then."

Her smile made his whole chest tighten. "I hope so."

He was totally gone over her, and he'd been careful to make sure she didn't know. That *no* one knew. The truth was, she was way out of his league. He wasn't near good enough for her. And she was also Tate's sister, which meant she was off-limits. But if by some miracle she ever indicated that she wanted him, all bets were off.

That hadn't stopped him from thinking about her, however. Or building up a database of sexual fantasies that had sustained him through several long and brutally demanding deployments in various hot zones overseas.

She didn't know it, but she'd gotten him through a lot of tough times just by living in his head.

The blare of an alarm cut through the air. *Aw, shit.* Mortar or rocket attack, probably. "Sorry, gotta go." Damn shit-tastic timing, as usual.

She nodded, a worried frown drawing her dark eyebrows together, and it didn't take a genius to know the alarm had reminded her of the day she'd been wounded. "Stay safe."

"Will do."

She put on a smile for him. "Bye. Miss you."

Shit. Hearing that made him ache inside. "Miss you too." More than she'd ever know.

He ended the call and jumped from his bunk, still thinking about her as the alarm blared in the background. And that he'd give anything for the chance to make her his.

CHAPTER TWENTY

Since the detective in charge of her case in Billings was currently swamped with higher priority cases, Avery had decided to continue investigating on her own for now and driven to Billings first thing this morning. Of the list of seven possible suspects she had to go on, she'd managed to narrow the field to three contenders as to who was stalking her.

The first two had been dead ends. The third…

A chiming through her vehicle's speakers alerted her of a call. Mason's name displayed on the dash. She smiled as she answered. "Hey."

"Just checking in. How you making out?"

She smirked at his choice of words. "I'm not."

"See? Shoulda waited and taken me with you. Then you'd be making out just fine."

"Riiiight, and I'd be getting so much work done, too." She turned right at the next intersection. "I'm close to my next stop. Call you later."

"Okay, hurry home. Miss you."

The sincerity and lack of teasing in his voice made her chest constrict. "Miss you too." And tonight, they needed to finally hash out exactly where they were going and make sure they were both clear about it before things went any further.

Ending the call, she pushed Mason temporarily from her mind and focused on the task at hand. Shannon Torbert was the last of the suspects Avery wanted to check out in person. Interestingly, Shannon hadn't been at work in the bank this past week. Something about a death in the family that Avery hadn't been able to substantiate.

She pulled up to the curb in front of the house Shannon was supposedly renting a basement suite in. There were no cars parked out front or in the driveway.

Avery got out and walked up the sidewalk to investigate. No one answered the front door, and when she checked in the windows all the lights were off. She headed around back next and rang the bell for the suite.

No answer there either, and it was also dark inside. Someone had brought in the mail recently, however, because the mailbox was empty and there were no newspapers on the doorstep. "So where are you, Shannon?" she murmured.

There was one more obvious place Avery wanted to check before leaving town. Just in case.

She started around the walkway, putting the pieces together in her head. The prison holding Mike Radzat was only six miles away.

Avery turned the corner of the house and stepped onto the driveway. Her gaze fixed on a silver compact car as it slowed near the driveway. The driver was a woman. Young. Dark hair.

Avery stopped. Their gazes locked for an instant through the side window.

Before Avery could get a good look at the driver, the car took off down the street with a screech of its tires.

"Dammit." She bolted for her vehicle, mentally cursing and wishing she had backup with her. She jumped behind the wheel and took off after the car, pulling onto the quiet street just as it turned the corner ahead.

Avery floored it and followed, doing everything in her power to keep the other car within sight. The traffic ahead picked up as the neighborhood transitioned into an area of higher density.

The suspect vehicle darted out to pass a slower-moving car, nearly collided head-on with a minivan before whipping back into the correct lane. Avery set her jaw and followed, but was forced to hit the brakes when someone turned onto the road in front of her.

She darted up a side street and turned an immediate left, hoping to catch up to the silver car, but she caught only a glimpse of it as it turned a sharp left and disappeared from view through the traffic.

Avery had no lights or sirens on her personal vehicle. Pursuing the vehicle in this kind of populated area was just going to get someone seriously hurt. So she pulled over, adrenaline still coursing through her, and dialed her contact at the Billings PD. "Hi, it's Avery. Can you trace a plate for me? It's in relation to Shannon Torbert."

"Sure, gimme the number."

After ending the call, she sat waiting, impatience pumping through her. She was ninety-five-percent certain it had been Torbert driving that car, and that she'd recognized Avery. There was no other explanation for why the driver would have taken off like that.

He called back a few minutes later. "Rental vehicle, from a local company. Name of the person on the rental agreement is Sharon Turner."

Which was real damn close to Shannon Torbert.

"Nothing flagged in the system when I entered that name."

Damn. "All right. Thanks. Will you try and contact her later?"

"Of course."

She ended the call and immediately called Mason to tell him what had happened.

"What are you gonna do now?" he asked when she was done. "Go back to her place and wait?"

"No. She won't go back there now." Not unless she was stupid, although given that she'd linked up with Radzat and had targeted a cop, maybe she was. "And she'll ditch the car."

She sighed and ran her fingers through her hair, suddenly tired now that her adrenaline level had dropped. Mason had kept her up until midnight. She'd been up since three to get out here, and had a six-hour drive ahead of her to get home again. "Just frustrating that I can't prove whether it's her or not."

"Sounds like it was. I'm just glad you're okay."

She smiled faintly, loving that he worried about her. "I'm fine. How are things there?"

"Great. Ric and I've been doing some work on the old barn on the property. Cleaning it out and getting it ready for demolition. You heading back now, then?"

"Yes. See you in just over six hours."

"Can't wait. Drive safe, and call me if you get tired. I'll keep you awake."

He was so damn sweet and caring underneath the bravado. "Thanks. See you soon."

It wasn't until she'd pulled onto the road that she realized her gut instinct had been to reach out to Mason rather than Tate, her fellow detective as well as trusted friend and partner.

That gave her a clear answer to everything she'd been questioning about her feelings for Mason.

She was in deep. Too deep to pull out of it now.

****

Shannon couldn't get her heart to slow down. Even after she'd ditched Avery and driven a few miles north to put some space between them, it was still knocking against her ribs.

Her palms were damp and her breathing was erratic. That had been way too close.

Her fucking *house*. How had the bitch figured out she was the one behind all this? Shannon had been careful through every single step. She'd only come back to Billings today to regroup, see Mike and get fresh clothes.

Tears of frustration and rage burned her eyes. She dashed them away with the back of her hand and kept driving. She couldn't go visit Mike now. Couldn't go for the foreseeable future, either, since now Avery might have the cops looking for her and she didn't have a solid alibi about where she'd been for the past week if anyone questioned her.

A road sign up ahead indicated the distance to the Interstate. East would take her toward the South Dakota border. South to Wyoming. Or west back toward Missoula, and Rifle Creek.

She pushed out a hard, shaky breath. Billings was no longer safe for her. Her instinct was to run. Get across the state line and find somewhere to lie low until she could make a decision about what to do next.

But if she did that, she would lose her man, and all the plans she'd made for their life together.

The tears came faster now, too fast to wipe away. She let them fall, let the rage inside her burst free, a scream tearing from her throat.

She wouldn't let this bitch cost her everything. Not after all she'd risked and all that lay on the line.

Her only choice was to stay and finish this. Risk it all and let the chips fall where they may. Her life was nothing without Mike anyway.

Since the other night, she'd thought of killing Avery

in so many different ways. Maybe making it look like an accident by cutting her brake lines. Ramming her vehicle off a cliff or high mountain road. But running her off the road wasn't certain to kill her. Shooting her in the face was looking better and better. Getting that close without being noticed was the problem.

Shannon still had the can of gas, however. If she could trap Avery somewhere, she could burn her to death. If not, she had a backup plan.

She opened the armrest and curled her hand around the grip of her pistol, imagining the moment when she put a bullet through Avery's head. If Shannon was going down, she was sending Avery to hell first. But she was going to need a new car, and help pulling the murder off.

Fortunately, she knew just where to look.

Resolved, she closed the armrest and turned left at the fork, heading for the highway going west to Rifle Creek.

CHAPTER TWENTY-ONE

Mason pulled open the front door for Avery before she could put her key in the lock, and took her in with a single glance. She looked tired, but not upset. "Glad you're back safe," he said, enveloping her in a hug.

She slid her arms around his ribs and leaned into him. "This is a nice homecoming."

Next to him, Ric was wiggling from the force of his tail wagging. "Hello, my sweet, furry prince," she crooned, reaching down to pet him. Ric's tail wagged even harder, knocking against the wall with rhythmic thuds.

"You're making me jealous of my own beloved dog." Mason curved a hand around the back of her neck and drew her in for a kiss. There was no stiffness or hesitation in her, she just melted into him, making his chest tighten. He wanted a future with her so bad.

When he ended the kiss, she inhaled and gave him a dreamy smile. "Did you cook again?"

"I did. You hungry?"

Her eyes gleamed. "Starving."

He was, too. "I'll feed you, and you can tell me all

about this female suspect." He led her into the kitchen and pulled the roasted chicken breasts and veggies out of the oven. "Go sit."

She did without arguing, watching him with a little smile on her face. "I feel so pampered."

He grinned. "Well, that was easy."

He dished up their dinner and carried it to the table, where Ric was already camped out, lying beneath it like a good boy. His chin was on his paws, but his eyes were trained on Avery in case she decided to sneak him something. "This is another one of my mom's recipes."

"It smells amazing." She took a bite, hummed in pleasure in a way that sent heat shooting into his gut. "Mmm, and it tastes even better. Is there lemon zest in it?"

"A bit. So, tell me about this suspect you went to find today."

"Shannon Torbert. Twenty-six, works as a bank teller in Billings. Never been married. Lives alone in the basement suite I checked out today."

"Ah, a fellow basement dweller with issues."

Her lips quirked. "Well, her issues have turned her into a psycho. I didn't know much about her background until this afternoon, but most of what Tate and my Billings contact found only substantiates what I'd thought. She came from a broken, abusive home. No father in the picture. Was taken into foster care when she was four, and got involved with petty crime in her teens, but probably before that."

Mason shook his head. "She sounds like me, except for the crime bit. That *would* have been me if it hadn't been for my mom."

Avery gave him a sympathetic smile. "But look what you've done with your life. You have so much to be proud of. *I'm* proud that you didn't let yourself become a statistic, when you were a kid, and after you were injured."

He squirmed a bit at the praise, but it also sent warmth through his whole body. "Thanks. Anyway, what else did you guys find out?"

"She met Mike Radzat online early this year, and she goes to visit him regularly. We think she's in love with him, and that him being denied parole might have set her off. She's looking for a target to hit back, and I'm it."

"Did you put out an alert for her?"

"Yes, but she's got at least one alias, and probably others we don't know about. If she's smart, she's already found another vehicle and maybe put on a disguise. And her crimes are such small potatoes compared to what's going on out there, the Billings P.D. can't devote much time or manpower to look for her. Right now, our best chance of locating her is when she messes up and uses a credit card we can track her with, or gets in contact with Radzat."

"She works at a bank, so we'll assume she's smarter than that. She'll make a cash withdrawal and use it sparingly."

"Right. She'll probably leave town now that she knows I saw her. Maybe try to go to another state for a while. But if she's in love with Radzat, she won't be able to stay away from him forever. So it's a waiting game."

"I feel better knowing she's probably running in the opposite direction from you."

"Me too." She finished her dinner a minute after him and pushed her plate away. "That was fantastic, thank you. Didn't realize how hungry I was." She stood with her plate, arching her back to stretch. "Or stiff from being in the car so long today."

He took the plate from her and ignored her protests as he carried the dishes to the sink. "Ric and I didn't get out for our usual hike today." He shifted his gaze to her. "Wanna go check out the property with me?"

"I've already seen it."

"Not with me."

A slow smile tugged at her lips. "You want to show me something up there?"

He smiled back, already planning it in his mind. "I do."

****

Not surprisingly, Rifle Creek wasn't busy tonight. A handful of people were out walking in the historic downtown district, exercising their dogs.

It had taken her a while to get everything organized, but Shannon was finally here. The bar parking lot only had a few vehicles in it. One of them was Ray's.

She reversed into a spot near his old truck and tugged the brim of her cap lower over her forehead. She hadn't bothered with a wig, instead tucking her hair up in a bun, and the cap covered it. Nobody here knew her except Ray.

Her eyes adjusted quickly to the dim interior. As expected, Ray was seated at the bar with a half-finished glass of beer. He had both forearms on it, his head and shoulders bent in a picture of dejection.

She slid onto the stool beside him. "Hey, Ray."

He lifted his head, blinked at her a couple of times. He was drunk already. She'd bet money he wouldn't remember her name even if he'd been sober. "Oh. Hi. Thought you left town?"

"Car broke down a few miles down the highway, so I came back here for the night." She ordered herself a double whiskey. It would help settle her nerves.

Shannon had barely resisted the urge to drive past Avery's house and check if she was home, wanting to wait for the best opportunity. Targeting her there was the most dangerous, because of that nosy neighbor and the probability that Avery's man would be there. Shannon wanted to be able to shoot her and get away.

"Ah." Ray took a sip of his beer as the bartender handed Shannon her glass. "You getting it fixed now?"

"Yes. I'll be gone for good as of tomorrow." She tossed back half the whiskey, wincing at the burn, but she needed some liquid courage right now. She also needed more intel. "So, Ray, you look upset about something. What's wrong?" Not that she cared, she just needed information about Avery and her man.

Ray sighed and set down his glass, shaking his head. "The property I told you about. Deal closed last night."

"Oh, no, I'm so sorry. Your family wouldn't listen to you?"

"No." He choked up, struggled to regain his composure before continuing. "Don't have any family left, now. They've all cut me off. 'Cept for Catherine, but she probably will soon too."

Blah, blah, blah. "The land sold to the people you thought it would? Avery's boyfriend?"

His eyebrows contracted in a fierce frown. "Yeah, him and Avery's partner." His jaw clenched. "It's all over. And now those heartless assholes are up there right now, gloating over their victory."

Shannon froze in the act of bringing the glass to her lips. "What? Who is?"

He waved a hand, growing agitated. "Them. Tate's friend."

To hell with Tate. "Who?"

"Avery's boyfriend." He shot her an annoyed look. "Mason something-or-other."

Her heart beat faster. "They're up at the property?" He'd told her all about it last time they talked. She knew exactly where it was, and how to get to the entrance.

"Yeah. Passed his red Jeep just before it turned onto the access road up there a while ago."

Shannon grabbed his arm, and his gaze snapped to hers in surprise. "When? How long ago?"

216

He frowned in confusion. "I dunno, maybe…twenty minutes ago?"

"Are you sure?"

"Pretty sure." He pulled his arm free, giving her an odd look. "What the hell do you care?"

"No reason. I just hate that they're up their gloating. Rubbing salt in your wound." It was perfect. A totally isolated location, and it was getting dark out. No one would even hear the shots up there. She had to get up there before they left.

Ray's face fell, his expression dejected. "It ain't right. It ain't right, but it's all over now."

It's not over. Not yet.

She left cash on the bar and hurried out to her vehicle. No one was in the parking lot when she got behind the wheel.

She glanced around once to make sure no one was watching before taking out her weapon. Her hands shook a little as she loaded a full magazine into it, and slipped an extra one in her pocket.

"Calm down," she ordered herself. She had to do this. For herself as much as for Mike. If she went to jail for killing Avery, so be it. She was prepared to go to jail to prove to Mike how devoted she was to him.

No, it wasn't over yet. But it soon would be.

CHAPTER TWENTY-TWO

"So what did you want to show me?" Avery asked him as they walked back to his Jeep.

Mason was glad they'd decided to come up here. The evening air was cool and damp, the scent of the forest filling their lungs, and he hoped it had taken Avery's mind off everything else for a while. They'd just played fetch with Ric for forty minutes, and he was finally getting tired, panting like mad as he trotted in front of them, his prize stick in his mouth.

"Not here. Up at the barn." He opened the back hatch and whistled for Ric, who leaped inside the back with a single bound. "Okay, buddy." He took the stick from him and tossed it aside. "You have some water and then sleep it off. We'll be back in a while." He shut the hatch and locked the vehicle, his pistol holstered on his hip in the unlikely event they ran into a bear or a cougar out here.

Avery glanced over her shoulder as they walked away from the Jeep up the slope. "He doesn't look tired anymore."

Mason looked back and grinned. Ric was sitting in the driver's seat, peering anxiously through the windshield at them with an expression of betrayal, his ears perked. *Dad, how can you leave me here by myself?* "He'll be fine. A few minutes and he'll curl up on his bed in the back for a nap."

"No, he won't. He'll stay on sentry duty the entire time we're gone."

Probably. "He'll be okay." He reached for her hand, her skin chilly compared to his. "You cold?"

"Just my hands."

He stopped and took her hands between his, rubbing them to warm them. "Hmm, I'll have to figure out a way to warm them up."

"In the barn, I'll bet," she said dryly.

"That's a great idea. Come on."

He led her up the incline toward the trail that cut through the trees, the changing deciduous trees glowing gold and orange amongst the verdant evergreens. The trail widened where the forest ended at the edge of the clear land, revealing the old, weathered barn a hundred yards or so in the clearing.

"You sure you need to demo it with machinery?" Avery said. "Looks like you could push it over by hand if you wanted."

He chuckled. "It's over a hundred years old, but she's still a sturdy old gal. I kind of wish we could keep her, but it's cheaper to pull it down and build new." He slid the panel door open and ushered her inside, then slid it shut. "Hang on a sec."

He'd left a battery-powered lamp on the shelf next to the door. He switched it on, giving them a little bit of light.

Avery turned in a circle, studying the space. "It looks more solid in here than the exterior does."

"Yep. A hundred years of weather will age a building. Now." He set his hands on her hips and spun her to face him. "I believe I promised to warm you up."

"You did." She looped her arms around his neck. "What did you have in mind?"

He brushed a kiss on her lips. Then another. Lingered as he wrapped his arms around her and pulled her flush against him, one hand sliding into her hair.

Avery hummed and parted her lips. He delved his tongue between them, touching hers. She squirmed and gripped the back of his head, sending a streak of heat straight to his gut.

He ran his free hand down her back, cupping one ass cheek and pulling her tight to the ridge of his erection. She moaned into his mouth and parted her legs, adding pressure and friction. But when he slid his hand up her shirt, she stopped him.

"My turn," she murmured, nipping at his lower lip before grasping the sides of his face in her hands and trailing kisses over his jaw.

Mason's pulse kicked hard as her hands roamed over his shoulders and chest, down his ribs to the waistband of his jeans. She gripped his erection through the denim, earning a low growl, then undid the fly and peeled the fabric down his hips. He sucked in a breath when her hand wrapped around the hot, throbbing length of his cock, her lips busy on the side of his neck.

His instinct was to take over. But the way she explored him, so intent on her task as she shoved his shirt up with her free hand and set her mouth on his bare chest, made him stay perfectly still.

He eased a hand into the silky strands of her hair, his fingers flexing. All his muscles pulled tight as her mouth moved lower, his heart thudding hard against his ribs. He'd imagined her on her knees going down on him at least a thousand times, and could hardly believe it was about to happen.

Her hand felt good on him, but when she nipped at his abs and sank to her knees in front of him, looking up at him with those pretty golden eyes, her lips inches away from the swollen head of his cock… She was his every fantasy come to life.

He stared down at her, dying a little as she leaned forward to touch her tongue to the flared head. His muscles grabbed, the air locking in his lungs. The hand in her hair tightened, the anticipation pushing the hunger higher and higher with every heartbeat.

Her lips parted. He felt the silky caress of her tongue as it swirled around him, then warmth as her mouth engulfed him.

Mason growled low in his throat as fire streaked up his spine. He clenched his fingers around her hair, pulling it. In answer, Avery sucked him deeper, her hand stroking up and down his shaft in the slow, decadent rhythm she set with her mouth.

The urge to close his eyes and throw his head back was strong, but he refused to miss a second of this. She was too gorgeous, too sexy as she sucked him off in the glow of the lantern, the wet sounds mixing with his harsh breaths. Pleasure flooded him, rising in an unstoppable tide.

"Does sucking me make you wet?" he murmured, his heart pounding out of control.

Her gaze flicked up to him but she didn't answer, flicking her tongue across the spot that made him shudder.

He tightened his hold on her hair. "Does it?"

She hummed around him, her head bobbing in a nod.

He gripped her hair and tugged gently, bringing that gorgeous, sultry gaze up to his, already on edge. "Stop," he commanded, his voice little more than a guttural growl. He was too close. A few more seconds and he'd be lost.

Avery eased off him, her expression confused. Mason grabbed her by the elbows and hauled her to her feet, crushing his mouth to hers. She opened for him, stroking his tongue with hers as he shoved her fleece and shirt up. He tugged the lace cups of her bra down, one hand splayed across her back as he bent to take a hard nipple into his mouth.

Her moan lashed across his nerve endings, his cock throbbing, desperate to plunge into her. But not until she was as hot as him.

He kept his mouth exactly where it was while he un-did her jeans and shoved them and her underwear down her thighs. She parted them as much as the fabric would allow, gave a shaky moan when he cupped her.

Fuck. She was hot and wet, melting against his fin-gers, and he wanted everything she had to give.

He caressed her clit, making her even wetter, then slid two fingers into her. Teasing the spot he would hit when he was finally inside her.

Avery gripped his head and rocked into his hand, de-manding more. He withdrew to stroke her clit, switching to the other nipple and lavishing the same attention on it until she was squirming in his hold.

He couldn't wait another second.

Straightening, he spun her around and pushed her forward until they came to the low cabinet built into the wall. He set a hand between her shoulder blades and pushed with firm pressure. "Down," he rasped out, and dug into his pocket for the condom he'd brought.

He rolled it on, desperate to get inside her, and the sight of her like that, bent over with her ass in the air, ex-posed and waiting for him made him dizzy. Stepping up close behind her, he spread one hand over the small of her back, then reached his other around to cup her silky folds.

"Mason," she said on a groan, rubbing her ass against his rigid length.

"Let me," he whispered, bending over her to kiss her shoulder, the curve of her neck, his tongue stroking while his fingers played with her clit. He was so damn hard, his whole body tight with a need that only Avery could quench.

When she was panting and moaning, he straightened

and grasped her hip, his fingers sinking into her soft flesh. With his other hand he guided himself to her folds, staring hungrily at the way she enveloped the thick head as he pushed forward.

She gasped and tried to push back for more but he stilled her with a solid grip on her hip and cupped her with his other hand, finding her swollen clit once more. Her plaintive moan went straight to his cock as he surged forward.

With one thrust he buried himself as deep as he could get, groaning in mingled relief and pleasure at being enveloped by her body. Slowly he withdrew and eased forward again, his shaft slick and shiny in the lamplight as he angled himself to stroke over her sweet spot, his fingers caressing her in a slow, steady rhythm.

He'd never felt anything this intense. The way she gave herself to him was so incredibly sexy, her needy moans rising with each stroke. His breathing was uneven, his heart racing as they both neared the edge.

She clenched around him and started coming, her soft, ecstatic cries of surrender filling his heart until he thought it would burst. Mason bent forward again, covering her back with his chest as he rode her, milking every ounce of pleasure he could out of her release before allowing himself his own.

He locked an arm around her waist and plunged deep, a shout tearing free as pleasure bombarded him, white hot, searing every nerve ending. Gasping, he rested his forehead against the top of her spine and just breathed her in, while the pulses gradually faded.

Their uneven breaths were the only thing that disturbed the silence. Mason kept his eyes closed and absorbed the blissful peace he felt, still buried inside Avery. He kissed her silken skin, up to her soft nape, his heart overflowing. "I love you."

Her muscles contracted as she turned her head to

look back at him. "What?"

Shit, he hadn't meant to blurt it out like that, especially while he was inside her. But he wasn't sorry, because it was true. He nodded, trailing his fingertips over the side of her face. "I do."

She straightened, forcing him to withdraw from her warmth, and turned to face him, her eyes searching his. "You do?"

He cupped the side of her face. "Yeah."

A startled smile tilted her lips. "I—"

Something flickered in his peripheral vision. They both glanced to the left.

She tensed, inhaling. "Do you smell that?"

The blood congealed in his veins, his heart seizing. *Smoke.*

Mason whipped around, his heart in his throat as that smell flooded his brain. Flames were already licking at the outside of the single window in the side of the barn, smoke pouring in through the boards.

Heart in his throat, Mason turned back to Avery as she got her holster in place, and shoved her toward the door. "Get out *now*."

She ran for the door, glancing back to make sure he was following. He was right behind her, adrenaline pumping through his system as past and present collided. The smell of the smoke, the hungry flames eating through the wood transported him back in time. He was pinned in place, wounded, every movement agony as he listened to his fellow soldiers' screaming as they burned in the shattered Chinook.

He shook it off, his heart slamming against his ribs. He had to save Avery. Had to get her out safely.

The glow was already brighter, the flames racing across the old wood, devouring it, feeding off it. Avery reached for the metal lever holding the sliding door shut, only to jerk her hands back with a cry of pain.

"What's wrong?" Mason demanded, pulling her back to look at her hands. The palms and fingers were bright red, seared by the metal.

"The lever. It's too hot." She grimaced.

Mason ripped off his jacket, wrapped it around his hands and reached for the lever. He pulled it, but nothing happened.

He set his jaw and leaned back, the muscles in his arms and shoulders standing out as he strained to open it. "Shit, it's stuck." His heart hammered against his ribs, fear gripping him.

Then he met Avery's gaze, and resolve hardened in his gut like steel. She was counting on him. Those men had burned to death in that helo because he couldn't get them out.

He would get Avery out of here alive, even if it meant sacrificing himself to save her.

AVERY SPUN AROUND, frantically looking for another way out. They couldn't get out the window, the flames were already too high and too thick. "Is there another door?" She hurried to the opposite side, searching for an exit in the wall. Her hands stung like hell and she could already feel the blisters rising. How had the fire started?

"No." He ran to the far end.

There was no gap in the wall, no loose boards that she could find to get through. The smoke was pouring in now, boiling in a black cloud against the ceiling. She coughed and bent over, putting the crook of her arm across her nose and mouth.

Mason was feeling along the end wall, trying to find a way out. She rushed to him, her eyes watering from the smoke. It was already burning her throat, filling her lungs. She coughed, sucked in a ragged breath and coughed harder.

"Here." Mason pulled off his shirt, ripped it in half and handed her one. She took it, wincing as her blistered palms and fingers burned while she tried to tie it around the back of her head.

He pushed her hands away and did it for her, then tied his half around his face. "Gonna have to break our way out. Stay back." He set her away from him, leaned back and drove the sole of his boot into the wall with a loud thud. The wooden boards shuddered but held.

Avery moved in beside him and timed a kick with his next, hammering at the old boards. Wood groaned and cracked, but held. Jesus, and here she'd thought the barn was in jeopardy of falling over.

Together they beat at the wall, over and over. Avery's eyes were streaming, sweat slicking her spine. She could barely see through the haze now, both of them coughing as the lethal smoke boiled around them.

Mason stepped back a few paces, then took a running start and drove his foot into the wall with a guttural snarl. This time a small hole appeared.

Avery's heart slammed in a desperate rhythm as she moved close and started kicking at the weak point with him. Together they managed to punch out a hole about three feet tall and two feet wide.

Mason grabbed one of the broken planks and started pulling on it with all his might, his muscles standing out, his forehead and temples streaked with sweat.

The board snapped free.

He staggered back a step, dropped it, then grabbed the next. Avery grabbed one too, but released it with a cry. Shit, she couldn't hold anything.

"I got it," Mason said, grunting as he pried another board loose.

Hurry, hurry, she urged him, desperate to get out of this deathtrap.

The board came loose. Mason grabbed her wrist and

shoved her toward the opening. "Go, now," he ordered.

There was barely enough room for her to squeeze through it. She struggled through the opening while Mason pulled on another board, the wood scraping at her.

Avery gritted her teeth, a cry locking in her throat as the wood suddenly snapped and sent her tumbling forward. Instinctively she threw her hands out to break her fall, wrenching a cry of agony from her as her blistered palms scraped across the ground.

She staggered to her feet and pulled the makeshift bandana off, turning just as Mason came through the opening. He yanked down his bandana and grabbed her shoulders, his watering eyes searching hers. "Are you okay?"

She was alive and mostly unharmed, so she nodded.

He put a hand on the middle of her back and started rushing her forward. "Jesus," he muttered.

She looked to the left, shocked to see how much of the barn was already engulfed in flames. A cough wracked her. She kept walking, a sense of numbness invading her. "How did it start?"

"I don't know, but let's get the hell out of here and call the fire department."

She hurried alongside him, both of them still coughing. The crackle of the flames made her skin crawl as they headed across the clearing for the trail. Then she heard another sound.

"It's Ric," she said, fear constricting her chest. He was barking frantically, trapped in Mason's Jeep.

Mason bolted forward, racing for the trail. Avery jogged after him, praying the dog was okay.

No sooner had she reached the start of the trail, when three shots exploded in the night.

She gasped as a streak of fire burned across her side, instinctively grabbing the wound as she fell.

CHAPTER TWENTY-THREE

Avery was down. She'd hit her!

Shannon ducked down out of sight in the shadows cast by the trees she hid behind next to the trail, her heart slamming against her chest. *Die, bitch.* She should have died in the fire. Shannon had been hoping to hear her screams.

"Avery!"

She whirled to the left and stared down the trail at Mason's shout and raised her weapon, prepared to fire once he came within range. He was the greatest threat to her now. She would kill him too if that was her only chance of escape. By the time anyone found their bodies, she would be long gone.

"I'm...okay." Avery's voice was weak and unsteady.

Shannon gritted her teeth, disappointment and fury lashing at her. Shit, Avery was down but not dead. Was she dying? Shannon wasn't sure where she'd hit her, or how many times.

Running footsteps pounded up the trail. Shannon hesitated, torn. Mason was racing toward them, but she could hear Avery moving around nearby, her pained groans music to Shannon's ears.

She'd come here to kill Avery. She and her lover had been oblivious that Shannon had been waiting in the trees to follow them to the barn earlier.

Hearing them fucking in there minutes later had made something inside her snap. She'd jammed a broomstick through the door handle to trap them, then doused the door and walls with gasoline, and set it ablaze before retreating a safe distance to watch the show.

Except the fire hadn't caught fast enough. They'd managed to escape, but Shannon had been ready and waiting when they came out.

She was going to kill Avery tonight one way or the other. She was so close now. One more careful shot and she could get out of here. Disappear and find a new town to blend into. She had a fake ID ready, and enough cash to get her through a few weeks until she could find work. It would mean a long separation from Mike, but he wasn't going anywhere and the sacrifice was necessary for them to be together in the end.

Another muted groan reached her, sounding farther away this time, near the spot where the trail opened up into the clearing, the barn still alight in the distance. Avery was trying to drag herself away.

Not happening, bitch.

Blood pulsed in her ears, louder than the crackle of the fire in the center of the clearing. Mason was getting closer every second, giving her only moments to make her move.

Resolve hardened in her gut like steel. She'd come this far. She was going to end this now.

Rising to a crouch, she kept to the shadows and ran

left, where she'd heard Avery moving. The light was almost gone now, the sky ablaze with the flames from the burning barn in the distance. Shannon used the extra light to scan the ground, searching for her prey.

She caught a flash of movement through the screen of trees. Avery's bright hair reflected the flames. She'd managed to get up. She was bent over at the waist.

Shannon put on a burst of speed, her breathing erratic. Another few seconds and she'd be within range.

Elation punched through her, better than the rush of any drug she'd taken. She stopped, her eyes trained on Avery as she raised the pistol to take the final shot.

****

"Avery!" Mason yelled again as he raced up the trail, weapon in hand, his heart in his throat. He'd barely made it to the Jeep to check on Ric before the shots had rung out. The smell of the fire still stung his nose, waking all the ghosts he fought to keep buried, his comrades' screams loud in his head.

He shook it away. Avery had answered his first shout saying she was okay, but she'd been hit, he knew it. The shots had come from up ahead and to the left, but he couldn't fucking see anything in the thick shadows of the trees.

He ran full out, ignoring the pain in his knees, his sole concern getting to Avery and protecting her. Ahead in the clearing, the barn was completely engulfed now, a wall of flame in the darkness to light his way.

His heart stuttered when he rounded the bend in the trail and finally caught sight of Avery. She was on her feet, but doubled over, facing away from him. Shit, how bad was she hit?

"Avery—" Another shot rang out. His heart lurched, and only started beating again when Avery didn't fall.

Mason locked down his emotions and raised his pistol, in operator mode as he searched for any sign of the shooter. He caught faint movement in the underbrush just inside the trees. Aimed. Fired.

A grunt sounded. The shooter dropped out of sight, melting into the shadows. He pursued his target, needing to take them out if he wanted to protect Avery.

The brush moved. He moved faster, adjusting his aim.

More movement, then the person dropped out of sight as the ground dipped into a gulley. Mason stalked forward, his steps almost silent, gaze trained on the dip.

He caught the faint sound of movement, and paused. The instant the shooter appeared, he fired, squeezing the trigger just as another shot rang out from his right.

The shooter dropped to the ground. Mason kept coming, ready to fire again. His eyes had adjusted enough to allow him to see his target.

A woman. And when her hand lifted, he didn't hesitate, pumping two more rounds in her chest and one in her head.

She was dead before her head hit the ground, her weapon falling with a soft thump.

Threat neutralized, Mason whipped around to find Avery standing twenty yards away, holding a weapon. She grimaced and dropped it, then fell to her knees, pressing one hand to her side.

Oh, shit, no. "*Avery*."

He holstered his pistol and ran to her, dropping down in front of her. Cupping the side of her face, he set a hand over hers and did a visual sweep of her, hindered by the darkness. "How bad?" He could feel the blood under his hand, smell it on the cool night air.

"Not bad. Just…hurts," she panted, her eyes squeezed shut.

It was a good sign that she could still talk. But he

couldn't see anything in here, even with the light from the fire. He needed to get her out of here and get the bleeding under control. "I'm gonna carry you out so I can get a better look, okay?"

She nodded, face strained.

Just as he reached for her, someone called out behind them. "Hello?"

Mason shot to his feet and drew his weapon, whirling to face the new threat. "Freeze!" he barked.

A figure appeared at the edge of the trees. A man. He stopped, raised his hands. "Don't shoot. I'm unarmed," he called out.

Mason stalked toward him, finger curved around the trigger. Avery was behind him. He had to protect her.

Within a few paces, the shadows retreated and the man's face became clear. "Ray?" he said in surprise.

"Yeah. Are you folks all right? I heard shots."

"Call 911. We need help."

"I already called 'em. Cops and fire department are on their way up."

Right on cue, Mason heard the faint wail of sirens off in the distance. "Avery's hit," he said, holstering his weapon.

"God dammit," Ray snapped, and rushed forward. "Where?"

"Her side. I need to get her out of here."

"I'll call for an ambulance."

Mason hurried back to Avery, who was still on her knees. "Ray's here. He called for help and it's almost here." He slid one arm around her back and the other under her legs, a twinge of pain ripping down his back as he lifted her.

"Good," she whispered, her breathing ragged as he carried her.

"I've got a med kit in the back of my Jeep," he said to Ray, who trotted along beside him, face worried. "Can you go grab it? And a blanket."

"Yeah, anything." He ran ahead.

"How you doing?" Mason asked Avery, trying not to jostle her. He needed to stop the bleeding and get her to the hospital.

"I'm getting pissed off," she muttered.

That made him crack a laugh. "Pissed off is good." Real good. It meant she wasn't going into shock.

The jingle of a collar reached him, then Ric appeared from around the bend in the trail. He must have jumped out the moment Ray opened the back. "Hey, buddy. You gonna help me look after Avery?"

"Hey, Ric," she gasped out. "Don't worry."

Ric ran anxious circles around them the whole way back up the trail, the sirens getting closer now. Ray was waiting near the Jeep with the med kit, a blanket already spread out on the ground.

Mason knelt and gently lay Avery down on it. She immediately curled up on her side, her hand pressed to her ribs, eyes squeezed shut.

"Let me see, Avery," he said gently, prying her hand away. Her palm and fingers were blistered and raw. The front of her shirt was soaked with blood but her breathing was clear.

"C-cold," she whispered.

"I know. I'll get you warm in a minute, but first I have to stop this bleeding." He pulled up her shirt to get a better look while Ray aimed the beam of a flashlight there for him. He bit back a curse.

The bullet had hit her between her hip and ribcage. It had gone clean through, the exit wound slightly larger than the entry. He applied a dressing to each and rolled her onto her back. "I have to put pressure on it," he warned, then pressed down with his hands on the entry wound.

She gasped and swore, her legs writhing on the blanket. "This sucks," she growled.

"I know it does. Help's almost here, and we'll get you to the hospital." His adrenaline level was dropping now, his hands a little unsteady.

It made him insane to see her hurting and bleeding, but he had to stay calm and not scare her more. He was worried about possible internal damage. The bullet could have hit an artery or her bowel or even kidney.

She panted, cracked one eye open to look at him. "The shooter...she's dead?"

He didn't let up on the pressure, sorry he was causing her more pain but determined to slow if not stop the blood loss. "Yes."

"Was it Sh-Shannon?"

"Yeah."

"Dammit, I knew that girl was up to no good," Ray said.

Mason glanced up at him sharply, his muscles grabbing. "What do you mean?"

"She was in the bar earlier. Asking questions about you both. Not the first time she done it, either. I mentioned you were both up here because I saw you turn off the access road on my way into town, but when she took off right away, I had a bad feeling. I called you, but there was no answer. So I tried to find her. I thought I saw her once, but lost sight of her and eventually came here to warn you."

Mason stared at him, raw fury punching through him. Jesus Christ, the woman had been hunting them and he hadn't even realized it.

Ray scrubbed his free hand over his hair, looking distraught. "I'm sorry. So damn sorry, I shouldn'a said anything. But I swear I didn't know she was coming up here to do anything like this." His voice caught.

Mason believed him. "She's not a threat to anyone

anymore."

"Thanks for c-calling for help, Ray," Avery rushed out, grimacing again. "I hate n-needles, but I think I need a f-few."

Mason lifted one hand from her wound to rub his thumb across her cheek. "Yeah, you will, angel eyes. But you're gonna be just fine, and I'll be there to hold your hand."

Because he loved her, and wasn't leaving her side until he knew for certain she was going to be okay.

CHAPTER TWENTY-FOUR

Avery cracked her eyes open when her hospital room door opened. *Oh, please, God, no more needles.*

She wasn't sure how much time had passed since she'd gotten here. They'd rushed her by ambulance to the trauma center in Missoula hours ago while Mason followed in the Jeep, and everything had been a whirlwind since.

Needles, tests and being rushed into the O.R. They'd whisked her away from Mason, and the next thing she knew she was on the operating table for emergency surgery.

Her heart squeezed when Mason stepped inside, his silhouette unmistakable even in the dimness. A quiet jingling told her Ric was with him. "Hey," she croaked out, her throat parched. Every time she drew a breath, pain streaked through the right side of her waist. "What happened to the part where you were going to hold my hand through everything?"

"Sorry, I wanted to be there when you woke up, but they wouldn't let me in the recovery room." He pulled the chair over to her bed, sat and reached for her forearm, curling his fingers around it because they'd bandaged both her burned hands. "How are you feeling?"

"Sore. Glad to see you. Lucky to be alive."

He leaned over her and smoothed the hair back from her face, his expression concerned. "What did the doctor say?"

"A nicked artery and intestine and some bruising, but my organs all seem okay. They stopped the bleeding in surgery. Now they're pumping me full of antibiotics and a little something for pain." Not enough, but better than nothing.

He stroked her hair. "Can I do anything?"

"You already are." She echoed the words back to him that he'd said to her the other night out on her deck.

He gave her a little smile, but his eyes were still worried. "Tate, Nina and Tala wanted to come down, but I told them not to yet. Maybe tomorrow."

"Did I hear Ric?"

"You sure did. Come here, buddy," he said, patting the side rail.

A second later, a handsome, furry face appeared next to her. His ears were up, his expression almost worried. "Hey, handsome." She reached up to pat him with her bandaged hand. "I'm so lucky to have you come visit me."

"I put on his therapy dog vest, and there was no problem."

She laid her hand back down, the constant burning in her palms and fingers from when she'd grabbed the scalding hot door handle right on the edge of unbearable. Second degree burns sucked. Singing the side of your finger on the toaster or oven rack was bad enough. Having both hands burned and blistered was awful.

The doctors had told her it would take a couple

weeks for them to heal, and that they'd probably remain sensitive for a long while after that. "How long are they keeping me here?" She already hated it.

"Maybe tomorrow night at the earliest."

She groaned. "I just wanna go home."

"I'll get you out of here as soon as possible, I promise." He leaned over to drop a kiss on her lips.

Avery gazed up at him when he pulled back. "You smell like the fire. And you've got soot all over you."

One side of his mouth pulled up. "I'll clean up later."

The half-smile didn't reach his eyes. And when she looked into them, her heart constricted. "Oh, God, the fire," she breathed. It hadn't even occurred to her how it must have affected him, she'd been too caught up in trying to get out. Of course it would have triggered all his demons.

"Yeah. I'm just glad we got out." He shifted in the chair. "You doing okay otherwise?"

She nodded, hating everything about this. To think that Shannon was psychotic enough to try and kill her because she'd testified against a convicted felon up for parole, was unreal. "The whole thing escalated so fast. Going from trashing a room and throwing bricks through a few windows to murder is a big jump. What in the hell triggered it?"

"Don't know, and don't care. I only care that you're okay." He cupped the side of her face in his palm.

Avery turned her cheek into it, feeling way better now that he was beside her. "Thank you," she whispered, her throat thickening.

His eyebrows contracted. "For what? You brought her down with me."

"But you ended it. So thank you."

He shook his head. "I'll do whatever it takes to keep you safe. Always."

Her chest tightened. This was the first chance they'd

had to be alone together since everything had happened. There was so much to process, so much to think about. And yet, in quieter moments, her mind kept going back to one thing.

"Mason."

"Yeah?"

"What you said in the barn. After…"

He didn't look away. "What about it?"

"Did you mean it? Or was it just a heat of the moment thing?"

His blue eyes stared directly into hers. "I meant it. I know it's fast, but I know how I feel. I love you."

Ohh… She swallowed, a tremulous smile forming on her lips. "You do?" Her throat thickened more, her heart beating faster.

A slow, gorgeous smile spread across his lips. "Yeah, angel eyes. I do."

"How can you know so soon?" Her feelings for him were powerful, but she was afraid to trust them.

"Because you're my light in the darkness. You see my flaws and accept me anyway. You make me believe in myself again." He shook his head, his expression earnest and his voice slightly rough. "And because… Because I feel totally safe to be myself when I'm with you."

Her breath hitched, a bittersweet pain lancing her chest. Of all the things he could have said, nothing could have prepared her for that. For this proud, strong man to admit something so deep and private, turned her heart inside out.

She blinked as tears scalded the backs of her eyes. Damn pain meds. "Good, because I love you too." It still scared her, but she had to let the fear go and reach for what he was offering.

He groaned and closed his eyes, bending down to press his cheek to hers, his hand now cradling the back of her head. "God, Avery."

KAYLEA CROSS

"This is all so fast. I swore I'd never let myself do this again. But all I know is, when I'm not with you, you're all I think about. You matter to me. I don't want to be without you."

He drew back, gave her a smile that eased the anxiety curling in the pit of her stomach. "You won't be without me, because I'm not going anywhere." He stroked his thumb down her cheek, his expression more tender than she'd ever seen it. "I love you, and always will."

She exhaled a shaky breath, covering a wince as her incision pulled. "So where do we go from here?"

"Home."

A smile spread across her face. She loved that he already considered her place home. She wanted to *be* his home. His safe place. Forever. "I like the sound of that."

"Me too, angel eyes." He dipped down to kiss her forehead. "Me too."

EPILOGUE

This was their first holiday season together as a couple, and so far, it was everything Avery had ever dreamed of and more.

"We're finally alone," she said to Mason, stretching her arms over her head as she lounged on the living room couch in her new satin robe. She'd left it open before coming in here, revealing the new, matching pink lingerie set she'd put on underneath.

Seven weeks had passed since the night Shannon had come after them. Her wound and hands were all healed up, and life was finally back to normal.

They'd just finished cleaning up after hosting Thanksgiving dinner here with Nina, Tate, Rylee and Tala. Avery had taken a quick bubble bath before putting her pretty new things on. The tree they'd all decorated together glowed softly in the corner, and the fire in the hearth gave the room a cozy atmosphere while the rain lashed the windows and pounded down on the roof.

"Think so." Mason carried two mugs in, the room filled with the sound of the rain on the roof. Ric trotted after him and went over to curl up on his bed by the fire with a contented groan, his eyes half-open.

241

"I love our friends, but I wasn't sad to see them leave." She wanted as much time alone with Mason as possible.

Now that he and Tate were ramping up the final stages for Rifle Creek Tactical, she didn't get as much time alone with him, especially on weekends, when she helped as well. Soon enough they would have all kinds of socializing to do, between various holiday events with her family, and both Braxton and Tala planning to be here for the Christmas holidays. Maybe it made her selfish, but Avery wanted to have Mason all to herself while she could.

"Careful," he said, handing a mug to her. "Let me know if it's too hot for your hands."

They were still sensitive to heat, especially her palms. She took it, inhaling. "Mmm, hot cocoa? With marshmallows. Yum."

"Mmhmm," he agreed, setting his mug aside as he knelt beside the sofa and placed a tantalizing kiss just above her navel, then over to the newly healed scar at the right side of her waist. He curled his hands around her hips, his palms warm from the hot drinks, his tongue caressing her skin just above the edge of the pink lace between her thighs.

Avery sighed and sank a hand into his hair, thankful to be able to run her fingers through it again without bandages or protective gloves in the way, and traced the fingers of her other hand over the JTF2 emblem on his right forearm. "Just thought I'd let you open a present early." She'd finally gotten the green light from the doctor this morning, so they could finally have actual sex again. Hence the fancy lingerie.

Avery couldn't wait to have him inside her again. They both needed it.

Mason looked up at her, his blue eyes glowing like flame. "Just one?" His fingers trailed ever so gently over the front of her panties, making her tingle and bite her lower lip.

"This outfit counts as one present."

"Best present I've ever gotten," he rumbled.

She'd gotten a pretty great present today herself, along with Thanksgiving dinner shared with her dearest friends. Tate had informed her that asshole Mr. Zinke was enjoying an extended stay in jail because his wife had decided to finally press charges. Not only that, she had also filed to divorce his abusive ass. Karma was so epic sometimes.

Avery liked to think she was enjoying the fruits of her own Karma too, totally free from the past with a new life, and a wonderful, caring man to share it with.

Mason was currently kissing his way up to her breasts as his fingers stroked the lace between her legs gently. Teasing her. Getting her all hot and wet because he loved revving her up almost as much as he loved exerting control in bed.

He put his talents to good use, taking his sweet time in teasing her, stripping off the lingerie inch by inch to replace it with his fingers and tongue.

She was breathless and pleading to come when he finally turned her over to drape across the padded leather arm of the sofa. She gripped the edge of it and let her head fall back as he surged into her from behind, working her body with steady, measured thrusts while his fingers stroked her clit, taking them both to heaven and back.

When they'd both recovered a bit, he stretched her out on her back once again and came down on top of her, lying together in a contented heap. Avery stroked his hair and back as the rain continued to fall outside their cozy cocoon.

Mason groaned and started to ease off her. She opened one eye when he reached down beside the sofa for his jeans, and let out a soft laugh. "Are you looking for another condom?"

"Soon. But no," he whispered against her lips, then eased off her. Cool air washed over her without his body heat to warm her, but the fire kept the chill away.

He took something from his pocket and turned back to her, and her heart stuttered at the look on his face. So earnest. His eyes intense.

Before she could ask if something was wrong, he cradled the side of her face in his hand, gazing into her eyes. "We've been through some tough times together, and we're stronger for it. I know you're scared of getting married again and being let down in the end. I know I'm not perfect, and that being with me isn't always easy. But I'm also the guy who will stand beside you no matter what comes, because I'll love you for the rest of my life." His other hand came up, and something sparkled in the light. "Will you marry me, angel eyes?"

Avery gaped at the diamond ring in his fingers, his words choking her up.

Her gaze shot to his, a flood of emotion pouring through her. She'd never expected this. Any of it. Not Mason, and not that she would ever give her heart to someone again.

But he'd won it completely, and she couldn't have given it to a better man. She loved him with everything in her.

She sat up to reach for him. "Yes." His strong arms engulfed her, the safest, most incredible feeling in the world. "And I'll love you for the rest of mine."

—The End—

Dear reader,

Thank you for reading *Lethal Temptation*. I hope you enjoyed it. Turn the page for a sneak peak at my next release!

If you'd like to stay in touch with me and be the first to learn about new releases you can:

Join my newsletter at:
http://kayleacross.com/v2/newsletter/

Find me on Facebook:
https://www.facebook.com/KayleaCrossAuthor/

Follow me on Twitter:
https://twitter.com/kayleacross

Follow me on Instagram:
https://www.instagram.com/kaylea_cross_author/

Also, please consider leaving a review at your favorite online book retailer. It helps other readers discover new books.

Happy reading,
Kaylea

Excerpt from

SILENT NIGHT, DEADLY NIGHT

Suspense Series
By Kaylea Cross

CHAPTER ONE

Emily Hutchinson grasped her husband's hand tight as they stepped out of the clinic into the pleasantly cool December afternoon air. A blanket of cloud obscured the sun, and the breeze held the edge of a bite to it. Neither of them said anything on the way to the parking lot, each of them caught up in their own heads, and right now hers was whirling like a tornado.

Anxiety burned in the pit of her stomach like battery acid, threatening to burn a hole through it. Her doctor had called last week to say that her blood work had come back abnormal, and had scheduled all the follow-up tests for today. Now all Emily could do was wait to find out what was happening.

Luke opened the SUV door for her, grim-faced and jaw tight, the gray light catching on the silver in his stubble. She slid into the passenger seat without looking at him, afraid to in case it made her burst into tears, and ordered herself to get a grip on her fear. He was her rock and the strongest man she knew, but she was his weak point. She had to hold it together for his sake, put on a brave face through whatever came next.

She took a deep, slow breath while he went around to the driver's side, pushing down the bubble of panic rising inside her. *Calm down. You don't know what it means yet.* But damn, she'd been doing so well.

This disease had taken so much from her already. Her uterus and right breast. All the side-effects from the chemo and radiation, the months of fear and uncertainty. Now it seemed it was back for more.

You can't have any more of me, she told it firmly, a hard seed of anger beginning to take hold. *I won't let you.*

Luke slid into the driver's seat and closed his door, shutting the two of them in and the rest of the world out. She pretended to busy herself with finding something in her purse, not quite having herself together yet, then a big hand reached out to capture her jaw and turn her face toward him.

She swallowed, a spurt of terror darting through her as she stared into those intense, dark-chocolate eyes.

"We're going to face this, and whatever else comes, together. Hear me? One day at a time, sunshine. We take each day as it comes."

In other words, don't leap ahead and think of all the terrible things that could be coming down the road. Which she'd already done, the instant she'd gotten that call from the doctor, and kept circling back to every day since.

She nodded and forced a smile, ignoring the sting at the backs of her eyes. More than anything she wanted to burrow into him and hide in his arms, but even Luke with all his strength and skills couldn't protect her from this. At least this time she would have him by her side, have him to lean on when it all became too much.

"Yeah," she whispered, her voice slightly rough. "And just in case I don't say it enough, I really love you, you know."

Raw grief flashed in his eyes for an instant before he masked it with his usual strong front. "I know. And I'll love you until the day I die."

I know. She gave him another smile and gently pulled from his grasp, clearing her throat as she faced forward once again, determined to focus on something other than the fear that her cancer had returned. Thank God she had something happy to look forward to. "We'd better get going, their flight just landed a few minutes ago."

Luke started the engine and drove out of the parking lot without another word. She punched a button on the dash to activate the radio, needing some kind of background noise to fill the silence. She had about twenty minutes to mentally shift gears before they reached the airport, northwest of the city.

Except… "Don't say anything to Rayne and Christa, okay? I want this to be a happy, stress-free visit for them. I've been looking forward to this for months."

He nodded once. "All right."

"Thank you." Dwelling on the future was pointless at the moment, she told herself. They didn't even know what they were facing yet, and wouldn't until these new test results came back. It was also possible that everything would be fine.

But it's never been fine before, has it? that insidious little voice in her mind whispered.

She blocked it from long practice and instead concentrated on the upcoming reunion. Their son and daughter-in-law had flown down from Vancouver to spend the holidays with them, and the rest of the crew was due in tomorrow so they could all have an early Christmas celebration together.

It was the first time they'd all been together since that harrowing time in Beirut when Luke had almost died saving her from the clutches of Tehrazzi. That fateful mission had changed her entire life for the better. It had brought Luke back to her, and he'd never wavered in his support of love in the year since.

Thankfully traffic was light and they made it to the airport in good time. Now that she'd made up her mind to put everything else aside, excitement bubbled inside her, pushing away the lingering fear and worry as she took Luke's hand and walked toward the terminal. With all the people she loved best in the world about to be staying in their home, she had lots to occupy her mind and keep her busy. Christmas was her favorite time of year. She wasn't going to let anything spoil it.

The arrivals terminal seemed busier than normal, no surprise given it was just a few days before Christmas. "Do you see them?"

"Not yet." Luke wrapped a solid arm around her shoulders and squeezed, and even though he didn't say anything else, she could hear his silent message. *It's gonna be okay, Em.*

She hoped so. And if it wasn't? She was going to soak up every single moment of joy these next few days brought, and all the days she had left.

"There they are."

She pushed onto her tiptoes to see over the crowd flowing around them outside baggage claim, then gasped, her heart flooding. A giant smile spread across her face and her feet were already carrying her toward her son. "You're here!" she cried.

Rayne and Christa both looked up, their faces brightening. It still amazed her how much he looked like his father, except for his hazel eyes.

She flew at them, earning laughs as she jumped into her son's waiting arms. Rayne caught her with a chuckle and hugged her tight. "Hey, gorgeous."

Ohhh, she'd missed him. So much. They'd gone way too long between visits, almost seven months this time. "Hi. I'm so glad you're here." She pressed her face to his shoulder and hugged him until her arms ached.

"Hey, where's mine?" Christa said next to him in her

adorable western-Canadian accent.

Emily let go of Rayne and reached for her daughter-in-law. "Don't worry, I've still got some juice left in these arms." She hugged Christa, her heart squeezing at the younger woman's genuine warmth. She'd fit into their family perfectly, and Emily couldn't imagine a better, more down-to-earth woman for her son. "I'm glad you're here too."

"So am I. I can't wait to spend Christmas with you guys." Christa rubbed her back gently, then pulled away to smile down at her, those pretty aquamarine eyes studying Emily's face. "You look so great."

"Well, thank you." *But I'm still here*, that awful voice whispered out of nowhere. *Spreading inside you. You can't stop me.*

She ruthlessly shoved it away. She was done with being a victim, and had too much to live for. If this stupid disease wanted her, it would have to fight her to the bitter end.

She hooked an arm around Rayne's waist, leaning her head on his sturdy shoulder while Christa hugged Luke. Luke was still a little stiff about it, but getting better. It always amused her to see him awkward with hugs when he was so incredibly affectionate with her.

"Y'all ready to get back to the house and have some good old Lowcountry cooking?" Emily asked. She'd made all Rayne's favorites, things she knew Christa liked as well.

"She's been cooking for days," Luke said.

"*So* ready," Christa answered, allowing Luke to take her suitcase. She came to stand on Emily's other side and linked their arms. "Rayne's been wondering if you made him coconut cake. Because lord knows I've tried to replicate it, but apparently only your coconut cake will do." She shot her husband a telling look.

Emily peered up at her son as he grinned at her and

shrugged. "No one makes it like you."

"That's true," she said, not feeling at all arrogant because it was the truth.

"So, when's everyone else due in?" he asked as they neared the terminal exit.

"Tomorrow," she answered, so happy she could burst. "And I can't wait."

****

Joe stepped into the light and folded his arms, standing only a few feet from the prisoner strapped to the chair. The man had already undergone twenty-one hours of captivity and interrogation. He hadn't broken yet. That was why Joe was here.

"Where is it?" he asked him softly, his breath misting in the cold air. His words carried through the empty room to be absorbed by the thick concrete walls. They were fifty feet below ground here in this secret facility where high value prisoners to the Agency were brought. There were no cameras or microphones down here. And no one would hear his screams.

The prisoner looked up at him through eyes bruised and almost swollen shut. Blood covered his face, his naked body covered with cuts and welts. "Where's what?" he slurred through battered lips, his words holding the faintest trace of an Arabic accent. Several of his teeth lay on the blood-spattered concrete floor.

Joe kept his expression impassive even as anger pulsed through him. "You know what. And I'm losing patience." He raised an eyebrow. "You've seen what happens when I run out."

A wheezy laugh answered, followed by a sharp wince as it pulled on the man's broken ribs. He drew in a shallow breath, his expression hardening, raw hatred gleaming in his slitted eyes. "I have n-nothing to s-say to you." His remaining teeth chattered, his body jerking with continual shivers.

Oh, you'd better. Joe leaned his upper body toward the prisoner and dropped his voice to a foreboding murmur. "You talked shit about sending those files to someone. That you planned to sell me out, but guess what? It's not happening. And you're gonna die either way." He thought the guy was bluffing—but Joe couldn't be sure.

Those swollen eyes focused on him, the defiance on that beaten face admirable, if pointless.

Joe smiled. A slow, savage smile as he let the anger flow, and straightened. "Now. If you want me to make this as quick and painless as possible, you'll tell me who you supposedly sent the files to." The asshole thought it was his insurance policy. That he could blackmail Joe with it and save his skin.

"If I don't check in with my c-contact within the next six hours, those f-files will be sent to all the national n-news networks, and the Director." He paused, pulling in a shallow breath.

"You think that's gonna save you?" Joe said with an incredulous laugh.

That stare never wavered. "You can k-kill me, but I'll t-take you down with me."

He chuckled softly. "Not gonna happen." If this asshole really had copied sensitive, incriminating files and sent it to someone, it would spell the end of Joe's and his accomplices' long and devoted careers to their country. It might even mean their deaths.

Fuck that. Joe had spent over twenty years serving his country, doing the shitty, gray-area things no one else had the stomach for. He and the others deserved more than a paycheck and a lousy pension plan for their service. He wasn't going down because of the piece of shit sitting in front of him.

Even as he thought it, alarm began to spiral up his backbone. Along with a gut-deep certainty that this interrogation was going nowhere. This asshole could have sent someone the files. Even after all the beatings, sleep deprivation and psychological torment, he still wasn't talking. He knew he was already dead, and still refused to talk. Torturing him further wouldn't do any good. He had no family or close friends to threaten him with. And he was too well-trained.

Because Joe was the best trainer in the biz.

In a single motion, he drew the pistol from the holster at the small of his back and put a bullet through the prisoner's forehead. The body slumped over in the chair, held in place by the bindings as blood poured into his lap and spilled onto the floor.

Joe holstered the weapon and turned, speaking to two of his men on the way to the door. "Get rid of the body. Then find if he actually sent those files."

Two hours later he got the grim news from one of his associates. CCTV footage of the prisoner putting a small envelope in a mailbox just down the street from the motel he'd been captured at yesterday afternoon. Which meant that whatever the envelope contained was well on its way to the recipient.

Cagey bastard had rightly sent a physical copy of the files to the recipient, rather than risking someone tracking it via email or in the Cloud.

Joe clenched his jaw and lowered his voice as he spoke into his phone. "Go back and tear apart every piece of evidence collected from his room. Find out who he sent that letter to, or we can all kiss our asses goodbye."

End Excerpt

About the Author

NY Times and USA Today Bestselling author Kaylea Cross writes edge-of-your-seat military romantic suspense. Her work has won many awards, including the Daphne du Maurier Award of Excellence, and has been nominated multiple times for the National Readers' Choice Awards. A Registered Massage Therapist by trade, Kaylea is also an avid gardener, artist, Civil War buff, Special Ops aficionado, belly dance enthusiast and former nationally-carded softball pitcher. She lives in Vancouver, BC with her husband and family.

You can visit Kaylea at www.kayleacross.com. If you would like to be notified of future releases, please join her newsletter: http://kayleacross.com/v2/newsletter/

COMPLETE BOOKLIST

ROMANTIC SUSPENSE
Rifle Creek Series
Lethal Edge
Lethal Temptation
Lethal Protector

Vengeance Series
Stealing Vengeance
Covert Vengeance
Explosive Vengeance
Toxic Vengeance
Beautiful Vengeance

Crimson Point Series
Fractured Honor
Buried Lies
Shattered Vows
Rocky Ground
Broken Bonds

DEA FAST Series
Falling Fast
Fast Kill
Stand Fast
Strike Fast
Fast Fury
Fast Justice
Fast Vengeance

Colebrook Siblings Trilogy
Brody's Vow
Wyatt's Stand
Easton's Claim

Absolution
Silent Night, Deadly Night

PARANORMAL ROMANCE
Empowered Series
Darkest Caress

HISTORICAL ROMANCE
The Vacant Chair

EROTIC ROMANCE (writing as *Callie Croix*)
Deacon's Touch
Dillon's Claim
No Holds Barred
Touch Me
Let Me In
Covert Seduction

9 798682 921379